'A DREAMSPINNER EXTRAORDINAIRE'

Romantic Times

'I'm sorry, but you'll have to continue your abstinence a little longer.'

'I think not.'

The next thing she knew, two hands were gripping her hips and drawing her forward. His rough cheek scratched against hers as his mouth sought and found her lips. Her heart had never pumped so hard. Her blood was racing, causing a tingling throughout her body.

She couldn't even find her voice when his mouth left hers to drift down to her neck. She could have demanded he stop what he was doing, could have regained some meager control of the situation, but she was too busy experiencing the uniqueness of having her whole body come wildly alive.

And then he was looking down, grinning at her.

'Still think me a ghostly being, lady?'

'SPIRITED CHARACTERS, CONTRASTING SETTINGS AND INTENSE CONFLICTS OF THE HEART . . . JOHANNA LINDSEY HAS A SURE TOUCH WHERE HISTORICAL ROMANCE IS CONCERNED'

Newport News Daily Press

Until Forever

Johanna Lindsey

CORGI BOOKS

UNTIL FOREVER
A CORGI BOOK : 0 552 14411 8

First publication in Great Britain

PRINTING HISTORY
Corgi edition published 1996

Set in 11pt Linotron Plantin by
Deltatype Ltd, Ellesmere Port, Cheshire

Corgi Books are published by Transworld Publishers Ltd,
61–63 Uxbridge Road, London W5 5SA,
in Australia by Transworld Publishers (Australia) Pty Ltd,
15–25 Helles Avenue, Moorebank, NSW 2170
and in New Zealand by Transworld Publishers (NZ) Ltd,
3 William Pickering Drive, Albany, Auckland.

Reproduced, printed and bound in Great Britain by
Cox & Wyman Ltd, Reading, Berks.

For Joe –
my Thorn, my Challen, my Falon, my James,
my Tony, and I could go on and on . . .

1

It was driving her crazy, to let that box sit there on the small credenza beside her desk and not open it. Roseleen White could have sworn she had more willpower than that, but apparently not when it came to her one and only passion. She still tried to ignore it, and the fact that she was glancing over at it every few minutes.

Time was getting away from her. She had to finish grading her students' papers tonight. Ordinarily, she would have taken the papers home with her, but she wasn't going home tonight. She was driving straight from the campus to her friend Gail's house, where she was spending the weekend. And she wasn't coming in on Monday either. A long-delayed dentist appointment had seen to that, so she had to leave the papers in her desk for the substitute to hand out on Monday.

The next three days had been perfectly scheduled, which was the way she liked her life to be. She hadn't counted on the delivery notice in her mailbox when she'd arrived home yesterday that said the long-awaited box had finally arrived from England, or the emergency last night when she'd had to take neighbor Carol to the hospital, which had kept her from grading the papers.

She'd stopped by the post office to collect the box on the way to the campus that morning and had even stuck scissors in her purse so she could open it immediately. But again, she hadn't counted on the long line at the post office that ended up giving her only enough time to get to her first class without being late. And she hadn't found a free moment since when she could have satisfied her curiosity.

Fridays were always her busiest days, with three classes in a row and the inevitable questions after each session from those students who didn't have to rush to their next class. She'd also had meetings today when she'd had to inform two of her students that they were failing the semester. Then, just when she thought she'd have enough time to grab a quick dinner and to open the box before she tackled the grading, the dean had sent for her.

She was still simmering over *that* meeting. Dean Johnson had said he wanted to break the news to her gently, before she heard it elsewhere, that Barry Horton was being offered tenure. Barry was the biggest disaster of her life, proof positive that a woman could be naive and gullible at any age. He was going to be her equal now.

The dean had been very diplomatic about it, but the gist of his summons was to tell her he hoped she wouldn't cause any trouble about it, that she wouldn't renew her old allegations against Barry. As if she would bring all that humiliation back to suffer through it again.

Now she was hungry, angry about Barry's undeserved good fortune, and unable to concentrate on the papers in front of her because that box was sitting there tempting her to open it. It had come down to a test of strength. She *wasn't* going to open it until the last exam paper was graded and . . . and to hell with that.

Antique weapons were her passion, the only thing that interested her besides medieval history, which was her field of expertise. Her father had collected them, an unusual hobby for a small-town reverend, and she'd inherited his collection when he died, and was slowly adding to it as she could afford to do so. Each time she visited England, she spent about as much time in antique shops as she did researching the book she was writing on the Norman conquest.

She'd brought the long box into her classroom only because she hadn't wanted to leave it in her car – or out of her sight, actually. She'd waited too long for its arrival. Three years of tracking down the owner after she'd first heard of the existence of Blooddrinker's Curse, the elation in finding out the ancient sword was for sale and that it wouldn't be sold at auction, where she knew the price would soar out of her reach. Then the frustration in trying to deal with Sir Isaac Dearborn, the eccentric owner. Another four months had passed in haggling over the price and the particulars, all of which she hadn't been personally involved in, because Dearborn simply wouldn't sell to her.

'No woman may own Blooddrinker's Curse,' she'd been told at her initial inquiry, and without an explanation. Dearborn wouldn't even answer her subsequent calls and letters. But David, her dearest David, the brother of her heart if not her blood, who had been orphaned as a child and taken in by her family, had taken up the gauntlet for her. And after four months and finally agreeing to Dearborn's unusual demands, David had managed the purchase.

She had been ecstatic when he'd called her from England to tell her he would be shipping the sword home to her, then amazed when he'd added, 'You can't reimburse me, Rosie. I had to sign a sworn affidavit that I would never sell the sword, or even bequeath it, to a woman. Nothing was said, however, about simply giving it away, so consider this your birthday present – for the next fifty years.'

Considering what the sword had cost, which would have taken every bit of her savings, plus a loan for another twenty thousand, she was definitely in David's debt, even if he had been joking about it being a birthday present. The cost of the sword was nothing to him, for he had married an heiress who adored him and lavished her wealth on him. His wife, Lydia, collected houses – mansions, actually – the way Roseleen collected weapons. But it was the principle, and the extravagance – Roseleen felt indebted, even if David had been happy to buy the sword for her. She was definitely going to have to do something really nice for him to make it up to him.

Having finally given in to the temptation, Roseleen felt her fingers trembling as she dug the scissors out of her purse. She glanced at the door to her classroom, considered locking it first, but then smiled to herself. She was getting a little paranoid. The campus was almost empty; only a few other professors and the drama class were here this late, rehearsing whatever play Mr Hayley had chosen for this semester. She wouldn't be interrupted, and even if she was, she had nothing to hide. Just because Dearborn had been so adamant that a woman couldn't own the sword . . .

Well, she owned it now. It was hers. It would be the prize of her collection, the oldest weapon in it, the oldest she could ever hope to find. She had craved it, sight unseen, as soon as she'd heard about it, simply because it *was* so old. She still hadn't seen it, not even a picture of it. But David had assured her it was in prime condition for its age, with very little corrosion – a miraculous circumstance, considering the hilt dated from the eighth century, the steel blade from the tenth. Apparently, every owner from that time on had taken superb care of it, as well as jealously guarding it from the public eye, just as she would.

Now, scissors in hand, she cut through the thick plastic shipping straps, then set them aside to open the box and dig through the straw packing. Beneath it was another box, this one of fine polished mahogany. She chuckled to herself, seeing the wide bow David had tied around it. Attached to the ribbon was a small key to unlock the box.

Carefully, she lifted the wooden box out and shoved the cardboard one onto the floor. The heavy weight that had forced her to use both arms to carry the shipping box into the classroom was still apparent in the narrow wooden one. A tug on the bow, and she had the key in hand. She was unknowingly holding her breath as she inserted it into the lock and heard the slight click as she turned it.

And then she was staring in awe at a stunning piece of history that was more than a thousand years old. The long, double-edged blade was chipped in only two places from corrosion, and blackened from age, but the silver-embossed hilt was so well-preserved it even shone in the light of her desk lamp. Embedded in its center was a round, murky amber gem the size of a quarter. Three smaller ambers graced the end of the curved pommel, and some kind of misshapen animal was etched around the grip, possibly a dragon or a snake. It was impossible to tell from its strange shape.

The craftsmanship was beautiful, the quality superb, to have survived so many centuries above ground, when usually only excavated artifacts were this well-preserved. It was Scandinavian in origin. She would have known that from the pagan style of it even if David hadn't told her. A sword made for a man of means. A Viking's sword named Blooddrinker's Curse.

Roseleen was a professor of history. The Viking Age might not be her favorite time period, but she was quite familiar with it and its artifacts. Vikings were renowned for giving their weapons names as unusual as the ones they gave themselves. Though she'd never heard a name quite as strange as Blooddrinker's Curse. Nor could she imagine why the original owner would have named it so. It was something she could only wonder about, the reason behind the name lost with the passing of centuries.

And she would wonder, because she was utterly

fascinated by this newest prize for her collection. How many lives had it taken? A few? Countless? The Norsemen were an aggressive, bloodthirsty lot, the marauders of the north seas, ancient hit-and-run artists. And the sword had probably been used in wars for centuries, since it hadn't been buried with its original owner, as was the Viking way. And why hadn't it been? Had that first owner lost it? Had he died not in battle, but peacefully perhaps, gifting his sword to another beforehand? Or perhaps he had died in foreign battle, away from his friends and fellow raiders, in a land that wouldn't observe his pagan customs.

She had endless questions that she knew would never be satisfied. Her frustration with that fact was mild, however, and nothing compared to her pleasure in being the sword's newest owner.

'Blooddrinker's Curse,' she said aloud, unable to resist any longer the urge to hold the ancient sword in her hand. 'You have been retired from what you were created for. You won't be spilling any more blood, but I give you my word you won't be neglected.'

Her fingers closed about the surprisingly warm hilt and lifted the sword from its bed of gold velvet. It was heavier than she would have imagined. She had to quickly bring her other hand up to support her wrist, or she would have dropped it. And as she held the weapon up in front of her, she barely heard the distant crack of thunder. But the lightning that flashed into the room from her bank of windows brought a startled gasp from her, and as if a dozen flashbulbs had gone off in her face, she was temporarily blinded.

The weapon started to tilt. She had to catch the long blade with her hand to keep it from crashing against the credenza. One of those jagged edges caught her finger and she winced, but that was nothing compared to the slamming of her heart because of the near-mishap. Though she could hardly see it, she carefully laid the sword back in its velvet bed, cursing the weatherman as she did so, for his morning prediction of clear skies for today and tomorrow. She didn't relish driving the three hours to Gail's house in the rain.

'Did you hear that, Professor White?' Mr Forbes, the night custodian, poked his head around her door to ask. 'Strangest thing.'

'There's nothing strange about an unexpected storm,' she replied.

She quickly closed the lid of the box, though she couldn't manage to lock it just yet. She recognized Mr Forbes's voice. Seeing him just then was impossible. Only the pool of light around her desk was visible, as the large black dots before her eyes obscured the rest of the room.

'That's just it, Professor. The sky's as clear as it's been all evening. There isn't a cloud in sight.'

She started to argue with the man, recalling now that clap of thunder just before the lightning, but her eyes, trying to focus on what she could see, touched on the exam papers lying ungraded on her desk. She didn't have *time* to debate the peculiarities of the weather, even if she cared to, which she didn't.

'I wouldn't worry about it, Mr Forbes,' she said, dismissing the subject. 'If the storm is blowing away before it even reaches us, that's fine with me.'

'Yes, ma'am,' was his reply as he closed the door again.

Hearing his departure, she took a moment to rub her eyes beneath her wire-rimmed glasses. When she looked down at her desk again, there were a few less dots moving randomly across its surface.

And then she was startled by another male voice, this one deep and unfamiliar, and with a distinct tone of underlying . . . Was it anger? Simple annoyance? Whatever it was, it caused a shiver to slip down her spine.

'You should not have called me, lady.'

2

Since the words she'd heard made not a bit of sense to Roseleen, she had to assume she'd misunderstood. 'Excuse me?' she said as she tried to focus on the shadowy form near the windows.

The light from her desk lamp didn't reach quite that far, and there were still a few spots before her eyes. All she could make out was a large shape, with the well-lit campus grounds apparent through the windows behind it. And as she stared, she noticed the silence. He hadn't answered her. He was just standing there, and another shiver came with the beginning of unease.

She shook it off, annoyed with herself. She was the professor here, the voice of authority. He had to be a student. And Mr Forbes was undoubtedly still within calling distance. But it was disturbing to think that she had been so distracted, she hadn't noticed when he entered the room.

And then she recalled what she had been doing just before Mr Forbes had interrupted her. With a touch of suspicion, she demanded, 'Just how long have you been hiding there in the shadows, Mr—?'

He didn't supply name, didn't answer at all. Her annoyance was focused completely on him now. She stood up to march to the door and switch on the overhead light so she could get a look at her visitor. Light flooded every corner of the large classroom now, and bathed the man's upturned face as he stared up at the light fixture on the ceiling. He was frowning, or was he just squinting?

And he was most definitely a surprise.

A jock, undoubtedly a football player, or soon to be one. Westerley's coach would sell his mother to get that body on his team, even if the man did seem a bit old for the sport, closer to her age or a few years older, thirty maybe. But still a jock, with muscles galore. She had a few in her classes, and for the most part they were more interested in cracking jokes and disrupting the class than in what she had to teach them.

But she was being unfair in stereotyping this man just because he was what her female students would call a muscle-bound hunk. What she found so surprising was the way he was dressed, or not dressed. And then she realized he had to be in costume, and she almost smiled.

The pants he wore were a rough textured leather or suede, made to resemble crudely tanned

hide. The coarse leather strips that criss-crossed
from his ankles up to just above his knees to hold
the material tight to his legs were in the medieval
style known as cross-gartering. A flap of the pants
material crossed over his loins to his hip, with an
extension that circled his back and came around to
join with another strip that tied off just below his
navel holding the pants to his hips. If there were
buttons or a zipper under that flap of cloth, they
were well-concealed.

Roseleen would have to compliment Mr
Hayley's new seamstress for her devotion to small
details. Those pants could have come out of a
museum. No belt loops, of course. And a belt
nearly three inches wide that also assisted in
keeping the pants in place, it fit so tightly to his
narrow waist. It was plain except for the large
circular buckle that was painted to resemble gold.
Hide boots, sewn on the outer seams like
moccasins, were tied off just above his ankles.

He wore no shirt – the reason for her first
surprise, having all those muscles so plainly
visible. Perhaps his costume wasn't quite finished,
or perhaps Mr Hayley's script called for a bare
chest. She had to allow that his was an impressive
bare chest, not overly bulging like that of a weight
lifter, but definitely well-developed, wide, and
finely sprinkled with light brown hair. And makeup had done an excellent job in giving him some

scars across his chest and thick arms, supposedly old battle wounds.

About his neck was a collar or choker of ancient design, a double tier of filigree in the shape of fat connected beads, again made to look like real gold. And he wore his light brown hair long, a bit beyond shoulder-length, which was likely why he'd been picked for the part. He personified an ancient warrior, a Saxon or . . . a Viking . . .

Another shiver passed down her spine. The coincidence was uncanny, that minutes before she had been holding an authentic Viking sword, and here was a drama student in what could definitely be a Viking costume.

And then his head slowly lowered and he was looking straight at her, likely with spots before his eyes, after staring at the light so long. But Roseleen felt something other than unease now. He had a face that was handsome in a harsh way, but that for some reason she found nearly mesmerizing. His brows were almost straight, and thickest toward the ends. His eyes were deep-set and a lovely shade of clear blue. Strong cheekbones surrounded a straight nose. His lips were on the thin side, and he possessed a very masculine, what could be called aggressive, square jaw.

He had the makings of dimples if he could manage a smile. It didn't look as if one would be forthcoming to soften his rather intimidating expression. He was not a happy man. That really had been annoyance or anger she'd heard in his tone.

The silence had gone on too long as they stared at each other. Roseleen was just about to repeat her earlier question when his eyes started a slow path down the length of her body, rested a bit too long on her exposed calves, then just as slowly traveled back up.

Her blush was instantaneous because men didn't do that to her. She downplayed her looks, a habit she had developed in high school when boys had started showing an interest in her. She had preferred not to be bothered then. She definitely didn't want to be bothered now. The way she dressed said so in capital letters.

The glasses she wore were made of ordinary glass; she didn't really need them. She rarely used makeup, and certainly never on campus. Her dresses and skirts she wore an exact inch below her knees, and she favored loose designs, either straight or belted below the waist, not just for unrestricted comfort, but so her curves wouldn't attract roving eyes. Two inches was the maximum she chose for her high heels, and always in plain, square-toed pumps that were as far from sexy as one could get.

She even wore her straight, auburn hair in an old-fashioned bun at her nape. Barry had once said he loved the natural, deep red tints in her hair. After they'd broken up, she had seriously considered dyeing it black.

She had just managed to recover from her blush when her visitor spoke again. 'You should have waited until you were properly dressed to call me, lady.'

Back came the blush, because he actually sounded . . . offended. She even glanced down at herself to see if one of the buttons on her blouse had come undone, if she had lost her belt without realizing it, or if one of her stockings was slipping. But no, she looked as neat and nondescript as she always did in her wrinkle-free polyester.

Her glasses had slid down her nose when she looked down. She jammed them back into place now and put on her sternest teacher-is-displeased expression.

'I'm not here so you can rehearse your script. The drama class is four doors down the hall if you missed it.'

She marched back to her desk and sat down, picked up the top paper on the stack in front of her, and pretended to read through it. But she wasn't reading it. She was waiting to hear the man leave. But she didn't hear him cross the room, didn't hear the door open and close. She was starting to feel uneasy again.

She gave up ignoring him and glanced back. He

was still there, but at least those disturbingly penetrating eyes weren't on her now. He was staring about her room with something that looked like fascination, as if he'd never seen classroom desks and blackboards before, let alone large maps of the world and flashy posters of medieval knights.

His eyes stopped on one of those posters and seemed to light up in recognition. 'Who has such talent, to create such a likeness of Lord William?'

In his questionable surprise, she detected a distinct foreign accent that she couldn't quite place. She followed his gaze to a poster of a man photographed in the long robes of the tenth century. 'Lord who?'

Those blue eyes came back to her. 'William the Bastard,' he said, his tone implying now that she shouldn't have had to ask.

There was only one William the Bastard who was renowned, the one who had changed the history of England, known also as William the Conquerer. How could anyone see a likeness between William as he had been depicted in the few tapestries that had survived from the eleventh century and that young poster hunk whose only resemblance was possibly in the brawn of his body . . . ?

Her brows snapped together. He was pulling her leg. Either that or trying out new lines that supported his character. She didn't appreciate either.

'Look, Mr . . . ?'

He didn't overlook the question in her tone this time. 'I am named Thorn.'

Roseleen stiffened. How many times had she heard the puns, 'Your bush could use a few thorns, Rosie,' or 'I'd like to be the thorn in your bush, Rose,' the crude, sexy innuendos of young boys that she'd thought she'd heard the last of after her college days.

It occurred to her then that this man wasn't a lost drama student. Someone had more than likely set him up to play a joke on her, and the only instigator that came to mind was Barry Horton. Perhaps it was his way of rubbing it in that he'd earned his professorship. And it made sense. The accent – Barry *did* associate with the few foreign teachers at Westerley and their friends. It probably made him feel sophisticated.

The anger she'd felt in the dean's office earlier returned in full force. That thief, that liar, that piece of – her father would be turning in his grave if he could read her thoughts. She squelched them, knowing that name-calling was beneath her. She couldn't help the glare, however, that she turned on Barry's idea of a joke.

'Mr Thorn—'

'Nay, Thorn is my given name. Thorn

Blooddrinker. Only you English put a *mister* before an honest name.'

My God, he'd heard her talking to the sword and was using it to further his joke. Her embarrassment was now complete, because he'd likely be repeating what had happened here, word for word, to her ex-fiancé.

'We *Americans* can settle for *just* mister, which I'm about to do. You can leave now, mister, and tell Mr Horton that his little joke is as immature as he is.'

'Thank you, lady. You are wise to send me back. Wiser still would be not to call me again.'

She snorted to herself. She wasn't even going to try to decipher those peculiar statements. She'd dismissed him. She proceeded to ignore him again, returning her gaze to the exam paper she was still holding. But she would be calling for campus security if he wasn't gone in the next two minutes.

And then she started again when another crack of thunder sounded in the distance. Recalling what had happened before, she quickly closed her eyes this time, but it only helped a little. The flash of lightning filled her classroom again, and was still quite bright through her closed eyelids.

There weren't quite as many spots before her eyes, however, so when she opened them, she was able to see outside her windows the campus beyond, which was still undisturbed by wind or rain. She frowned. The stillness meant nothing, of course. Within seconds, a downpour could occur. Damn weatherman. Was it too much to ask for an accurate forecast with today's technology? Apparently the vagaries of Mother Nature refused to cooperate.

But at least a glance around the classroom showed her that her unwelcome visitor had departed. She got back to work, blocking out the picture of Barry Horton laughing when he learned how well his little joke had worked. She was still as gullible as when he'd first met her, when she'd believed all his lies and professions of love.

Her only consolation from that debacle was that she'd stuck to the morals her father had imparted to her. Barry Horton might have gotten a ring on her finger, he might have stolen two years' worth of her research, but he hadn't managed to get into her bed. Perhaps she'd known, on a subconscious level, that he wasn't sincere. Or perhaps her heart hadn't been involved as much as she'd thought. But at least she did have that one fact to be grateful for. Small consolation, considering what she'd lost, but better than nothing.

3

'Well, are you going to show it to me or not?'

Roseleen grinned as she joined Gail at the foot of the bed where the long wooden case had been laid on top of a bedding chest. She had arrived so late at her friend's house last night that there had been no time for them to talk. They'd just finished breakfast now, and she'd told Gail that the long-awaited antique had finally arrived, that she even had it with her. Gail knew all about the sword, but then Gail knew everything about Roseleen.

They had grown up together in the same small town in Maine, attended the same schools, even the same college. For as far back as Roseleen could remember, Gail had been a part of her life and her very best friend. No one knew her better than Gail, not even David, because she didn't share all confidences with him, whereas she did with Gail.

They weren't at all alike. Roseleen was auburn-haired, with chocolate-brown eyes. Gail was blond and blue-eyed. Roseleen was tall, bookish, and basically shy, while Gail was short, had been chubby all her life, and was afraid of nothing. They complemented each other, because what one lacked in personality, the other possessed.

Neither had dated much in high school, Gail not for lack of trying. She'd just had a little problem with rejection that had come too often because she hadn't been remotely pretty in her teen years, retaliating with deadly insults that had kept any boys who might have been interested away.

Roseleen, on the other hand, just hadn't had time for boys. She'd known what she wanted to do with her life, and getting the best grades was part of it. Unfortunately, her intelligence wasn't on the remarkable side, so she'd had to study much harder than everyone else to get the grades *she* wanted. She was where she was today because she had worked toward it all her life. But all that studying hadn't allowed for an active social life.

Gail had grown into a little beauty, still on the chubby side, but she was now comfortable with that, and it showed. She had dropped out of college to get married after her second year. It had been the third marriage proposal she'd received.

Roseleen would never have considered doing such a thing, even if she'd had some offers. She didn't have any. Boys came to her to help them study. The few she had dated found out quickly enough that she was all for having a good time – if it didn't include groping in a backseat. Since they'd rather be groping, they found other girls to date.

The first man she had ever taken a real interest in had been Barry Horton. Gail had feigned a collapse when she'd been told, screaming, 'Finally!' because Roseleen was twenty-six at the time. He'd started teaching at Westerley the year after she did, and she was drawn to him because of their common interest in history.

Westerley, along with a number of other prestigious schools, had courted her during her last year of college, because of her outstanding grades. She had chosen Westerley because it was in a small town, which she preferred, because it was only a three-hour drive from where Gail had moved to, and because she'd been promised tenure within her first year there – if she fulfilled all expectations, which she did.

When she began dating Barry not long after he joined the staff, she found out that not all men were interested in groping first, conversation second. Barry wooed her intellectually, which was why she'd liked him so much, and why it hadn't taken her long to think she was in love with him.

His proposal had come much later, but not long after she'd agreed to marry him, he'd stolen her research notes on the book she was writing about the Middle Ages. She hadn't even known it, had been devastated to think that two years' worth of work had been accidentally tossed out in the trash as he'd suggested, until her book was published a year later, under Barry's name.

He'd done his best to get her to marry him before the publication date. But she'd put it off for one reason or another – if she were fanciful, she'd think a fairy godmother had been guiding her in those days, to keep her from making an even bigger mistake.

She'd taken Barry to court, of course, and had nearly lost her job because of it, because the dean had recommended she drop the case and she'd refused. She'd lost the case, but only after it was implied that she was the bitter, deserted lover, a vindictive woman merely trying to get even. Lies, all of it, except maybe for the bitter part, but she'd been unable to prove otherwise. Barry got to reap the rewards of her work, but she'd learned a valuable lesson from him. He'd taught her never to trust a man again.

That had been six months ago. Since then, she had seriously been considering giving up her tenure at Westerley College and moving elsewhere. She didn't even want to be in the same state as Barry Horton anymore, let alone the same campus, where it was inevitable that she would run into him frequently – and he could get away with tasteless little jokes like the one he'd pulled yesterday.

She would make her decision this summer,

when she visited Cavenaugh Cottage in England, her one legacy from her great-grandmother. She had been going there each summer ever since it had become hers five years ago. It was there that she did most of her research. It was there that she'd first heard about Blooddrinker's Curse.

Now, as she opened the box that contained the sword, she was experiencing the same anticipation and excitement that she had felt last night. But she felt something else too, that prompted her to tell her friend, 'Look, but don't touch.'

Gail laughed. 'You sound like you're talking about a man, Rosie.'

Roseleen snorted. 'You know me better than that.'

But Roseleen couldn't imagine why she'd said what she did. It had just come out automatically – and it smacked of possessiveness, something she'd never experienced before. She was proud of her collection, yes, but she didn't guard it jealously.

But instead of amending her statement, she offered instead, 'This one is so old, I worry about it even being exposed to the air, let alone the oil in our hands. Silly, I know; it's survived this long. But I won't stop worrying until I get it safely behind glass.'

'I don't blame you. A deadly thing like that definitely needs your protection.' Gail said it straight-faced, but after a second, they were both laughing. 'It is beautiful, though, isn't it? It almost compels you to want to touch it – hurry up and close the box before I can't resist.'

Gail was teasing, but Roseleen did close the box and lock it. If anyone was under a compulsion, it was she, for the urge had been there again, to lift the sword in her hands – the same powerful urge she'd felt last night. She decided she was being fanciful again. There was no other explanation.

'Now, speaking of "knowing you better than that," ' Gail said, 'trouble is, I do. You've got the antique sword you've been after for nearly four years now, your career is just where you want it, so *when* are you going to do something about your nonexistent social life?'

Roseleen flinched mentally, having known this subject would pop up eventually while she was there. 'I tried that, remember?'

'Come on, Rosie, not every man you meet is going to be a jerk like Barry. And you tried an intellectual. Now how about a sportsman or even a laborer, a man who works with his muscles instead of his brain, someone who won't give a hoot about the book you're writing so you won't have to worry about that again – and will toss you into bed on a regular basis, emphasis on *toss*, by the way.'

Roseleen had to smile. Gail did like her macho men. But she hedged. 'It hasn't been long enough since I ended things with Barry—'

'It's been *too* long—'

'I've been looking—' Roseleen began to lie.

Gail's snort cut in this time. 'Where? On campus? You don't *go* anywhere else. And look at you. You're working too hard, Rosie. You've got bags under your eyes, for crying out loud. All work and no play—'

'Oh, stop. I'm sure you're going to mother me to death this weekend, and force me to sleep half the time I'm here.'

'Are you kidding? I'm going to be dragging you to every social event I can think of. *One* of us is going to find you a man. You can catch up on your sleep when you go home. And you better. Next time you visit, I don't want to see you looking like you're about ready to keel over.'

Roseleen sighed. 'Maybe I have been putting in a few too many hours on my book lately, on top of the schoolwork I bring home. But the semester is almost over. I'll get all the rest I need in England this summer.'

'Oh sure,' Gail said skeptically, knowing Roseleen too well. 'Between hunting down new antiques over there and doing your research, you'll be running yourself ragged as usual. When does that leave time for a social life, let alone some needed rest?'

'I'll get the rest, I promise. As for the social life . . . I'm still not ready to take that risk again, Gail.

Maybe when I get back from England.'

'And what if you come across the ideal man in England? Don't go putting this on a time schedule like you do everything else.'

'*Okay* – I'll keep an open mind about it,' Roseleen said, just to end the subject. 'If I bump into Mr Wonderful, I won't ignore him.'

'You promise?'

Roseleen nodded grudgingly, not that it would matter. The few men she had been really attracted to over the years had barely noticed her. And besides, she just wasn't ready for another relationship, not when it would involve trust, because Barry had depleted all the trust she had to spare. Maybe someday . . .

4

'I can't believe you brought it with you,' David said as he filled his glass with Scotch at the small bar in the corner of the spacious drawing room. 'If I had known you were going to do that, I would simply have shipped it here to Cavenaugh to await your arrival.'

Roseleen couldn't quite meet her brother's gaze and toyed with the ice in her tea instead. She wasn't going to own up to the power that sword seemed to have over her. He'd never believe it, and she couldn't put a name to it anyway. She had simply been unable to leave Blooddrinker's Curse behind in the States.

She'd missed her first flight to England and had arrived in London a day late, because after she had left for the airport the first time, she'd turned around and gone back home to get the sword. For some unaccountable reason, she felt as if she had to keep it near her, at least have it in the same country that she happened to be in.

But David was due some sort of explanation, so

she said now, 'I wouldn't have been able to wait that extra month until the summer break allowed me to come here, just to have my first look at it. And it isn't all that odd that I'd bring it with me. Considering how valuable it is, and the fact that security systems aren't infallible, particularly my system, which is so outdated, I would have spent my entire vacation here worrying about it.

'Besides, I had new neighbors moving in next door that I hadn't met yet. Their moving van arrived only a few days ago. And you know how new neighbors always make me nervous. You never know if you're getting the next serial killer or your next best friend.'

He grinned as he lifted his glass to toast her. 'I was only teasing, Rosie. I know how eagerly you awaited that sword. I wouldn't be surprised if you tucked it into bed with you each night.'

He was still teasing, but she had to fight down a blush, because she had come close to doing just that on a few occasions this last month. Her attachment to this particular antique was absurd, unhealthy even.

She had other old weapons; the previous star of her collection dated from the fifteenth century, a magnificent foot-long dagger whose scabbard had two pockets to hold two tiny jewel-hilted eating utensils. She loved that dagger, but she'd never had her emotions thrown into such turmoil over it, as was happening with Blooddrinker's Curse. She was treating the sword as if it were her child, for God's sake, worrying about it being out of her sight, fretting over anyone else's touching it, fearful that it might get damaged or lost.

She had been in a state of panic nearly the entire flight over, imagining it being thrown around by careless baggage handlers, despite the fact that she'd crated it with such meticulous care. And getting through customs had been a nightmare, waiting for some stranger to insist on opening the crate and – but she'd been lucky. The sword had passed through unmolested, only one of her three suitcases drawing inspection. But she was definitely going to ask David to send the sword back to the States for her on his wife's private jet. She wasn't going to go through that nerve-wracking experience again if she could help it.

David would probably say that what she was feeling was perfectly normal, after she'd waited years to obtain the thing. He would even assure her that it was only temporary, that her worries would settle down, given a little time. She wasn't going to give him a chance to say so. She just couldn't bring herself to admit to what had the earmarks of an obsession, even to this brother of her heart. She didn't understand it, so how could she expect him to?

She offered him a smile to acknowledge his

teasing, and waited for him to join her on the sofa. He'd picked her up at the airport that morning and had driven her straight to Cavenaugh Cottage. His wife, Lydia, was presently in France meeting with the decorators who were handling her newest acquisition, a chateau near Troyes. Lydia wasn't expected back until the end of the week, so David would be spending a few days with Roseleen at the cottage.

Though there was no reason for them to resemble each other, not sharing the same blood-lines, merely the same household as children, ironically, there was a slight resemblance between Roseleen and David. Anyone who saw them together would swear they were brother and sister, and they didn't bother to correct the misconception.

That David had retained the name he was born with, David Mullen, only made people assume that Roseleen had married at some time or other. It was the fact that their last names were different that had allowed David to step in to deal with the sword's previous owner, when Roseleen had failed to get anywhere with the man.

They both had deep, clear chocolate-brown eyes without a fleck of gold to lighten them. And although David's dark brown hair lacked the soft reddish highlights that Roseleen's had, they both had high cheekbones, the same oval shape to their eyes, and brows that slanted at the same angles, and they were both tall and slim of build.

She had been five years old when David had lost his folks and had come to live with her family. He had been only seven at the time. As far as she was concerned, he was her brother, and he felt exactly the same way. Still, there were certain things you just didn't feel comfortable discussing with siblings, or best friends for that matter. That you might be having a nervous breakdown was one of them.

Not to change the subject, but to redirect it, Roseleen said, 'I feel somewhat guilty about owning Blooddrinker's Curse, you know, because of its beauty and historical value. I keep thinking it belongs in a museum, where everyone could have the chance to be awed by it.'

David lifted a brow, a grin lurking in his expression. 'Thinking about donating it?'

Roseleen laughed. 'Not on your life. I'll live with the guilt, thank you.'

'As it happens, I mentioned that to Sir Isaac – after the sword was in my possession. The old guy really was eccentric. He said he couldn't trust it to a museum, where some woman might get her hands on it.'

'Did he ever tell you why he wouldn't sell it to a woman?' she asked.

'He said he didn't know.'

'*What?*'

David chuckled. 'That was my own reaction. But Sir Isaac claims his father left him the sword, with the dire warning that if he didn't want to spend eternity suffering the agonies of the damned, he'd make sure no woman ever got her hands on it. Apparently, Dearborn's father had had to sign an affidavit similar to the one I signed when he first came into possession of the sword, and the owner before him as well. Dearborn had no information earlier than that – at least about the previous owners. But I'll tell you something, Rosie, Sir Isaac didn't come right out and admit it, but from the way he acted and the things he said, I'd swear he really believes that sword is cursed.'

'Just because of its name?'

David shrugged. 'You have to admit it's strange, all those owners being so fearful and protective of the sword. That fear had to be based on something.'

'On legend, no doubt, that is centuries old and so obscure, it didn't survive the last few. You know how superstitious and fanciful medieval folk were. Pagan gods, sorcerers and witches, demons and devils, even elves and fairies, all held great significance back then, because the people really believed in them. And that sword has had a thousand years to gain notoriety. It's too bad the curse or whatever superstition was attached to it didn't get passed along with the sword. I'd give anything to know what it was.'

'Whatever it was, it's a pretty good guess that it involved a woman, or women.'

Roseleen nodded in agreement. 'Which is strange in itself, if you think about it. Historically, with only a few exceptions, women aren't usually associated with weapons of any kind. Queens might have commanded armies, but they didn't bear arms themselves.' And then she grinned. 'Again, with a few notable exceptions.'

'Ah, now I have it. Did you get the urge to go to war when you touched the sword?'

She laughed and was still smiling when she answered, 'Not war, actually, though I did have the urge to use that sword on old Barry when he arranged for a rather tasteless joke on me to celebrate his obtaining tenure.'

David frowned, since she hadn't mentioned that to him before. She'd almost forgotten the incident herself and was no longer embarrassed to relate what had happened.

'What'd the bastard do this time?' David demanded.

'Somehow he must have found out that I'd finally gotten the sword, or was soon to receive it, because he sent a young man to me dressed in Viking costume, who was very good at pretending to be the real thing. He called himself Thorn Blooddrinker.'

'*Thorn* Blooddrinker?'

Her expression suddenly mirrored his own disgust as she recalled *that* part of the joke. David knew about all those crude rosebush innuendos associated with her name that she'd endured over the years. But no one had ever actually tried to claim that his name was Thorn. After all, what parents in their right minds would stick their son with such a name?

'Exactly,' she said. 'It's my guess that Barry had been planning his little joke for a long time, and he happened to see me lugging the sword into my classroom the day it arrived. I didn't have enough time to take it home after picking it up at the post office. If he saw me with that crate, it wouldn't have been hard for him to guess what it was, and that would have given him ample time to set up the joke for that evening.'

'Just what one might expect from a man devoid of principles and—'

'Shh,' she cut in when he started getting red in the face. David despised Barry as much as she did. 'He'll get his one day – somehow. I'm a firm believer in justice catching up to those who escape it the first time around.'

Roseleen changed the subject then, until David got his anger under control and put all thoughts of Barry Horton from his mind. When she had him laughing again, an easy enough task – she had a droll sense of humor that only those close to her ever saw – she got back to the subject that she was presently fascinated with.

'So tell me, why did Sir Isaac sell the sword at all, if he was so worried about some silly curse?'

'Because he *was* worried about the curse. He doesn't think he has too many years left, and he has only daughters who will be inheriting his estate. He wanted it sold and away from them before he died.'

She shook her head. 'It's amazing that someone could believe in curses in this day and age.'

'Ah, but to your benefit,' he said, grinning. 'If Sir Isaac didn't believe that the sword is cursed, then he never would have sold it. Yet here we sit, proof that there's nothing to fear from it. The curse, or whatever it is, hasn't caught up with me for turning the sword over to a woman, and it doesn't look like you've turned to stone yet, though I do notice a gray tinge on your—'

He stopped, laughing, when she tossed one of the sofa pillows at him.

5

When Roseleen had inherited Cavenaugh Cottage, she had imagined a quaint, cozy little two- or three-room house covered in English ivy. It had been a shock to find instead a fourteen-room house that fit her description of a mansion, replete with a carriage house converted to a four-car garage, a separate caretaker's house more the size of what she'd been expecting, and four acres of land.

She had been fortunate that John Humes and his wife, Elizabeth, had more or less come with the house. They had worked for her great-grandmother for nearly twenty years, and although they weren't young anymore, they took excellent care of the house and grounds.

The cottage was over two hundred years old. That it had been thoroughly refurbished in the last ten years was the only reason Roseleen hadn't been forced to sell it yet. She'd never be able to afford the repairs on such a large house when they became necessary, as they were bound to, nor

44

would she let it fall to ruin just to hold on to it. But that day hadn't come yet, and in the meantime, she enjoyed the house for its historical beauty, if not its great size.

She hadn't known her great-grandmother, Maureen, very well. The lady had come to the States to visit her grandson's family only twice when Roseleen was still a child. Her own family had never been able to afford the luxury of a trip to England. But all of Maureen's personal belongings had come with the house, fascinating journals from her younger years, an attic full of antique furniture, outdated clothes and jewelry. It had been a treasure trove for someone who loved old things as much as Roseleen did.

She had taken the master bedroom for herself, a room that was bigger than her living and dining rooms combined at home. Even the bed in it was an antique four-poster, the handmade comforter probably fifty or more years old itself. Except for the belongings she had brought with her, and the typewriter she had bought during her first trip to England and left here for her research, everything in the room was older than she was – in particular, Blooddrinker's Curse.

She glanced at the wooden case as she passed through the bedroom to the bath. The urge to go straight to the box and open it wasn't as strong here as it had been in the States. For an entire month, she had fought that urge, determined not to let it control her. Only when the urge wasn't as strong would she allow herself to look at the sword.

Today had been the only exception. When she'd unpacked it here at Cavenaugh, she'd had to make sure it had survived the flight without any damage. But she still hadn't touched it again. That was the strongest urge, the one she fought the hardest.

Fighting her desire to touch the ancient weapon had become part of her obsession. She'd even refused to put the sword in the expensive glass display she'd had made for it, which was presently hanging in the center of her collection at home, just waiting for her newest acquisition. She wouldn't put Blooddrinker where she could view it at any time – until she no longer wanted to view it *all* the time.

The bathrooms in the cottage had been converted to modern plumbing some time during the present century. The master bath had both a shower and a tub. As much as Roseleen liked a good soak, she was too tired to indulge in one tonight. Jet lag was catching up to her. She was surprised she'd lasted through the evening. Even David had already gone to bed.

So she was in and out of the shower in fewer than ten minutes, and with a thick towel wrapped around her, she headed for the old-fashioned wardrobe to search out one of the nightgowns she'd unpacked earlier. She tossed a baby-blue silk one on the bed, where it settled in a pool next to the mahogany sword case. She was still too damp to slip into silk yet, so she moved to the vanity to brush out her hair first.

In the mirror, she could see the bed, and the case lying on it, and it occurred to her suddenly that she had no desire to open it just then. She was probably too tired. Or maybe the sword was more comfortable here in England, back where it came from, and so was exerting less power over her – oh, God, she was getting fanciful again, attributing feelings and motives to the sword now. This was *her* problem, all in her mind, and she *would* beat it.

But she had promised herself that she could examine the sword again, once she wasn't feeling compelled to do so. She smiled at her reflection in the mirror, in no hurry to claim her reward, and relieved that it was so. But even if she was feeling indifferent due to exhaustion, a promise was a promise. So when she finished with her hair, leaving it loose and flowing down her back, she fetched the key from her purse and moved to the bed.

In only a few seconds, the sword was in her hand again, the hilt as warm as she remembered it had been the last time she'd held it. And then strangely coincidentally, she heard something she remembered hearing before, a crack of thunder in the distance, and even though the room was well-lit, there was a slight flash as lightning illuminated the backyard on which the two windows in the room faced, penetrating even the curtains covering them.

She glanced toward the windows, frowning, because if a storm was coming she'd have to close them. The windows had no eaves to keep the rain out, not with the mammoth attic above this floor, which had ceilings high enough for it to be converted into an entire third floor if she had the inclination or the wherewithal to do it.

But her eyes didn't quite reach the windows, and a small shriek of fright accompanied the sight of a man standing in the corner of her room. And not just any man. It was *him*, the one who called himself Thorn Blooddrinker – Barry Horton's idea of a joke. Impossible! She blinked, but he was still there. And her beleaguered, tired mind just wouldn't accept it.

Barry wouldn't carry a joke this far, to include paying for this man to come all the way to England. Would he? On the other hand, if the man had been scheduled to come there anyway, for some other reason, then Barry would jump at the chance to continue his little joke, since it had worked so well the first time he'd arranged it.

It was definitely the same man who had shown up in her classroom that night. His face, his body too, for that matter, were unforgettable, and just as fascinating as she'd found them before. She was attracted to him on a purely physical level, and not at all happy with that realization.

It wasn't something that happened to her often. The few times she'd been drawn to a man because of his looks, nothing had come of it, because the attraction wasn't mutual. And there had always been that tiny bit of curiosity in wondering what it would be like, having the chemistry just right. But not with *this* man.

He was dressed a little differently than before. Not in a normal fashion, however. He was still in costume, but – tattered was how she would describe his new apparel.

The pants and boots were the same as before, or very similar, but he was wearing a long-sleeved tunic now in a somewhat white color, loosely belted about the waist and completely ripped down the front. It took her a moment more to realize that the dark spots she was seeing on the cloth could be blood, and another moment for her to register that there was blood trickling from the corner of his mouth.

He'd been fighting, and the moment she drew that conclusion, another leaped into her mind. 'Oh, God, you didn't hurt David when you broke in here, did you?'

'David? It was my brother, Thor, I was beating. 'Tis rare he will fight me anymore. Send me back *now*, woman. I wish to finish—'

She had failed to note that the anger was there again in his expression. She couldn't mistake it in his voice, however, because his unusual accent was more pronounced with it. Joke or no, it was disconcerting to have a man of his size in her bedroom, and sounding so vastly annoyed – with her. She would, in fact, have been truly frightened, if she weren't so angry herself.

So she cut him off with 'Put a lid on it, mister. I don't care how long it took you to rehearse those lines, you're not playing to an appreciative audience. This foolishness has gone too far. I'll have you and Barry both brought up on charges if you persist—'

He did some interrupting himself. 'You summoned me, lady. I do not come willingly to your command.'

Her eyes narrowed on him. 'So you're not going to drop it? Do you really think I find this amusing? Barry has misinformed you if he told you I would.'

His expression suddenly changed to one of curiosity. 'You have berries that speak here?'

That caught her off-guard. 'What?'

'I am partial to blue.'

'Blue—?'

A sound of pure frustration escaped her when

she realized he was talking about blueberries. But before she could verbalize it, he said, 'On second thought, lady, if you have summoned me for a bedding, my brother can wait.'

He was staring at the towel around her as he said that, and the few inches of her upper thighs that were visible to him from where she stood on the other side of the bed. Her face flooded with color over what he had just plainly insinuated.

She had been holding the sword so that it rested against the mattress. It was purely an instinctive reaction for her to lift it up in front of her. His reaction was demoralizing.

He laughed, his head thrown back, the sound one of genuine amusement.

And when that amusement wound down, he was still grinning at her. He *did* have dimples, she noted irrelevantly. And he didn't mind telling her what he found so funny.

'My sword cannot draw my blood. Only the gods can do that now – and Wolfstan the Mad, if he ever finds me.'

Roseleen heard nothing beyond the words 'my sword,' and every bit of the possessiveness that she had developed for the weapon in question came rushing to the fore. 'Your sword? *Your* sword! You've got two seconds to get out of my house, or I'm calling the police!'

'No bedding then?'

'Get out!'

He shrugged. He grinned again. And then he disappeared before her eyes – and again, thunder cracked in the distance with a flash of lightning on its tail.

For five minutes, she continued to stare at the space where he had stood. Her heart was pounding. Her thoughts were frozen. Her skin was covered in gooseflesh.

When her mind began to function again, she carefully put the sword away and tucked the box beneath her bed. She put her nightgown on, yanking the towel out from under it only after it fell to her knees, something she'd never done before – or felt she had to do.

Her eyes kept returning to that empty spot in the corner that remained empty. Even after she crawled into bed, she still sat there and stared at it for a long while. She didn't even consider turning off the lights that night.

When she did finally lie back against her pillows, it was with a weary sigh. In the morning, she'd have a logical explanation for what had just occurred. In the morning, she wouldn't be too tired to figure it out. Just now, all she could think was that she really was losing her mind.

6

A dream. Roseleen had her explanation for what had occurred last night – or rather, what she'd thought had occurred. Somehow her subconscious mind had combined her curiosity about the sword with Barry's joke to give her some answers, but as dreams go, she hadn't gotten around to asking any questions.

A dream. It was the simplest explanation, and the most logical. It was a shame, though, that the one time she got a handsome man into one of her dreams, she had to go and get all huffy and send him away. Curiosity about the sword wasn't the only curiosity he could have appeased, and he'd been willing to appease that other curiosity. He'd even mentioned it: bedding her. All she would have had to do was say, 'Yes, that would be nice,' and . . .

She smiled to herself, thinking about it. You couldn't find much safer sex than sex in a dream. Morals, guilt, regret, even your own personality, all could be set aside while you enjoyed doing something that you wouldn't consider doing outside a dream. But she, of course, had to remain true to form and bring her morals, her indignation, and her testy temper along in what had to be one of her most unusual and interesting dreams ever. Truly a shame.

Roseleen was satisfied with her explanation – but only after she'd spent an hour thoroughly searching the bedroom for wires and hidden cameras that might have been capable of projecting a lifelike image into her room. She found nothing out of the ordinary. She hadn't really thought she would.

Getting that complicated was beyond Barry Horton's imagination, after all, not to mention that he was too tightfisted to cover the expenses for the kind of sophisticated equipment it would take to pull off such a hoax. His idea of an extravagant gift during their courtship was to bring her whatever flowers happened to be in bloom on his route to campus. Heaven forbid he should ever enter a florist's shop. The less it cost, the better, was his motto.

Obviously, his joke had begun and ended in the States, a onetime shot for him to get a good laugh. But she supposed it had made a bigger impact on her than she'd thought, for her to dream something similar a month later, and to have her subconscious recall every exact detail about Barry's handsome accomplice.

David was leaving her his London car for the duration of her vacation, which meant that she had to take him to the train station tomorrow. Today he was accompanying her to the next town, where there was a large grocery that imported many of the American staples they were both used to at home. She drove in order to get used to driving on the opposite side of the road again, with someone in the car to remind her if she happened to forget, which she usually did for the first few days each time she came here.

On the way back to the cottage, she decided to tell David about her strange dream. When she finished, he was grinning at her.

'Blooddrinker's original owner, and you kicked him out before you could ask him about the curse?'

'I didn't realize I was having a dream, David. I thought I was experiencing another break-in by Barry's friend, who only *pretends* to be the owner of that sword.' And then she grinned herself. 'Besides, had I asked him, whatever answer he gave would actually come from my own subconscious, and I still haven't a clue what that supposed curse is all about.'

'Ah, but it would have been interesting to find out what your subconscious would have come up with for a plausible answer. An amazing thing, the subconscious. Those who believe in reincarnation say every life you've ever lived is buried some-where deep inside it.'

Roseleen rolled her eyes and ended up swerving off the curve on the narrow country road. By the time she got the car back in her lane and they both finished laughing over the minor mishap, she said, 'It's bad enough that we're discussing a ridiculous curse. Let's leave reincarnation out of it, if you please.'

'By all means, but you know, that thunder and lightning you mentioned wasn't part of your dream. I was just dozing off myself last night when it woke me.' She was starting to frown when he added, 'But then sounds that we hear while we're asleep can be transferred to our dreams.'

'True,' she replied, yet his remark made her realize something that hadn't occurred to her before. Both times the Viking had appeared to her, in her classroom and in her dream last night, it had been right after she'd touched the sword. And she'd been under a damn compulsion to touch that sword ever since she got it. Was it possible—?

She shook herself mentally to stop the fanciful direction her thoughts were taking. And to prove just how fanciful they were, as soon as they reached the cottage, she left David to bring in the groceries while she marched straight upstairs to her bedroom. Without any hesitation this time, she slid the box out from under her bed, placed it on the mattress, and opened it, then lifted the hilt of the sword just enough to get her fingers around it.

The thunder cracked. She didn't look toward the windows to see if lightning was going to follow. She looked straight at the corner where Thorn Blooddrinker had stood last night, and there he was again, this time with a fat poultry bone in his fist that was heading toward his mouth.

Oh, God, this wasn't happening. She didn't have the ghost of the sword's original owner standing in her bedroom, in broad daylight. Not a pretend Viking, but a real one. A real *dead* one. A ghost. She didn't believe in ghosts – but what else could he be? And somehow, he was connected to the sword . . . *his* sword. No, this simply *wasn't* happening.

His eyes were already narrowing on her in that accusing way she was beginning to realize meant he didn't appreciate being there. 'You have taken me from Odin's feast, lady. Send me back, or feed me, for I have a large appetite that needs appeasing right quickly.'

'Go away,' she said in a very, very small voice.

His eyes narrowed a little more. In one bite, he ripped all the meat from the bone he was holding, then tossed the bone behind him, where it hit the wall and fell to the floor. He didn't disappear. He stood there and chewed the meat, then licked his fingers.

'If I did not enjoy one of Odin's feasts so well, I would stay, for you are vexing me sorely with these summonings. But I give you fair warning, lady. You can send me back and I will go – but only because I choose to go. If I chose to stay, there is naught that you can say or do to be rid of me.' And then he grinned suddenly, again showing her those beguiling dimples that sent a giddy rush of feeling straight to her belly – a sensation at odds with her present fear. 'Summon me again, lady, and I may prove it to you.'

He was gone, just as he'd come, instantly, no slow fading away, wisps of smoke, or eerie sounds one might associate with ghosts – unless one could associate thunder and lightning with ghosts, because *those* both came again with his departure. But he was definitely gone and Roseleen was left staring at the poultry bone he'd left behind, still lying on the floor where it had fallen.

A ghost who could leave things behind? A ghost who could eat – with a large appetite? But she didn't believe in ghosts any more than she believed in curses.

She started to laugh, but it ended in a groan. She was still dreaming, obviously. She let the sword drop back onto the velvet lining, slammed the box shut, and curled up on her bed – to hurry the process of waking up.

7

Roseleen went downstairs in somewhat of a daze, holding the poultry bone, which had still been in her bedroom when she woke from her nap, between two fingers as if it were a dead rat she had to dispose of. She was heading for the kitchen to do just that, and that's where she found David, starting to prepare their dinner. His back was to her, and an array of vegetables was spread out on the counter beside him.

Seeing him, she said the first thing that came to her mind. 'Pinch me, David. I think I'm still dreaming.'

He turned, took one look at her, and said, 'For God's sake, you look like you've seen a ghost.'

She almost laughed, had an hysterical urge to do so, but managed to restrain it. That he happened to choose *that* phrase to describe her pallor was just too ironic for her present state of mind. But fortunately, his eyes dropped to what she was holding so far out in front of her, and he added, 'Did Elizabeth's cat misplace that?' jolting her back to what was sane and rational.

Of course, another logical explanation. Elizabeth Humes had a cat that got into the house occasionally, and cats loved bones just as much as dogs did, poultry bones in particular. She wasn't going to quibble about the fact that she hadn't seen that bone until she'd seen it in *his* hand. Obviously, she must have noticed it before she took the nap she just woke from, but was too tired to register what it was, otherwise, it wouldn't have been included in her dream.

Now she walked over to the kitchen trashcan and dropped the bone into it. She was smiling when she asked David, 'Need some help?'

He grunted at the way she had of ignoring subjects she didn't want to discuss. She treated them as if they hadn't been mentioned.

'I'm glad to see some color back in your cheeks, but what I need is to hear why you were so pale a second ago. You're not getting sick, are you, Rosie?'

'No – at least, I don't think so.' And then she shrugged, deciding it wouldn't hurt to admit, 'I just had another dream, this one almost identical to the one I had last night, with that Viking ghost, Thorn Blooddrinker, materializing in the corner of my bedroom again, the sound of thunder accompanying his appearance.'

'Why do you call him a ghost now?'

60

'He's a thousand years old,' she replied, 'and yet he's showing up in this century, even if only in my dreams. What else would that make him?'

'Immortal?' She gave him the snort that remark deserved, which made him chuckle before he asked, 'So, did you question him about the curse this time?'

'I was too frightened by his appearance again even to think of the curse. I simply told him to go away. But – he did volunteer a warning before he vanished, something about how I could send him away and he would go, but only because he wanted to go. If he chose to stay, he said there was nothing I could do to get rid of him.'

'At least until you woke up.'

That simple statement brought a wide grin to her lips, and some very definite relief. She hadn't realized she was still wound up so tight with nervous tension until it drained from her now.

'It's too bad I didn't think of that while I was having the dream.'

'Now that you have, maybe it will occur to you next time, and you can—'

'I do *not* intend to have that particular dream again, David,' she interrupted him, her tone more determined than certain.

'*If* you do, keep him around long enough to find out about the curse. I'm curious to know what your subconscious will come up with for an answer.'

61

Roseleen wasn't. Her conscious thoughts had become too fanciful as it was, since she'd had that first dream. She would just as soon not know how much more fanciful her subconscious could get.

'And by the way,' David continued, 'I wouldn't be surprised if it wasn't the thunder this afternoon that triggered your dream again. The storm that didn't show up last night has arrived, if you haven't noticed.'

She hadn't noticed, but she looked out the kitchen window now to see that it was indeed raining, and no small drizzle but a downpour. Her smile, on the other hand, was as bright as sunshine.

'I never thought I'd welcome the sight of rain,' she said, 'but I have to tell you, having thunder and lightning show up in cloudless skies twice lately was beginning to get a little spooky. At least this time it appears to have heralded a perfectly normal storm.'

He burst out laughing. 'Getting a little superstitious, are we?'

She blushed slightly but still grinned. 'Maybe just a little.'

Somehow, she managed to put thoughts of ghosts and Vikings and thousand-year-old curses from her mind for the rest of the day, so she could enjoy David's company while she had it. It wasn't easy.

She would be starting her research next week. She had museums to visit, as well as bookstores, the older libraries with their wealth of books no longer in print, and, of course, ancient battle sites. She had no time to devote to the analysis of dreams that couldn't *really* satisfy her curiosity about that curse. Whatever answers her subconscious could come up with wouldn't be the real answers, and . . .

Roseleen still ended up giving it some thought later that night while she lay curled up in her bed, trying to sleep, but knowing it would be impossible with that one little kernel of doubt still floating around in her head – what if she hadn't been dreaming?

It was a very big *if*, one that her logical stick-to-the-facts mind was leery of exploring, because if she hadn't been dreaming, and she hadn't found anything to prove that she was the victim of a hoax, then she'd been talking to a ghost. And that led to a wealth of other questions.

Thorn Blooddrinker had left each time she'd told him to leave, but what if what he'd told her was true – that he could stay if he chose to? What did she know about ghosts, anyway, except that she didn't believe in them, or she hadn't believed in them. Was that the curse on the sword, that its original owner came part and parcel with it?

The previous owner had been warned about

eternal damnation if the sword fell into the hands of a woman. Because only a woman could 'summon' the ghost? Was she going to be stuck with a ghost for as long as she owned the sword? That possibility was terrifying and fascinating by turns. If she had to be stuck with a ghost, having one as handsome as—

She groaned into her pillow. She wasn't *really* starting to believe this nonsense, was she? But what if . . . what if Blooddrinker really was a ghost, a thousand-year-old *Viking* ghost . . . ?

Her heart started pumping as another possibility occurred to her. Had he been a witness to all the centuries since his death? Could he tell her about the Middle Ages in actual detail? Give her facts that were unknown? Actually assist her in her research?

The mere possibility of *that* was so exciting to her, she started to throw off her covers to get the sword, but stopped herself with another groan. It had to be her exhaustion. She really should have gotten some rest before she came to England, instead of promising herself that she'd rest once she was there. That was the only reason she could think of for why she was letting her imagination run amok like this.

Well, there was one other reason, her enthusiasm for historical research. But still, that was no excuse for getting so fanciful. There were no such things as ghosts. Curses weren't real either, for that matter. Weird dreams were, however.

But it was time to forget them. She'd had the right idea to begin with. Just stop thinking about it, get some much-needed rest, then tackle the research she wanted to get done while she was here. If she did that, she heartily hoped there wouldn't be any more dreams to disturb the peace she intended to nurture this next week.

8

Roseleen was taking the longer, more scenic route back to the cottage after dropping David off at the train station, simply because of his parting remark. He'd warned that if she didn't relax and have some fun, she'd end up collapsing from exhaustion. She did agree with him, but good intentions or not, it wasn't long before all those 'what ifs' from last night came back to haunt her. And here she'd been patting herself on the back for putting those dreams out of her mind so she could enjoy her last few hours with David.

Of course, it was easy to forget troubling experiences when you had a companion to talk and joke with about other things. But now that she was alone, Roseleen's thoughts veered with amazing swiftness right back to the crazy theory she had come up with last night – that Thorn Blood-drinker was an actual ghost, rather than merely a dream.

There was really only one way to test the theory, and once that thought settled in her mind, the nervous excitement that built up within her was impossible to tamp down. She'd do it. She'd touch her sword again someday anyway, so why wait and wonder needlessly?

She no longer noticed the scenery as other things occurred to her. If – and it was still a very big *if* – her ghost did appear again, and did decide to stick around for a while as he'd threatened to do, how was she going to control him? But his sticking around wasn't a likely possibility. She was counting on the fact that he didn't like being summoned by her. Each time she'd done so, he'd insisted that she send him back to wherever it was he resided when he wasn't haunting.

She would just have to assure him that she wouldn't keep him for very long, only long enough for him to answer all her questions. She was hoping he'd simply cooperate with her.

But regardless of whether she could control him, she was determined now to summon him again – if he wasn't just a dream. The things he could tell her about the past were too important not to take that risk.

There was no changing her mind this time, and she'd never driven as recklessly as she did in returning to the cottage once her decision was made. And as soon as she got there, she fairly flew up the stairs to her bedroom.

The only precaution she took was in locking the

door and hiding the key, so the ghost couldn't escape from her room until she explained things to him. Or at least she hoped he wouldn't be able to escape. If he could walk through walls and doors as ghosts were reputed to be able to do, then there wasn't much she could do about restricting his movements.

She was still out of breath when she dragged the sword case out from under the bed and opened it. This time she stared right at the corner before she touched the warm hilt of the weapon. She was also wincing in expectation of hearing that loud crack of thunder.

The thunder came – and so did Thorn Blood-drinker.

It was true! Roseleen's heart was pounding almost painfully. This couldn't be a dream. Dreams weren't controllable like this, couldn't be summoned at will. But her ghost could.

He was dressed almost formally this time, or what would have passed for formal in his day. His dark blue tunic was finely embroidered with gold thread about the neck and down a V that opened to the middle of his chest. A short cape with the same embroidery was attached to his wide shoulders with large gold discs. His boots seemed of a better quality than before; at least the sewn seams weren't as visible this time. And the belt that girded his narrow waist was much fancier, this one set with gold discs that matched those on his shoulders.

He actually seemed more handsome to her each time she saw him, and she was still sounding a bit breathless when she said, 'Hello, Thorn Blood-drinker.'

Her voice instantly drew those clear blue eyes to her, and his sigh could be heard across the room. One of his hands even raked through his long curly mane in a clear sign of exasperation. Roseleen almost smiled. Her ghost didn't want to be here – again.

And then his eyes pinned her to the spot. 'You have mastered your fear of me, I see.'

That wasn't at all true, but she didn't bother to dispute it at the moment. She offered an apology instead. 'I'm sorry if I've taken you from some sort of . . . special occasion. I won't keep you long this time.'

'Keep me?' His frown came immediately. 'Lady, do you toy with me now?'

That frown of his, so intimidating, had Roseleen stammering her assurance, 'No – truly, I – I'm just curious about you. And I want to know how it's possible for me to summon you here as I have.'

'You already know how 'tis possible,' he said in a grumble. 'You hold my sword in your hand. You know this gives you the power to summon me.'

His eyes dropped to the sword as he said it. That possessiveness of hers reared up, and she let go of the weapon and quickly closed the case on it before she said, 'I understand that much, but . . . you've asked me each time to send you back. What happens if I don't?'

His expression said he *really* didn't like that question, yet he didn't deny her an answer. 'You draw me here with my sword, lady, so only you have the power to send me back. 'Tis my choice if I go or stay, yet by the same token, I cannot leave if you do not bid me to.'

'In other words, the choice is yours if I want to be rid of you, but the choice is mine if I don't?'

His nod was curt, angry. He didn't seem to like her having that control over him, any more than she liked being powerless if he chose not to obey her orders – *if* he was telling the truth about it.

She supposed she'd find out if he decided to stick around, or leave before she told him to. In the meantime, she was going to satisfy her curiosity, and that could take hours, days even.

With that in mind, she offered, 'Would you like to sit down?'

There was a comfortable reading chair set between the two windows, another chair at her desk. He chose to saunter to the bed and sit on it instead, right next to the sword case. She immediately snatched the box out of his reach and slipped it back under the bed. Her action brought a slight twist to his lips that might have passed for a grin, but she wouldn't stake her career on it.

He sat sideways on the bed so he faced her where she stood on the opposite side. His eyes briefly moved down her body, taking in her loose sleeveless blouse and baggy slacks, which were not at all becoming, but then her clothes never were. When she was home alone, she didn't wear her hair so severely, but she'd just returned from dropping David off, so her hair was in the tight bun that the outside world always saw, and her glasses were firmly in place.

For a moment, she thought he might be trying to find the woman he'd seen before in the short wrapped towel and flowing auburn hair, but his expression wasn't revealing his thoughts at the moment. Hers likely was. Having him this close to her was truly disconcerting. He really was a big man or, rather, a big ghost. And every bit of him looked hard, solid . . . dangerous. Looked that way, anyway. For all she knew, there might be no substance to him at all, and in that case, he could hardly be dangerous.

That thought had her asking bluntly, 'What is it like, being a ghost?'

His laughter came instantly. 'I am as flesh-and-blood real as you are, lady.'

It was a moment before anger took the place of

her surprise. 'You can't be. You're a ghost.' Now she was really confused.

She had been counting on hearing him tell her about the centuries she was an expert on. She would have been able to tell by his answers if he was being truthful – or if this *was* some kind of elaborate hoax.

He was still amused; at least the lingering smile said so. 'You are not the first to accuse me thusly, yet have I already told you that only the gods can draw my blood, and Wolfstan the Mad. I look forward to the day he finds me again.'

She was still angry, yet she was too intrigued by that last statement not to ask, 'You want to die in battle with him?'

Arrogance entered his tone. 'I mean to prove he is no match for me.'

'Then you can kill him as well?'

He sighed. 'Nay, he is already dead, killed by the witch Gunnhilda just so he could bedevil me. He hates me for that, and in that no Viking can blame him. Gunnhilda denied him Valhalla with her curse.'

'Valhalla? Wait a minute . . . Odin's feast? Yesterday, you said I took you from Odin's feast – in Valhalla?'

'Where else?'

'Give me a break,' she said, feeling utterly exasperated. 'Valhalla is a myth, just as Odin is, and Thor, and—' She stopped when she recalled what he'd said the night before last, that he'd been fighting Thor – his *brother*, Thor. She threw up her hands in disgust at that point. 'That does it. If you're going to tell me you're a Viking god, then I have nothing more to say to you. My beliefs have been stretched enough in accepting the possibility that you might be a ghost, but I draw the line at mythical gods.'

He was laughing again, almost rolling on the bed with it, his amusement was so strong. That his humor was at her expense had her cheeks flushing with color.

Tightly, she said, 'Is that a yes or a no?'

He had to wind down to mere chuckles before he could manage, 'I am no god. I might have had a small following of worshippers who knew me and knew I could not die, but 'twas the curse's doing, and before my brother took pity on me and granted me entrance to Valhalla.'

'But you *are* saying your brother is a god?'

'He was worshipped much longer than I. Unlike my name, which has since been forgotten, his name has survived in legend.'

She detected a little resentment there, and couldn't resist asking, 'That annoys you?'

'Would it not you?' he demanded. 'There is naught he can do that I cannot do, and I even best him more often than not when he will agree to fight me. Yet 'twas my misfortune to earn Gunnhilda's curse.'

Roseleen sighed at that point, realizing that she'd been snared into taking what he was saying as fact. 'Gunnhilda the witch – you're asking me to believe in witches and Viking gods now, and I simply can't—'

'Lady, your beliefs are no concern of mine. I do not need to prove what I say. That I am here is sufficient—'

'*If* you are here,' she corrected. 'I'm about ready to doubt that again.'

That earned her a grin, and it was still there as he stood up and started walking around the bed toward her. Roseleen's heart jumped up into her throat.

'Ah – I think it's time for you to leave,' she got out as quickly as she could, but not quick enough.

'I thank you for giving me the means to do so, yet I am not ready to depart your time.'

He was standing right in front of her as he said it, mere inches away. She enjoyed being a bit above the average female in height at five feet, eight inches, yet he stood a good nine inches over her – a fact she was most aware of now that she had to look up at him. And then she nearly fainted as she saw his hand coming toward her face.

She squeezed her eyes shut and stopped breathing. She expected – she didn't know what. A haunting experience? Something really terrifying. All she felt was her glasses sliding off her face.

' 'Tis strange to me, this jewelry you wear. What is it called?'

Her eyes flew open. He was staring at her glasses. Merely the way he held them, his fingers grasping the lens rather than the rims, proclaimed his lack of familiarity, if his remark hadn't.

No attack. No cold chills one might expect from a haunting presence standing so close to her. She let out her breath slowly.

'Glasses,' she said.

His eyes came back to hers and stayed there. The glasses he tossed over his shoulder, much as he had the chicken bone, not caring where they landed.

'Ornaments are meant to enhance, lady. Why do you wear jewelry that does not?'

'Glasses aren't jewelry,' she started to explain, but she ended in a gasp, because he was reaching toward her face again. 'What—?'

She didn't finish. He didn't answer. His hand had already reached what it was after, the tight bun at her nape. He tugged at it once and dislodged the metal bobby pins that held it, sending her hair unrolling down her back. He grasped the mass of it and brought it forward to drop over her left breast. Too close to that same breast, he found a bobby pin to pluck out and examine. She had a feeling it would go the way of her glasses when he was done looking it over. She was right, and now his eyes were back on her.

'Better,' he said as he slowly looked at each one of her features, then again at the long length of auburn hair that fell to her waist. 'I am pleased that you showed me what was before hidden. I think I will not mind so much, your possession of my sword.'

She would have had to be dense not to realize he was alluding to seeing her wrapped in no more than a towel, and the outlandish assumption he'd made at the time, that she had summoned him to bed her. Hot color was back in her cheeks. But before she could even think what to reply to his remark, he was reaching toward her again.

The narrow shoulder of her sleeveless blouse had drawn his fingers this time. 'How does this strange tunic come off?' he asked.

That third leap and drop of her heart had her answering huffily, 'It's a blouse, and it's not coming off. If you think I'm going to stand here while you examine everything I'm wearing—'

'Nay, your raiments interest me not,' he interrupted, though he was tugging now at the narrow piece of material his fingers still grasped. 'I can see now 'twould be a simple matter to tear it from you. If 'tis your wont to save it, lady, say so now.'

Her heart was back in her throat and staying there. He couldn't mean what that sounded like.

'You've taken off enough already, Thorn. Nothing else is coming off.'

He responded by hooking the thin piece of material on her other shoulder beneath two of his fingers. There was a slight pull on each shoulder as both his hands curled into fists, then a swift jerk. The thin summer blouse ripped straight down the center in both front and back, coming away in two pieces that now hung from her arms.

In her shock, she heard his disappointed sigh. 'Now what is that contraption that binds you?'

Her bra. He was staring at her bra, and she could see it in his expression, the moment he decided he had figured out how to get rid of that too.

Her arms came up immediately to cross in front of her. Pillaging and raping might have been standard practice in his time, but this wasn't his time, it was hers.

Sternly now, and desperately trying to overlook the fact that she was standing there only half-dressed, she said, 'I don't know what you think you're doing, but you can't do it. You can't just take anything you want here. You have to ask – and my answer is no.'

He merely grinned at that. 'Then why would I be so foolish as to ask?'

'You're missing the point—'

'Nay, I understand you plainly. You wish me to

77

grovel, yet that I will not do. The last wench to possess my sword also uttered such nonsense. But you, lady, were warned that I have a large appetite.'

'For food,' she quickly reminded him.

'And fighting . . . and women. And it has been too long ere I have enjoyed the pleasures of a comely wench.'

'I'm sorry to hear that, but you'll have to continue your abstinence a little longer.'

'I think not.'

He sat down on her side of the bed then, and the next thing she knew, two hands were gripping her hips and drawing her forward between his spread legs, closer, then closer still, until she lost her balance and fell toward him. She heard his laugh just before her chest collided with his, and then he rolled, placing her beneath him on the bed.

Stimuli came at her in waves – his weight, very real, very solid, very heavy; his rough cheek scratching against hers as his mouth sought and found her lips. There was nothing even remotely insubstantial about the body pressing her down into the mattress. And the lips moving over hers were the most sensual she'd ever tasted.

The fear she still felt had to be contributing to the riot of sensations going on inside her. Her heart had never pumped so hard. Her blood was racing, causing a tingling feeling throughout her body. And when his teeth tugged at her lower lip just before he sucked on it, she came damn close to . . .

She couldn't even find her voice when his mouth left hers to drift down to her neck. She could have demanded he stop what he was doing, could have regained some meager control of the situation, but she was too busy experiencing the uniqueness of having her whole body come wildly alive.

And then one side of her bra was being pulled down. He was using his teeth to do it. His large hands were gripping her sides, near her breasts, but not quite touching them. That his fingers were so close was driving her crazy. But when her breast popped free, the edge of the lacy material beneath it now, pushing it up, her nipple puckered immediately. No sooner did she gasp at the tightening there than her breast was surrounded by the heat of his mouth, completely surrounded, and being slowly drawn on.

She moaned, arching toward that heat. She couldn't help it. The chemistry was right. For the first time, it was exactly right, and she was combusting. And then he was looking down at her, grinning down at her actually.

'Still think me a ghostly being, lady?'

It sank in slowly, finally reaching her befuddled mind, but when it did, she felt – she wasn't sure what, but it wasn't nice. He'd done what he just did merely to prove to her that he could. He wasn't actually going to rape her – or make love to her, however she chose to look at it. And now that her senses were returning to normal, she didn't know if she should be disappointed or relieved.

'You have been twice warned, wench. Summon me again, and you will see to my needs, all of them.'

'I'm supposed to offer you a fight also? Do I get to use your sword for it, or do you?'

She could have said the devil made her say that, but the fact was, she was getting angry. How dare he put such a price on the information she wanted?

And he had the nerve to answer her with 'There is only one sword I will wield against you.'

That grin of his was back in spades. 'Viking crudeness I can do without, thank you,' she replied stiffly. 'And you've worn out your welcome, Thorn Blooddrinker.'

She pushed against him as she said it. It was galling to know that she couldn't have budged him if the decision hadn't been his to move off her. But he did move, until he was sitting on the edge of the bed again. There he glanced back at her, his eyes holding hers with an intensity that stopped her breath again. But then his gaze dropped to her breast, which was still exposed, and she realized that she hadn't moved a single limb yet herself.

She groaned and scrambled off the bed, yanking her bra back into place, and practically ran for her wardrobe across the room. Behind her, she heard his deep laughter. The sound sparked her anger like nothing else could. But before she could turn around to blast him with what she was now feeling, the thunder cracked in the distance.

She didn't have to turn to know he was gone. Her shoulders slumped with . . . relief, of course. Yes, definitely relief. She wasn't going to bemoan missed opportunities. Dealing with a thousand-year-old jerk was more than she was capable of, obviously. He could rot in his mythical Valhalla before she'd be foolish enough to summon him again.

9

For five days, Roseleen managed not to think about Thorn Blooddrinker's ultimatum. She tried not to think about what he'd done to her on her bed too, but that wasn't as easy to ignore, when what she'd felt during those few minutes had been so wildly exciting, so uniquely pleasurable, she simply couldn't get it out of her mind. She could blame her fear for the heightened feelings she had experienced, and yet – she'd be lying to herself if she tried to deny that he had aroused her in a really big way.

And she still didn't know *what* he was.

It had been easier to accept that he was a ghost. Other people believed in them, swore they'd seen them. She'd merely been in the skeptical show-me-before-I'll-believe-it group. Even an extraterrestrial being was more plausible because, again, so many people believed they were real. But an immortal? Someone who could live a thousand years and not show a gray hair for it? Someone who claimed to live in a mythical heaven exclusive to Vikings? No way.

Then who was Thorn Blooddrinker? An

eccentric practical joker who could afford the kind of expensive imaging equipment that could fool her into thinking he could appear and disappear because of a cursed sword? He *was* real. There was nothing ghostly about that body that had covered hers, or that mouth that had felt so hot and . . .

She knew how she could prove it. There could be equipment set up in her room, in every room of her house, for that matter, even in the car she was using. She wasn't going to tear her house apart looking for it. That wouldn't be necessary. She'd just take her sword out to a secluded part of the countryside where nothing else was around.

And if he did show up again? That would prove . . . at least that he wasn't a high-tech illusion. It still wouldn't prove exactly *what* he was, but that was just one of the many things she still had to question him about. If he showed up, if she was actually willing to risk it again, she'd have his ultimatum to deal with first, and that was the only thing on her mind now.

Summon me again, and you will see to my needs, all of them.

The mere thought of it, seeing to his needs, *his sexual needs*, caused a hot fluttering deep in her belly. It almost made her wish that she wasn't burdened with the strict morals her father had imparted to her. It even had her questioning her state of virginity, when she never had before.

After all, how many other twenty-nine-year-old women could claim they'd never made love with a man? She'd have a hell of a time finding one in this day and age.

The sixties and seventies had been responsible for the sexual revolution. In the eighties, women had gained power and made strides toward attaining equality, and the process of changing people's attitudes about women's role in society had continued. Women had gained a lot, there was no question of that, but they'd lost true 'gentlemen' in the process.

Barry was a prime example of the kind of man that had replaced the gentleman. He'd never opened doors for her, or seated her at a dinner table before he seated himself, or insisted on unlocking her door the few times he'd seen her home. Usually, he hadn't even walked her to her door when they'd dated. He would simply meet her wherever they were going, *and* expect her to pay her own way. And she'd thought nothing of it. She was a child of the seventies, after all, even if she was very old-fashioned in one aspect of her life.

That one aspect had made her nervous, and embarrassed, when she had thought she was going to marry Barry. She'd dreaded the prospect of explaining her unusual condition to him on their wedding night. The irony was, men no longer expected to marry virgin brides. Disbelief was the very least she could have expected from Barry. Laughter and ridicule were also possibilities. No, she definitely had not been looking forward to justifying her morals.

And he had never questioned her refusal to sleep with him. He'd put it down to her reserved nature – he'd said as much – and she'd let him think that's all it was. Of course, he'd never been that hot to get her into bed anyway, and she should have questioned that herself, though she'd merely been relieved at the time that he wasn't pressuring her or getting angry, as some other fiancé might.

But the situation with Thorn Blooddrinker was different. She'd been given an ultimatum, and she didn't like that at all. The prospect of making love with him might be consuming her thoughts and playing havoc with her body, but the fact was, he'd put a price on what she wanted from him. She'd have to pay with her body to get the information she craved, and she found that degrading, sordid, absolutely unacceptable.

If it had been anything else he was demanding, she wouldn't have thought twice about it. That would have been no different than buying a research book, or paying for a guided tour of a historical site. To be fair, he deserved *something* for what she would get from him. But her body, her virginity in particular? That was asking too much, and she knew damn well that he knew it, that he had named that price because he didn't want to be summoned again.

Finally allowing herself to think about her dilemma and get angry about it all over again, she soon figured out a way to get around it. After all, two could play the game of threats and ultimatums. And almost immediately after the solution occurred to her, she packed a very large picnic basket, grabbed the sword case, and was soon driving out into the country.

It took her a while to find the perfect setting, and she almost missed it because it was so perfect for her purpose. Between two fields of golden wheat and down a gentle slope that hid it from the road was a small, lush meadow. It was richly dotted with wildflowers, had a few low-branched trees thick with summer leaves for shade, and was disturbed only by flitting butterflies and a soft afternoon breeze.

With nothing but nature in view, it could have been a scene from any century, which was why it was ideal. She didn't want her Viking distracted by the twentieth century. She wanted his undivided attention – at least until they got the bargaining out of the way.

It took her two trips to the car, because the large basket and the sword case were too heavy for her to carry at the same time, but soon she had a blanket spread out beneath one of the trees, the basket open to reveal the mountain of food she'd stuffed into it, and the sword case open too, though she was careful not to touch the weapon yet.

The food was a consolation prize. Thorn wasn't going to be happy with her when she was done giving him *her* ultimatum, so she figured the least she could do was assuage *one* of his needs. Satisfaction of the other two needs he professed to having he would have to do without, since she wasn't going to barter on the intimate level he'd had in mind when he'd threatened her, and in this century he'd have a hard time finding the kind of battle he was used to.

She grinned to herself, thinking of that. Poor man. He really was going to get the short end of the bargain she was going to propose. And then it hit her suddenly that she really was expecting another appearance, was practically taking it for granted. And there weren't any hidden gadgets out there. If he came with his thunder and lightning, she really was going to have to accept the fact that he was—

She groaned to herself. She didn't want to think about that, didn't want to face facts that were just too implausible to credit. There *had* to be another explanation, one that didn't demand she suspend all known beliefs, and she was determined to find it.

She reached for the sword but didn't quite touch it, because her heart was suddenly beating erratically, her blood started rushing, and deep inside her – dear God, just the thought of seeing him again was arousing her. No man had ever had this kind of effect on her before. She didn't *have* to bargain with him. She could just – no. No. Not in payment for information she wanted, and not with a man she wasn't even sure, yet, was real.

She took a deep breath, pulling her emotions *and* her body under control, and slipped her fingers firmly around the sword hilt. As usual it was warm, another thing that defied logic. The metal should have been cold and warmed only to her touch, but not this sword.

The sun was out. If there was lightning, she didn't see it, but there was no mistaking the crack of thunder. Yet she didn't see Thorn Blood-drinker. She swung around quickly, but he hadn't appeared behind her either. And she felt . . . crushed, devastated with disappointment. It was as if she had just lost something very, very dear to her, and she felt the urge to cry, to scream even. But she didn't. She dropped the sword and pushed back the realization that the whole thing had been just a hoax, some cruel joke played by . . . whoever the man was who had invaded her bedroom. She wasn't ready to deal with that yet, or how it had been accomplished, or why. She was too—

'You surprise me, lady. I would have thought you would prefer a bed.'

10

Roseleen slowly tilted her head back on her shoulders, and there he was, Thorn Blooddrinker, sitting on one of the lower branches in the tree above her. His legs were swinging back and forth, reminding her of a little boy. But there was nothing childlike about the smile he gave her. It was broad and distinctly wicked-looking, telling her exactly what he was thinking – that he figured his long abstinence would soon be over.

For a moment, she stared at him blankly, while her emotions readjusted from dejection to – well, she certainly didn't feel dejected now. Acute nervousness would be an apt description of the feelings that were quickly taking over.

Had she really thought she could handle this man? He came from a race of the most aggressive, warminded, barbaric men history had ever produced, men so arrogant that they believed in a heaven that was exclusively for them, and could only be entered if they died in battle, with weapons in hand. That alone said so much about the way they must have thought, the way *this* man thought.

She'd be running for her car in a moment, if she didn't curb the direction of her thoughts, so she blurted out, 'How did you get up there?' and hoped the question would distract him from *his* thoughts as well.

The very loose, thin white tunic he was wearing wasn't tied at the neck and nearly slipped off his shoulder as he shrugged in response. A good portion of his chest was bare, and his dark brown leggings were tucked into soft high boots that were cross-gartered to his knees. He would have looked very casual, almost harmless, if there weren't a scabbard attached to his wide belt. It was empty, but the vicious-looking, long-bladed dagger right next to it kept her from being relieved about that.

And then she had an answer from him, of sorts, 'You may summon me, but I choose where to set my feet, and I chose not to set them down for the moment.'

That he would be setting them down right in front of her when he got around to dropping from that tree made her leap up and move out of his jumping distance. His laugh was soft, knowing. He knew exactly what she was feeling, how apprehensive he made her. Hardly conducive to a good bargaining position – for her.

She was wearing a long, ankle-length skirt

today in a blue and yellow floral design, with a yellow silk tank top that she hadn't bothered tucking in or belting, and sandals. She would have worn long sleeves if the weather weren't so warm, so this was as close as she could get to what he was more accustomed to seeing women wear. After all, women's knees hadn't made an appearance out of the bedroom until this century, and it wasn't until the last century that a few had bravely worn men's pants. And she had no idea in *what* century he'd last been summoned – another thing she meant to find out.

She was wearing her glasses like battle armor, and her hair was even more tightly bunned than usual, just for good measure. She'd known she had been taking a risk that he would feel challenged to remove her glasses and hairpins again, but getting the message across that she had no intention of deliberately trying to attract him was more important.

Now she squared her shoulders and tried to correct the cowardly impression she'd just given him. And in the tone that managed to get two-hundred-and-fifty-pound jocks sitting up straighter in their chairs, she said, 'I wish to talk to you, Thorn.'

He wasn't impressed. In fact, his expression, just before he pushed off of that tree limb, said he was amused. 'You may do so – after.'

He'd dropped to the ground about six feet away from her, but unfortunately, that wasn't where he stayed. But she stood her ground as he approached. Running just wasn't going to lend conviction to her ultimatum, which had to come out immediately, before he closed the gap between them.

'One more step, and you'll never get back to where you come from.'

He stopped, about two feet away from her, within reaching distance, but he didn't reach. Instead, he was looking at the ground between them as if he expected a trap to open up there and swallow him whole. Since it appeared to be no more than it was, soft grass with a few pink flowers, he looked elsewhere, all around him in fact, and his very tenseness told her he wasn't discounting the possibility that an entire army was hiding in the wheatfields.

Without looking at her, still trying to find the tip of an arrow or the flash of a sword, he said urgently, 'Explain, lady. What will keep me here?'

She considered running then, because after what she *knew* he'd just been thinking she was certain he'd be enraged by what she was about to say. She said it anyway.

'I will.'

His eyes came slowly back to her. At first, they were confused, then merely curious.

'You will? How will you?'

She had to clear her throat to get out, 'By not saying the words that will release you.'

Still he showed no anger. Actually, he seemed amused. 'So you would keep me with you?'

The conclusion he'd drawn startled her, and she narrowed her eyes on him to show that she didn't share his amusement. 'I don't think you understand. All I want from you, Thorn, is answers to my questions – and for you to keep your hands to yourself. If we can agree on that, you'll be back where you came from in no time at all.'

'I cannot agree to that.'

For some reason, she hadn't expected a flat refusal and it threw her into a panic. 'Why not?' she demanded, her voice rising.

'Because I want you.'

The effect of those simple words was dramatic. Roseleen's knees almost buckled under her. She made a sound very like a groan. And what his penetrating blue gaze was doing to her insides . . .

'And you want me,' he added.

'That's not – that's beside the – I *can't* agree to your terms!'

His expression hardened. 'You would hold me here and not see to my hunger?'

'I anticipated your hunger. There is a basket behind you, full of food.'

' 'Tis not that hunger I refer to, lady, and well you know it.'

There was anger in his voice now, and plenty of it. Oddly enough, it bolstered her own courage.

'Your hunger for food is the only one of your needs I am willing to satisfy,' she told him firmly. 'I'll provide you with that and a bed to sleep in – the operative word being *sleep*. What *you* were suggesting is out of the question. We barely know each other.'

'I have tasted you and found you to my liking. What more need I know?'

It was happening again, spirals of heat turning in her belly. But there was also heat in her cheeks. He was barbaric in his bluntness. She wondered if he even knew how to approach a subject with tact.

'Then let me rephrase that,' she said. '*I* barely know *you* – and don't bother mentioning taste again. That subject is no longer under debate. You'll keep your hands *and* your person off me, or – or you'll never see your Valhalla again.'

'My person?'

She was amazed that she'd finally managed to sound stern and unaffected, especially since she was now dying of embarrassment. 'Your body,' she clarified, and even more color flooded her cheeks, then more still when he threw back his head for a hearty laugh.

' 'Twas wise of you to mention both, lady. Very well, I will not jump on you. Give me leave now to depart, and I will answer your questions.'

That was too easy a turnabout. 'I'm supposed to trust you? I don't think so. I'll give you what you want just as soon as you give me what I want.'

'And I am to trust you?'

'At the moment, Thorn, I believe I hold the upper hand. I really don't want to keep you long. I just want my curiosity satisfied – fully.'

'And will you appease mine?'

She had gotten his agreement to her terms, but she didn't relax until she heard that. Appease his curiosity? Just what the doctor ordered. Finally, something that she could offer him in return, to assuage the guilt she was feeling for coercing his cooperation.

'Certainly,' she said, and even gave him a tentative smile. 'What would you like to know?'

'In what time do you live?'

'This is the twentieth century.'

He snorted, looking around. ' 'Tis not much different from the last century I was summoned to.'

Since that was just what she had hoped he would think when she had found this meadow, she made no comment to that and asked instead, 'What year was that?'

'Seventeen and twenty-three 'twas named, and I like these new times not – unless . . . Have you a war for me to test my skill in?'

Now why wasn't she surprised that that was one

of his first questions? She shook her head mentally. Vikings, always eager for a fight. She was going to have to keep that in mind at *all* times.

'I'm afraid modern wars are not what you would be used to, Thorn,' she was forced to tell him. 'The weaponry you may have encountered in the seventeen hundreds, pistols and explosives, are much more sophisticated now.' She could see that he wasn't quite following her, probably because he didn't understand the words *sophisticated* and *explosives*, so she added, 'Swords are no longer used. No one likes to get that close to the enemy in a war these days, and besides, this country happens to be at peace.'

The word *peace* apparently didn't please him. His disappointment was obvious. 'And what country is this, that you have brought me to?'

'England.'

At that he grinned. 'The English, they are never long at peace.'

History supported that statement, so she was compelled to point out, 'Since a third world war would likely wipe out the human race, countries are a bit more diplomatic nowadays, England included.'

'There was a *world* war? And I missed it?'

She rolled her eyes over this new disappointment he was displaying. 'You wouldn't have liked the last one, or the one before it. Forget it, Thorn, you aren't going to find a handy war around here.'

And to make sure she got his mind off battles, she added, 'It's been more than a couple of centuries since you were last summoned, and a world of differences has taken place since then. At no time in history has change ever been so dramatic as in this century. Some changes you'll like, most you probably won't. For instance, what you were thinking of doing to me is illegal without my permission.'

'Illegal?'

'Against the law.'

He grinned now. 'I make my own law, lady, with my sword arm to back it up.'

She shook her head at him. 'Sorry, but you can't do things like that here.'

His expression said he'd do things however he pleased. She decided they could go round and round with that subject and get nowhere. She didn't want him arrested, she merely wanted some answers from him. And besides, she never should have introduced *that* subject again.

But he changed the subject himself. 'I have already seen some of these differences you mention. That painting of William, 'tis amazing how lifelike it was.'

Hearing that, she could no longer doubt that his first appearance had been in her classroom in the States. Not that she was still doubting his existence. He was real enough. But the questions of why and how still boggled her mind.

Her own questions would have to wait, however, because it had already occurred to her that if she got him interested in this time period, then he wouldn't mind sticking around long enough to share his knowledge of the past.

So she said, 'That wasn't a painting, but a blowup of a photograph,' and when he just stared at her blankly, she added, 'Come, I'll show you.'

She moved back to the blanket and knelt down in front of her purse to search through it. She didn't notice that he had come to hunker down right next to her until she lifted out what she'd been looking for, her wallet, and turned to find him – mere inches away from her.

He wasn't watching what she was doing, he was staring at her face, and for a long moment, she got caught by his eyes, and couldn't manage to break the contact. The heat she'd felt earlier was back again, and so was the churning in her belly. She imagined lifting her hand to his cheek, then wrapping it around his neck to draw his lips to hers. Her breath suspended. She could almost taste him . . .

Roseleen snapped her eyes shut. Dear God, she had to be crazy to want to keep him around when he had such control over her body – no, she corrected herself, she had to be crazy not to put into action what she'd just imagined. She groaned inwardly at such contradictory thoughts. If only she'd been raised differently, if only he were a *normal* man, unable to disappear and appear at the whim of a sword.

When she looked at him again, he was grinning at her. He knew. He knew exactly what he'd done to her, and he was the very image of a man confident that he'd be getting what he wanted in the near future.

'You had something to show me, lady?'

Did she? Yes, the pictures in her wallet. Think of that, think of astounding him, think of keeping him so bedazzled with modern wonders that he would have no time to work his sensual magic on her.

She opened her wallet, then the snapshot section of it, and practically shoved the first picture under his nose, then flipped another over, then another. 'These are photographs of people I know, my parents; my brother, David; Gail, who's my best friend; Bar – damn, I can't believe I still have that one in there.' She slid out the snapshot of Barry, which she'd forgotten until now, and began ripping it into little pieces. 'Shows you how often I look at my own snapshots,' she added in a grumble.

'Why would you do that?'

She leaned over to shove what was now no more

than rubbish in her hand, to the bottom of the picnic basket, before she answered him. 'Tear up a picture? Because I can't stand the man in it.'

'But 'twas costly, was it not?'

'Not at all. What I was trying to explain to you is that the poster you saw in my classroom the night you first appeared was no more than an enlargement or blowup of a photograph similar to these. No artist painted it. And it certainly wasn't William the Bastard who posed for it. Photos are taken with a camera, a little boxlike device that's been around for more than a century now, and I certainly wish I had an instant one here to show you, because it could produce your own image—'

She stopped because he was no longer listening to her. Possibly there had been too many words that he didn't understand, so what she'd just said made no sense to him. Or possibly something else interested him more, because he was, without permission, rummaging through her purse.

Her perfectly normal reaction was one of indignation, yet she had to clamp down on her lips to contain it. Whatever interested him could only be to her ultimate benefit. She had to keep that in mind too, and keep a lid on her temper.

Getting angry with a man who likely personified male chauvinism would be a pure waste of time. After all, his attitudes toward women would be as medieval as he was, and she knew exactly where women were placed in his day and age – right alongside the cattle and the stock of mead, as no more than property. Actually, women had had even less value than salable goods back then.

So would he care if he offended her? Would he care if she showed her temper? Not even a little. She almost smiled. Dealing with him was going to be a history lesson in itself. She supposed she should be grateful that she knew history so well, knew historical attitudes, so she could adjust her own thinking accordingly. Otherwise, she had no doubt that she'd spend all her time with this Viking being outraged, and that would get her nowhere.

So she held her tongue and waited to see what would gain his interest. Her purse-size perfume spray? Her tiny solar-powered calculator? Maybe the little packet of tissues she'd picked up at the airport?

What came up in his hand was her lipstick, and he examined the white metal tube thoroughly, from every angle. Of course, that would interest him, since metal was related to weapons. He even flicked it with the nail of his forefinger to assure himself it was metal. And then the top separated slightly, enough for him to notice, and his eyes widened as he pulled it off the rest of the way.

He was fascinated all right, and she found out why immediately as he stared into the empty well of the top and tried to get his large finger inside it. He couldn't manage that, of course.

'So thin, this metal, and perfect in its roundness and texture,' he said in an excited voice. 'Your blacksmiths are ingenious, lady!'

She couldn't help smiling at that. If a little thing like a lipstick could amaze him, he was going to go into shock when he saw his first television, or – God help him, an airplane would blow his mind.

'You'd have a hard time finding a blacksmith these days, Thorn. They kind of lost their importance when the horse did – never mind, you'll find out about *that* on the way back to the cottage.'

And she was suddenly looking forward to getting him into her car. Would it frighten him, or simply awe him? Or would he relate to it instead as transportation to get him into a battle more quickly? She was going to start laughing if she didn't stop imagining how he was going to react next, and get the image out of her mind of him wildly waving a sword out of an open window as he raced past tanks and mobile rocket launchers.

'As for metal,' she continued, 'it can be made into just about any shape or size now, just like plastic and fiberglass and – anyway, factories produce the parts, other factories put them together, and the results are the conveniences of the modern age, which we who live here pretty much take for granted. You'll be seeing many of these modern wonders for yourself. Just don't ask me to explain how things work. Technology is not my field of expertise.'

To that he merely snorted, and she had to allow that she might not be making much sense to him again. He was back to examining what he was holding, and only now did he notice what was inside the base tube.

Roseleen grinned and suggested, pointing, 'Hold this part, and turn the bottom.'

He did, and his eyes flared as the colored stick shot out of the tube, then disappeared back into it again when he turned the base in the opposite direction. In and out it went for nearly a full minute as he played with it just as a child would with a new discovery.

But finally he got around to asking, 'What is this used for?'

At least this was an explanation she could handle, and on a simple level that he could easily grasp. 'To give color to the lips, women's lips that is.'

'Why?'

Her smile was self-directed. 'I've often wondered that myself. It's just one of the many cosmetics women use to enhance their looks.'

He glanced at her lips then, and stared at them for so long that the heat started generating in her belly again. She couldn't believe how easily he could turn her on, but that's just what his eyes were doing to her.

She was about to turn away in the interest of sheer self-preservation when his gaze returned to the mauve lipstick, and he remarked, 'You have not used this.'

Somehow, she got her voice to respond, breathless as it was, 'No, I rarely do.'

He handed it to her. 'Show me.'

It was a command. He actually expected to be obeyed without an argument. She didn't care at the moment. She'd do anything to get her mind off how tempted she was to throw herself at him.

Briskly and efficiently, she smoothed the lipstick over her lips, rubbed them together, then, because she'd done it without a mirror for guidance, automatically ran a finger down the center of her top lip to erase any color that might have strayed from the lip line.

When she glanced back at him, she was met with the pointed question, 'What does it taste like?' and she knew in what direction his own thoughts had just gone – if they hadn't been there already.

'You're not finding out,' she replied, her voice sharp with warning.

He responded by taking the lipstick from her again and slowly, too slowly, running it down the

104

center of his tongue. All the while, he watched her staring spellbound at his mouth.

Finally, his lips curled, and as her eyes jumped up to his, she heard him say, ' 'Tis not – distasteful, but I would rather taste you.'

She groaned and in desperation dragged the picnic basket over to him. 'Here, eat!' she fairly shouted. 'I'm going for a walk.'

Walk, hell, she practically ran in the opposite direction, deeper into the meadow, and his laughter followed her every step of the way.

11

Thorn watched her while she wandered about the meadow. He wanted to see her hair loose and blowing in the breeze. He wanted to see her lips parted for him again, and that sensual heat in her eyes that she could not hide. He wanted to feel her softness beneath him again, and to know that she very much liked being there.

She fascinated him with her desire and her denial of it. None of the other women who had possessed his sword had ever denied themselves the use of his body. They had either wanted him or not, but they'd never said nay when they had.

Gunnhilda would be turning over in her grave if she knew just how much he wanted this woman who was now in possession of his sword. His pleasure was not what the old witch had intended when she had cursed him and bound him forevermore to his own weapon.

Her curse had placed him in the power of women, at the mercy of women, subject to their whims. Gunnhilda had known he would hate that above all else, and in that she had been correct.

He still hated it, yet was there now a compensation for all those years of fury – this woman, with her strange words and her strange name, Professor. He had fought what she made him feel, because he liked it not, her control over him, no more than that of the others. But he was through with fighting it. He'd been able to think of nothing but her since he'd first tasted her. He had no intention of leaving her this time, did she bid him to or not.

She was different from the others, there was no denying that. She did not want the use of his sword arm to kill her enemies. She did not insist that he pleasure her, just the opposite. She did not treat him as her personal slave. But then, she did not know yet that part of the curse compelled him to do her bidding. That it would not let him lie to her or harm her. That she had much more power over him than she realized if she would not release him. Once he was released, however, the power was his to command.

The others had known, and he had despised all of them, for they had made full use of the curse's power. Even those few who had been timid at first soon gained confidence and became avaricious when they realized what he could do for them.

But most of them had been rich, and spoiled, and corrupt before they'd gained possession of the sword. One had even killed to possess it, knowing its secret. She had herself died when her husband found out she meant to replace him with a younger noble of higher rank. But then, she had made the mistake of not commanding Thorn's silence when she'd ordered him to kill her husband.

Unfortunately, Thorn would have killed the man. The curse would allow him no other option, since he had been directly commanded to do so. 'Twas not that he minded killing. In fact, he much enjoyed a good fight, whether for a noble cause or simply to test his skill against others. But he despised murder, and fighting a man as old as that woman's husband had been would have been naught but murder.

He liked to think Odin had intervened that time because it had not come to that. He'd enlightened the man with the truth first, and since the greedy, foolish woman had been there, wanting to witness her husband's death firsthand, she had died instead, which immediately had ended her power over Thorn, and that, fortunately, had saved the husband. And Blooddrinker's Curse had not come into the hands of another woman for nearly four hundred of these mortal years after that summoning, not until the last time, in 1723.

He did not care to remember that time. None of the times were worth remembering, except perhaps Blythe's summoning. The cause she had embroiled him in had been just, and she'd wanted no more from him than his fighting alongside her liege lord in order to protect him. Thorn had been sorry to leave that time and the friends he had made there.

Each summoning thereafter, he had tried to return to that time. Odin had assured him 'twas possible. But the women who controlled him would not oblige him that luxury, since they would have to accompany him. They were too fearful that they would become lost to their own time. And giving him what he wanted had never been their priority.

With this woman, he was hesitant even to broach the subject. She was too quick with her denials of what he wanted, of what even she herself wanted. And she was disbelieving of the curse, and of where he resided when he was not with her, so how could he convince her of the one benefit, as he saw it, that the sword was capable of? And even if he could convince her, why would she grant him that benefit?

'Twas the first time he had ever been doubted. After all, everyone knew of the existence of witches, and a witch's curse was a fearful thing indeed. All and sundry knew that – at least, everyone in the past knew such simple things. He had to wonder why this woman did not. Did witches no longer exist in this time? Had they finally been destroyed? Or were they merely more secretive these days?

Whether they still existed did not really interest him. He had already tried to have the curse broken by another witch, one reputed to be more powerful than Gunnhilda, and had been told how foolish he was to suppose that another witch would help him, even if she could. 'Twas only the woman who interested him now.

The curse *could* be broken, however, yet its power kept him from saying so. Gunnhilda herself had taunted him with that knowledge. Only if he were asked could he explain how 'twas possible to give him back control of his own destiny. And none of the women who had ever controlled him had bothered to ask if the curse was breakable. Releasing him from this bondage had been the last thing on their minds. Only using him had interested them.

Thorn noticed that every so often, the woman bent to pick a wildflower. Not once had she looked his way. But Thorn still could not take his eyes from her.

He ate the food she had brought, but he knew not what he was eating. He would merely reach into the basket and take whatever came to hand. If he occasionally found himself chewing something that was, in fact, unchewable, he would simply spit it out. 'Twas not worth the effort to examine it, when he would much rather be watching her.

He would have her. He had not the least doubt of that, was doubtful only of when it was going to happen. He knew not yet what she wanted from him, what her 'curiosity' would entail, yet was she determined to keep him here until she had it, whatever it was.

She had called his bluff right handily in that. Courage she had in abundance. Even fearful of him, she had stood her ground, even without knowing that he couldn't hurt her.

From the sword, she had full power over him at the moment. But she also held him in her own power because he wanted her. He never thought it could happen, but just now, he did not mind in the least being so completely bound, as long as it was by her.

12

Roseleen couldn't believe it. She'd actually left Thorn Blooddrinker behind with his sword. If he had possession of it now, she couldn't imagine how she'd get it back. And what if his possession of the sword ended her control over him? Could he just leave then, and take the sword with him?

The moment she realized what she had so foolishly done by putting some distance between them so she could cool off, she ran all the way back to him. She wasn't expecting to find the sword still in its case, the blanket and the surrounding area littered with discarded food, and Thorn looking up at her as if he were starving, when she could see very well that he'd gone through every bit of the food she'd brought along.

It was his hungry expression that twisted her tongue and had her saying in a rushed garble, 'I thought you might have . . . Don't you know better than to . . . Stop looking at me like that.'

When he dropped his gaze, her urge was to have it back. Oh, God, she didn't know what she wanted. Yes, she did. She wanted to share his knowledge of the past. She had to concentrate on that, and to stop getting fried by his glances.

To help accomplish the latter, she focused on the mess that he'd made, clicking her tongue as she started picking up what he'd tossed into the grass. 'I know perfectly well that cleanliness wasn't on anyone's high-priority list in your day, and you've never heard of litter control or five-hundred-dollar fines, but really, Thorn, you're going to have to become acquainted with rubbish cans while you're here. Today, we like to leave our environment the same way we found it, and that means picking up after ourselves.'

'Are you chastising me, lady?'

She glanced at him sharply, but his expression was now only curious, the blatant need of a moment ago gone, or – hidden. 'I wouldn't dream of—' she started, but suddenly changed her mind. If she was going to spend time with him, she couldn't be worrying about offending him over small matters, when she had so many other worries to deal with. 'Yes, I believe I am chastising you. No more tossing things over your shoulder when you're done with them. You put them back, give them back, or throw them away, whichever is appropriate.'

'Throw away is just what I did, as you can plainly see.'

He did sound indignant, not because she was scolding him, but because she hadn't explained properly, so he must have felt he'd been unjustly scolded. She sighed. Was she going to have to think about everything she said before she said it? That was going to be an impossible task.

'I'm sorry, "throw away" today is just a shortened way of saying toss it in the nearest rubbish can. And since there isn't one handy, for now we'll just put everything back in the basket and take it with us, so we leave this place as we found it.'

'The creatures of the wild will not thank you, lady.'

She heard the scolding tone in his own voice, and sat back on her heals, shaking her head. So there was a reason for his slovenliness? He liked to feed wild animals. That was so sweet and generous, traits she would never have associated with a Viking, that it disconcerted her for a moment.

And she almost hated to admit, 'I don't believe England has any more wild animals, Thorn, at least, not the kind you're probably used to. So let's humor me and clean up here, all right? You can just gather up the blanket with whatever's on it and jam the whole thing in the basket, while I get the rest of this stuff.'

She snatched the sword case off the blanket

114

first, in case he took her literally. But with it in hand, she owned up to what had made her run back to him.

'I thought you might have taken the sword, but you didn't even touch it, did you?'

He had already risen to gather up the blanket, so he wasn't looking at her when he answered, ' 'Tis my greatest wish, to have the sword returned to me, yet I cannot touch it without your leave.'

'You can't, or you won't?'

'The curse will not allow it. Only you can place the sword in my hand.'

She hoped he was telling the truth. That would certainly relieve one of her worries.

'And if I let you hold it?'

He was looking at her now, and so intensely that she caught her breath. 'Then the power would be mine to control. Would you do this for me?'

'If it would let you disappear on me again, no way,' she said with several shakes of her head. 'The sword belongs to me now, Thorn. I'm not giving it up.'

He looked so crestfallen, she almost said, 'Here, take it.' She had to will away the urge to do so, unable to understand why she even had the urge.

'*Would* you be able to disappear?'

'If you gave complete power to me by relinquishing your claim on the sword, aye. If you merely give me the use of it, nay, I still could not depart, do you not give me the words to allow it.'

He'd made her curious once again about the intricacies of the strange curse. 'What if I did just *lend* you the sword temporarily, not to keep, mind you, but then inadvertently released you? Would you take my sword with you, so I could never summon you back?'

' 'Tis not possible, lady. I could go, but the sword would not go with me. Only if *you* agree to go with me would the sword stay in my hand.'

Her, go to Valhalla? she mused. Be surrounded by brawling, drunken Vikings in Odin's mythical feasting hall? Not in this lifetime or any other, thank you.

She realized he could just be telling her what she wanted to hear. He could be lying. She had no way of determining the truth until it was too late, and he and her sword were gone. But, of course, that's if she was willing to believe that his home was Valhalla, that he was exactly who he said he was. *How* could she believe that? *How* could she believe what was happening? She pinched herself hard and definitely felt it. There had to be some logical explanation for all of this.

Facts. She needed facts, proof, and she intended to get it. The information she was going to get from him about the past could be verified, at least most of it could, and he would have to pull that information from his memory. That would prove, or at least support his claim that he'd really lived in those times, or been summoned to them.

'That's enough of that subject for now,' she said as she tossed her first handful of scraps into the basket, then went back for more. 'And by the way, I'm not comfortable with the "lady" you keep calling me. I know it's a title of complete respect where you come from, but some Americans tend to give it a different meaning, especially in moments of frustration, and anyway, my name is Roseleen. You may call me—'

'Rose?'

He laughed as soon as he said it. She blushed profusely. That even a thousand-year-old – whatever he was, could see the connection between their names . . . Or was that what was amusing him? She decided to find out.

'Care to share the joke?'

'Joke? Nay, 'tis only that I thought "professor" was your name. What then, do you profess to, that you are called professor?'

She grinned now at herself for drawing the wrong conclusion. He didn't see the connection between their names, and she wasn't about to mention it herself.

'History,' she answered. 'I went to college to study it, now I teach it.'

'All history?'

'I'm most familiar with the Middle Ages, particularly the eleventh century.'

He was still grinning himself. 'Aye, I know that time well. I much enjoyed their wars.'

Hearing that was nearly as thrilling as – well, not quite *that* thrilling, but damn close, and Roseleen was filled with excitement. She had a thousand questions for him. But somehow she was going to contain them until they got back to the cottage and she had a notebook in hand.

Yet her smile was generous when she said, 'I can't tell you how glad I am to hear that, Thorn, and I'm going to want to hear much, much more about it later.'

'I could show you—'

Misunderstanding, she cut in, 'Demonstrations won't be necessary, just facts.'

She didn't see the disappointment on his face because she was staring at what she'd just picked up, a sandwich wrapped in cellophane with a single bite taken out of it. That the bite went right through the cellophane had her turning back to him to ask, 'You couldn't figure out that the wrapping had to come off of this before you ate it?'

He was standing there watching her complete her task, having just completed his. He spared only a brief glance at what she was holding, though, before his blue eyes came back to meet hers and stayed there. His shrug was so slight it was barely noticeable.

'I was looking at you, not at what I was eating,' he told her. 'And be warned, Roseleen. I like looking at you.'

The heat came flooding back, and she groaned inwardly. How could she get him to stop saying things like that, and stop looking at her like that? She knew she couldn't. She'd already stated her demands. No touching. She had nothing more to bargain with now.

And besides, she was the one insisting that he stay, keeping him here against his will, more or less. She couldn't deny him *everything* that he liked. So how was she going to survive what he was doing to her?

She probably wasn't going to survive it at all.

13

Roseleen held her breath when they reached the top of the slope and Thorn got his first look at her car, or rather, David's car. It was a brand-new sedate, shiny black Ford, custom made for an American driving in England so that the driver's seat was on the left. But there was nothing pretentious about it. Lydia might ride around in her Bentleys and limousines, but David preferred not to announce the size of his wallet by the make of his car.

And Thorn Blooddrinker didn't look amazed or dumbfounded by it.

He had stopped to stare at it, but only for a moment. Actually, it was the utility poles that had caught his interest. He was staring at them with a good deal of curiosity.

Roseleen couldn't help it, she was quite disappointed by his reaction, or lack of reaction. Of course, he didn't know yet what a car could do.

She perked up with that thought, and even volunteered before he asked, 'Do you remember the light you stared at on the ceiling in my classroom, Thorn? It was powered by electricity, and those lines you're looking at now are what transport the electricity to wherever it's needed. No more smelly oil lamps and candles – except for when there is a power outage.'

His gaze came to her, so full of questions that she sighed. 'Don't ask me to explain electri—'

He cut in to ask, 'This power outage, would it work on my sword?'

That's all that caught his interest? She shook her head. She was being more surprised than he was.

'No,' she said, 'whatever power the sword has is of a supernatural nature. The power I was referring to comes from electricity and makes things of a mechanical nature work. You'll see a lot of those things when we get back to the cottage. But there are other sources of power too, batteries, gasoline – and you're about to discover one of the things that gasoline gives power to.'

She continued on to the car, put the sword in the backseat, then opened the trunk for him to set the basket in. She was still waiting for his reaction, and when it came, it sounded merely exasperated.

'What *is* this thing?'

'You've been in the seventeen hundreds. You've seen the exquisite paintings from that period, so you must have seen a few carriages while you were there. The eighteenth century was known for some of the fanciest—'

His impatience interrupted her, 'What has that to do with this thing?'

'This is an automobile, or in more modern terms, a car. When it was first invented, though, it was known as a horseless carriage. That's why I mentioned carriages, for you to understand the transition.'

'Horseless carriage? It does not move then?'

'It moves.' She grinned. 'Feed it gasoline, and it will take you just about anywhere.'

' 'Tis *alive*?'

She winced mentally. She was going to have to do better on her explanations. Cute remarks like 'feed it' could only confuse him more.

'No, it's not alive. It's one of those unusual things that metal can be shaped into these days. It's a modern carriage, Thorn. Come, I'll show you what has taken the place of horses, and makes it possible for this thing to move.'

In a few moments, she had the hood open and kept the rest of her explanation brief, 'This is an engine. The gasoline I mentioned is what makes it work, giving it "horsepower." That power turns its wheels so that it will move. Are you ready for a demonstration?'

'I wouldst prefer a horse, lady.'

That he was calling her *lady* again showed his

confusion, doubt, and very likely unease. Had she really been looking forward to putting him through this? But she wasn't going to walk the three miles back to the cottage just to keep him comfortable with what was familiar to him.

'Horses are used today only for pleasure, not for transportation,' she told him. 'When people want to go somewhere, they go in cars or – well, let's stick with cars for now, and this one will get us home in just a few minutes, if we'll just get *in* it.'

To that end, she took his arm and led him around to the passenger side, opened the door, but still had to practically shove him into the vehicle. Moving the seat back to give him more room for his long legs made him growl, and she had to go through another explanation about comfort, convenience, and power seats.

When she finally got into the driver's seat, she was no longer hoping he'd be amazed, she just wanted to calm his unease, and so she warned him, 'The engine is going to start working now when I turn this key. You'll be able to hear it working, so don't be alarmed by the sound. And please don't be alarmed when the car starts to move. That's what it's supposed to do. Okay? Ready?'

His nod was curt, stiff. He was holding on to the edge of the seat with both hands and looking straight out the windshield at the long road before them, the landscape broken only by an old barn in the distance. He was about as tense and wary as a man could get.

Roseleen sighed. She thought briefly about delaying their departure so she could explain some more, but figured nothing was going to make his first car ride easier for him. So she turned the key. But she had forgotten about the radio that she hadn't bothered to turn off. It came on now with the purr of the engine, and Thorn's wide blue eyes shot right to it.

'It talks? You said 'twas not alive!'

She couldn't help it. His tone was so accusing and disgruntled, his expression so comical in its mix of outrage and awe, she had to laugh. The station she'd previously been listening to was having a newscast, so they were only hearing a single voice speaking, but that was enough to make him think she'd lied to him.

'That isn't the car speaking, Thorn, it's a radio. It plays music, and there are lots of different kinds to choose from.' She switched through two noisy rock stations until she found something mellow. 'See? A radio is just another convenience, this one for our entertainment.'

He didn't appear to be listening to her, was still staring at the radio, and probably trying to decide whether he should believe her. She rolled down the windows to let some of the heat out of the car, but he didn't even notice, so rapt was his attention on the radio.

Roseleen decided to get them home, the sooner the better. But when she put the car into gear and stepped on the gas, he shot half out of his seat, and her own reaction was to slam on the brakes, sending them skidding several feet in the dirt beside the road.

At that point, she didn't know what to do to calm him down, and she needed to calm down herself, because his nervousness was making her jumpy. And then she did know what she could do. That that particular solution came to her so readily could only be because she'd been thinking about it ever since he'd reappeared, but she wasn't going to berate herself for that. Help was help, and she needed some to get his mind off the terror of his first experience with a car.

So she turned to him, leaning toward him and putting her hand at the back of his neck to urge him to meet her halfway. His eyes came to her instantly at her touch, questioning, then suddenly heated when he figured out the answer for himself. But he didn't move an inch toward her. He was going to make her move some more and do the kissing as well because he probably wasn't taking any chances with their bargain.

But that was okay. She wasn't thinking about

bargains right now. She'd found an excuse to kiss him that her morals couldn't quibble over, and she was going to do it quickly before she could change her mind.

So she did scoot over more, and she even wrapped her arms about his neck. And between a few brief kisses to start, she said, 'Relax. This doesn't have to be a terrible experience for you. You should be enjoying your first ride in a modern vehicle.'

And then she was kissing him deeply, and he was no longer uncooperative. In a second, he had complete control of that kiss, and though she'd intended to make it brief, he had other ideas about that.

His tongue was as aggressive as he was, delving, toying with hers. *Toying* wasn't the right word. There was a savageness about his kiss that proclaimed his hunger, and it must have struck a chord in her, because she was kissing him back with equal fervor, as if she couldn't get enough of the taste of him.

Roseleen had no idea how long that kiss went on. She was in a daze when it ended, and for the long moments it took her to catch her breath. Somehow, she'd ended up half on his lap with his arms holding her there. She was surprised only that she hadn't been tossed into the backseat.

Of course, Thorn wouldn't know about the

backseat of cars, and she'd sworn she'd never find out about them firsthand herself. If he had known, though, she couldn't see herself objecting, and that frightened her. Considering how totally she'd been lost in that kiss, she could have been deflowered and not realized it until it was over with.

She wouldn't look directly into his eyes. She was afraid she'd still see the hunger there and go right back to kissing him.

She managed to find her voice. 'There, I think we're both a bit more – relaxed.'

Relaxed just wasn't the word for what she was feeling now. Nonetheless, she tried getting off his lap, but he wasn't releasing her.

She had to look at him now. Thankfully, the fires in his eyes were banked – somewhat. But his gaze was still intense, too intense for her to hold it for long.

'We need to be going, Thorn.'

'What I need—'

'Don't say it,' she cut in quickly before he could. 'I kissed you to get your mind off the car, but our bargain still stands.'

'Nay, it does not stand the same, for I am touching you, with my hands.' His hips suddenly moved against her buttocks before he added, 'With my body. You will have your questions answered, but you will not deny me again, what you have yourself just invited.'

She was blushing profusely by the time he finished. He was right; by kissing him, she had invited his touch – at least he was going to see it that way, no matter what she might say to the contrary. So it would be pretty hypocritical of her to tell him again to keep his hands off her, but she'd have to. Just not right now.

'We'll discuss that later. Let me go now, so I can drive us home.'

He did, instantly, and she made quick work of getting back behind the wheel. As for getting them onto the road, that went *very* slowly. And she didn't glance his way to see how he was taking it this time. She'd just as soon not know.

It wasn't until a few minutes later, with the wind stirring her hair, that she realized she wasn't wearing her glasses, and her hair was hanging down her back. Again, he'd taken off her glasses and freed her hair, and without her even knowing it. She imagined her glasses had probably been tossed out the open window. She tried to remember if she'd brought another pair with her, but couldn't recall packing one.

Not that it really mattered. It was just his high-handedness that she found so vastly annoying. He didn't like her glasses, so the moment he'd had an opportunity to get rid of them, he'd done so, and to hell with what *she* had to say about it. But then that was so typically medieval. Women's opinions hadn't counted for beans back then. Men had made all the decisions, controlled every aspect of their lives.

She shouldn't be annoyed. Thorn was merely being himself, a medieval male. Just because he'd been summoned into the twentieth century didn't mean he was going to change any of his habits or be any less domineering than he—

She'd been so distracted by her thoughts, she hadn't noticed the vehicle coming down the road at them. Oh, God, a truck. A *big* truck. She'd forgotten to tell Thorn that these power-driven horseless carriages came in different shapes and sizes. And a swift glance at him showed his tension was back, and even worse, his fingers were wrapped white-knuckled around the hilt of his dagger.

'Close your eyes,' she suggested.

She hadn't really expected him to do it, but he did. It didn't seem to relieve his tension, only seemed to make it worse, so she quickly added, 'It's not going to hit us. It's just going to pass us on the other side of the road and be gone in a few seconds.'

'Roseleen, release me.'

Oh, God, why hadn't *she* thought of that, to spare him this terror? 'All right, you can go. I'll call you again when there aren't any—'

'I thank you,' he said stiffly, 'yet 'tis my eyes that needs be released.'

'What?' He didn't repeat himself, and the truck sped past them, taking her own anxiety with it. 'You can open your eyes now, Thorn. It's gone.'

His eyes opened, and he turned to glare at her. 'Never deny me again the opportunity to face danger, woman. Wouldst you make of me a coward?'

'What are you talking about? And why didn't you go when I gave you permission?'

'For what reason would I leave, when you are here?'

14

The dining room was a picture of old-world elegance. Dark wine fabric adorned the walls, overlaid with rich mahogany wainscoting. Candlelight reflected off hundreds of prisms in the large chandelier overhead, the crystal glasses, the polished silverware. Mrs Humes had outdone herself, because Roseleen had told her there would be a guest for dinner.

Roseleen was sitting across from that guest now, and feeling much more at ease. He'd wanted to explore the house when they finally got to it, and she'd agreed – up to a point. She hadn't wanted him to find the kitchen, with its wealth of electrical appliances, and it had been a chore, steering him away from that area.

Thankfully, the rest of the house was very old-fashioned. So it wasn't very different from what Thorn had experienced at his last summoning. What he was most fascinated by was the light switches. He wouldn't pass through a room without turning them off and on a number of times. The television he'd walked by, barely noticing it. She wasn't about to turn it on for him. Maybe in a few days, once he was more comfortable with this time period, but not so soon after the harrowing car ride.

She might have been able to keep the television and stereo system off, but she'd forgotten about the telephone. It had rung while they were passing it, and Roseleen had automatically picked it up and started talking. It had been David, calling to let her know that he was flying to France to meet Lydia for the weekend.

Thorn had stared at her through the whole conversation – hearing only her end of it, of course, which had prompted a twenty-minute explanation after she'd hung up, about the wonders of communication, and how people could now talk to others who were far away, even on the other side of the world. He'd looked at the thin wire connecting the receiver to the unit, then the equally thin wire connecting the unit to the wall jack, and snorted. He wasn't buying it.

Modern plumbing, however, he'd accepted without a hitch, at least he did after he'd flushed the toilet about ten times, and burned his finger under the hot-water faucet. The shower he'd wanted to try out immediately. She'd managed to convince him to wait until after dinner. As for the portable hair dryer that he'd picked up and turned on before she could explain its use, well, it was now in the rubbish can, quite broken from its crash to the floor.

Now she watched him handling a knife and fork by her example, and she couldn't help smiling. He was doing quite well, actually. At least he'd been willing to try it her way. For someone who was used to eating poultry gripped in his fist, that was saying a lot.

'You have mentioned Americans – twice now,' he said around a mouthful of Yorkshire pudding. 'What are they?'

He'd been so avidly interested in the food on the table, in everything on the table, for that matter, including the salt and pepper shakers, that she hadn't expected dinner conversation from him. The subject he'd brought up seemed harmless enough for their digestion though.

'Americans are the people who took over North America and wrested it from English control,' she explained. 'Afraid you missed that war too.'

He gave her a sour look for that. She laughed. She'd actually just teased him and gotten away with it. She must be feeling more comfortable with him, to have even dared. And that was surprising, considering the last remark he'd made in the car.

For what reason would I leave, when you are here?

She'd gone utterly still, not because she'd lost

133

control of him and their bargain, if he really had no intention of leaving, but because of the way it made her feel hearing those words. Frightened and elated, a complete contradiction in emotions. But then he'd been confounding her emotions ever since his first appearance.

She shied away from delving too deeply into the reasons for that, and to get her mind off it, she decided to get him to appease her curiosity about another matter. She still had so many questions, about his sword and its unusual powers.

'By the way, Thorn, why would the last owner of the sword think he would be damned if the sword should fall into the hands of a woman?'

His eyes lifted from his plate a bit, just enough to see her, and if she'd ever seen a smug, self-congratulatory grin, that Viking was wearing it. 'My warning must have worked with Jean Paul.'

'Jean Paul?'

'The oldest son of the last woman who gained possession of my sword. She was dying. He was due to inherit Blooddrinker's Curse.'

He was making light of it. He even shrugged. She wasn't going to let it drop.

'Do you have that power, to actually damn someone?' she asked.

He merely smiled. Was he teasing her now? Was a Viking capable of teasing?

'Stupid question,' she said, more to herself than

to him. 'You assured me you're not a god.' And then another thing occurred to her. 'Does the sword give me any other powers that I should know about?'

The smile he'd been wearing went from pleasant to positively beaming. 'It did.'

'Did? Not does?' She frowned. 'What's that supposed to mean?'

'The power was yours to command me. I could not lie to you, hurt you, or refuse to do your bidding. Thus did you have complete control over me.'

She stared at him incredulously. No wonder he had closed his eyes in the car when she'd told him to, and literally had had to get permission from her to open them again. The thought of having this Viking utterly in her control was mind-boggling. But he was speaking in the past tense.

Her eyes narrowed on him suspiciously. 'Are you telling me that I had that power, but now I don't?'

It seemed impossible, but now his smile was even more smug and triumphant. 'Indeed. When you released me, you lost that power over me.'

Roseleen sat back with a sigh. She ought to be angry that she'd missed out on something like that, and also that he hadn't bothered to mention it sooner. But of course he wouldn't volunteer that kind of information. Why should he? She had been worried about bargaining with him, while all along, he would have been compelled to do anything she told him to do. Yes, she ought to be angry, but she wasn't, because she didn't really *want* that kind of power over him or anyone else. But having him released from it . . .

She had to wonder now what else he wasn't bothering to mention. 'Are there any *other* powers related to the sword that I should know about?'

'That you should know about? Nay, all other powers are mine.'

'Like what?'

He put his fork and knife down before he said, 'Give me the sword, and I will show you.'

'Yeah, right.'

Sarcasm that blatant was kind of hard to miss, no matter what century you came from. 'You have a reason to deny me even temporary use of the sword?'

He sounded offended, so she replied carefully, 'Don't get me wrong, Thorn, but you *are* able to leave now whenever you like, and I have only your word for it that the sword won't leave with you. I'd rather not put your truthfulness to the test quite that way, if you don't mind.'

'Think you that I would lie to you?'

'You didn't lie to Jean Paul about damning him for all eternity?' she countered.

After a long, disconcerting moment in which

she couldn't believe she'd said that, and he apparently couldn't either, he was suddenly laughing. He even picked up his glass of wine and offered her a silent toast.

And to enlighten her as to the cause of his humor, he said, 'Methinks I like it that you do not believe me.'

Roseleen blinked. 'You do? Why?'

'I am under no compulsion to answer that.'

She frowned at that answer, and that pleased-with-himself grin that he was sporting again, until it occurred to her, 'You're getting even with me for teasing you, aren't you? Go ahead, you might as well admit it.'

'Roseleen, were I to "get even" with you, you wouldst not be in doubt of it.'

She was definitely getting annoyed with him, and she wasn't even sure why.

'Just how *would* you get even with me, then?'

That had him laughing again. She started drumming her nails against the table, her annoyance rising several notches. He noticed, stared at her fingers for a moment, then his eyes came slowly to hers with an intensity that stilled her immediately.

'Mayhap I should show you,' he suggested, his voice husky and sensual.

It became instantly clear how he'd get even with her. He'd dominate her sexually, totally. He'd make mush of her will, until she was eager to do anything he wanted, and she knew now just how easily he could do that. She was rendered breathless just imagining it.

'Stop it,' she said.

One of his brows quirked slightly. 'What?'

She considered changing the subject. She really ought to. But that feigned innocent look he was giving her brought back some of her annoyance.

'You know exactly what. I've asked you not to look at me like that.'

'Do all women of your time expect their men to do their bidding?'

Talk about a loaded question. There were a dozen ways she could answer it. She decided the safest route was not even to try.

'Never mind that. We had a bargain. Are you going to honor it?'

'The bargain included not looking at you? Odd, that I have no recollection of that.'

He was toying with her and apparently enjoying it. And he hadn't answered her question. She was starting to get a little nervous. She really should have changed the subject, but it was too late now.

'The bargain, Thorn. Will you honor it?'

'Did you?'

The blush came, and with it, some indignation. 'I was trying to relieve some of your tension and stress' – damn, he wouldn't know what *stress* was –

'to help you get through your first car ride. I even gave you permission to leave so you wouldn't have to endure it anymore, when I swore I wouldn't. I think you should be thanking me instead of giving me grief.'

'Thank you,' he said with a brief, *really* condescending nod.

She realized then that he was deliberately not answering her. He wasn't going to. He was going to leave her wondering, and nervous, and . . . She glared at him. He gave her a smile in return.

Dinner, of course, was ruined for her, her appetite replaced by a knot of consternation in her belly, or was it . . . ? No! She was *not* pleased that he considered himself no longer restrained from taking whatever he wanted.

She stood up, bracing her hands against the table as she leaned forward. 'I hope you remember what I said about the law, and what is and isn't permissible around here, because I'm going on record right now in telling you to keep your distance from me. And don't ask me to elaborate, you know exactly what I'm talking about. If you're going to help me with my research, I'll meet you in the library in one hour. If not, I'd appreciate it if you'd leave my house.'

She had to congratulate herself on getting that out through the growing lump in her throat. She didn't think he'd stay, despite what he'd said earlier, and her disappointment was choking her again.

Had she thought about it, she'd know that the lost opportunity for research material couldn't possibly account for the emotional turmoil she was presently experiencing. But she didn't think about it. She merely noted as she left the room that he made no reply at all.

15

It was one of the worst hours Roseleen had ever spent, waiting to see if Thorn would leave or if he'd show up in the library. She tortured herself by not going to the library to wait for him, where he might have shown up sooner than at the end of the appointed hour – if he was going to – and relieved her mind about it. She locked herself in her room instead, and paced, and berated herself over and over again for giving him an ultimatum like that.

When was she going to get it right, in her dealings with him, that he wouldn't think like a twentieth-century man, or react like one? It was no wonder he hadn't answered her. She'd probably shocked him again with what he would consider her outlandish audacity. Women in his day just didn't make demands or issue orders to men, not unless they were wearing crowns and sitting on thrones.

When she finally dragged herself downstairs to the small library at the end of that hellish hour, she found it dark, but that was no more than she'd been expecting. Even if he'd wanted to stay, he would have gone, just to prove that he wouldn't be dictated to by—

'Where is the switch to supply the light, Roseleen? I could not find its location.'

She nearly jumped out of her skin at the sound of his voice. With the light from the hall behind her, she located Thorn in one of the three easy chairs the room contained. She quickly crossed to him and turned on the reading lamp next to his chair. Her heart was pounding hard, and not just from the shock he'd given her, but also from his presence.

But he wasn't interested in her reaction to the fact that he hadn't left after all. She was jumping around with delight on the inside, while all he did was peer up under the lampshade where her hand had gone to turn it on.

'I assumed this was a light source,' he said. 'Yet did I not find a switch like those others on the walls.'

'No, it's different on lamps. You don't flip the switch up or down, you turn it.'

His look was reproachful now, as if to say she should have mentioned that sooner. She couldn't believe they were even having this discussion about light sources, let alone that they both sounded so calm.

But she was too anxious to ignore the subject on their minds, at least on *her* mind, for very long. 'I really thought you'd leave.'

'And give you the opportunity to make bargains again when you summon me back? Nay, the control is mine now, and I mean to keep it.'

She went very still. How was it she hadn't thought of that before now? She had put herself through hell for nothing, worrying about his leaving, when it would have been better for her if he had left. Then she would have had the upper hand again.

But she had completely forgotten about the power she possessed through the sword, power that wouldn't be hers again until he did leave. Now – now she still didn't know what he intended, but the fact that he was under no restraints was definitely upsetting her nervous system.

He wasn't exactly jumping on her, however. He seemed perfectly relaxed, with no sexual tension that she could detect. Maybe he would still abide by the bargain – no, it had been based on her releasing him, and she'd already done that. Why should he abide by it?

She was the one now who wanted to avoid that particular subject, so she quickly introduced another, 'Where did you learn to speak English so well? When you were last summoned?'

'I was forced to learn it after my third summoning brought me to this country, and in later years, I learned the Norman's French.'

'But that would have been Old English, which is certainly nothing like the English language that has been around for the last half-dozen centuries. I spent a semester studying the old tongue myself back in college. It's so archaic, it's like a foreign language. And that doesn't explain how you speak modern English now.'

'I had tutors.'

'Excuse me?'

Her surprise prompted a grin from him. 'Jean Paul's tutors,' he clarified. 'His mother insisted. She wanted there to be no misunderstandings when she . . . spoke to me.'

A picture came to mind of him sitting at a child's desk in some stuffy attic, which was where the children of the English upper crust tended to be taught in those days, with a stern-faced *male* teacher standing over him with a ruler in hand. She almost burst out laughing.

She restrained that urge, but she couldn't hold back the smile. 'You obviously had an excellent teacher.'

His grin widened a little. 'Aye, she was most diligent in her efforts.'

She was surprised again – big time. 'She? Don't get me wrong, I'm not doubting you, but women teachers were rather rare in the seventeen hundreds, if not nonexistent. How did you come by one?'

'The wench was an upstairs maid who sneaked into my bed each—'

She interrupted him before her cheeks got

redder than they were. 'Never mind, I don't want to hear the details. Your actual *tutor* was male, though, wasn't he?'

'Aye, and a more disagreeable creature never lived in any century. However, his attitude much improved after I broke his nose.'

So simply he mentioned that, as if it were nothing out of the ordinary. 'Do you do that a lot?' she ventured hesitantly. 'Breaking noses, that is?' When his grin started, she quickly amended, 'Forget I asked. I'm sure I don't want to know just how many you've broken.'

'In Valhalla, a feast would not be complete without a fight or two. 'Tis good sport.'

At least he wasn't giving her specific numbers, but since he hadn't dropped the subject, she was curious enough to ask, 'You participate in those fights?'

'Always,' he replied with a pleased grin. 'And I never lose.'

Bragging? Why didn't that surprise her? As big and brawny as he was, he probably had a lot to brag about.

But she reminded him, 'I thought you said you lost to your brother occasionally.'

'When Thor accepts my challenge, 'tis official with Odin presiding. And Thor is presently not welcome in Odin's hall. They are feuding – again.'

Was she really interested in the doings of

mythical gods – that she didn't believe existed? She really ought to keep in mind that Vikings were known for tall tales – and bragging. Spinning yarns that would captivate their listeners was part of their daily life. They certainly didn't have television to entertain themselves.

That thought made her smile, and so she allowed herself one more question on the subject. 'What are they feuding about?'

Thorn shrugged. 'It does not take much, with those two. On this last occasion, I believe my brother insulted Odin's feet.'

Not exactly what she was expecting to hear, and now she just had to ask, 'What? Did Thor say they were too big or something – how *do* you insult feet?'

'By calling them too puny to leave a noticeable mark behind. He was more – explicit – in the saying of it, than I would care to repeat for your ears.'

She almost laughed. She could just imagine how colorful the invectives of a Viking god could get.

'Thank you for sparing me—' she began.

But she was cut off when Thorn shot out of his chair, heading for one of the windows, and asking on the way, 'From what does that sound come?'

She followed him to the window, but she didn't hear any sound that was out of the ordinary . . . and then she did. An airplane, and a commercial liner by the sound of its jet engines. It was a sound a lot of people just tuned out, because it was so common.

But someone who'd never heard it before, or anything like it, would notice it immediately.

And Thorn had not only heard it clearly, he'd now found its source and demanded, 'What *is* that?'

She glanced around his shoulder to see what he was looking at, and was thankful it was dark and the plane was merely outlined against the moonlit clouds. Seeing it clearly would probably put him into shock. Yet this was still going to take a great deal of explaining.

Roseleen opened her mouth to begin, but suddenly thought better of it. She figured she'd have a nervous breakdown if she ever tried to get him into an airplane, so she wouldn't be trying it.

And instead of explaining *that* particular modern wonder, she said with a shrug, 'It's a bird. We grow them bigger these days.'

The look he turned on her was incredulous, either because he didn't believe her, or because he did. She wasn't going to ask which. She steered him away from the window instead, adding, 'Don't worry about it. They don't attack people. They're really quite harmless – as long as they don't crash,' she added to herself, and to get his mind onto something else, 'About that research I mentioned . . .'

He stopped abruptly. 'Aye, I must own up to being curious. What is it that you cannot find, that you wish my help in searching for?'

'I beg your pardon?'

'You wish to re-search for something.'

From his stance and expression, she gathered that he really liked the fact that she needed his help. He'd also stressed the word enough that she realized he was making two words out of one and so was missing its meaning.

But before she could correct him, he asked her, 'If I find what you have lost, would you be willing to grant me a boon for it?'

Was he trying to bargain with her now? Another way to get her into bed with him? She put her correcting on hold to find out.

'All right, I'll bite,' she said, crossing her arms over her chest in the same manner that he was doing. 'What is it you want?'

'The return of my sword.'

It was a bit deflating to hear that, when she'd been anticipating a quite different answer. 'I've already told you I won't—'

'What then do you want for it?' he cut in, frustration in his tone now. 'Would you like riches? Slaves? Give me the sword, and I will grant your greatest wish.'

'So now you're a genie who's going to drop a pile of treasure at my feet?' she snorted.

At that he grinned. 'Nay, I would rob one of the king's tax collectors.'

'What king?'

'Any English king you like.'

'Any one? You're not making sense, Thorn. England is ruled by a queen now. And besides, I wouldn't sell that sword for any price.'

He looked disappointed, extremely so. He tried to hide it, but it was kind of hard to miss, with those drooping shoulders and that frowning countenance. But that was too bad. He wasn't going to sweet-talk her out of Blooddrinker's Curse, no matter how strong an urge she felt to wipe that frown from his face.

'Can we get to that research now? And it doesn't mean that anything is lost. Research is a thorough gathering of information on a particular subject.'

He grunted. He didn't seem at all interested in her explanation, and was obviously still thinking about his sword. But he did offer a token reply. 'I doubt I would be very skillful at the gathering of information.'

'No, I don't want you to gather it for me, I want to get it *from* you. Your knowledge of the past, Thorn. I'm hoping it will aid me in researching the book I'm writing.'

'My knowledge? And if I choose not to give it?'

The sexual tension was there now, and so potent, she had to take a step back from him. 'You can forget *that*,' she said, her eyes narrowing on him in a warning.

He didn't bother to play the innocent and ask

what she was referring to. He grinned instead, his mood much improved now, whereas hers had just gone sour.

'You are certain, Roseleen?' he asked, his voice lowered to a husky timbre.

'Damn certain,' she shot back, ignoring the leap in her belly that reacted to his sexy tone. 'If you don't want to help me, that will be too bad. It will simply mean that we have nothing further to discuss.'

Now he laughed. 'You think to dismiss me again? You will find that not so easy to accomplish. But I did not say I would refuse you the knowledge you seek. You have yet to tell me what that knowledge is.'

Suddenly faced with his cooperation, she wasn't sure where to begin. But her excitement was building, mixed with her relief. And then she remembered the poster and knew exactly where to start.

'When you saw that medieval poster in my classroom that night, and you thought it was William the Bastard, it seemed as if you'd actually known him – personally. Were you ever summoned during his day?'

He was surprised, then seemed excited himself. 'I have met him, aye. Would you like to?'

16

Would she like to meet one of the greatest kings of England? The question so surprised Roseleen that for long moments she simply stared at Thorn. And she could blame that surprise for the ridiculous question that came out of her mouth next.

'Do you mean you can bring the ghost of William of Normandy here?'

'Nay, but I can take you to him, when he was flesh and blood.'

Hearing that, she sighed. These ups and downs of excitement and disappointment were becoming tedious. Take her to him? What he was suggesting wasn't possible and she told him so.

'That isn't poss—' she began, but stopped herself.

What was she saying? *His* being here wasn't possible either, yet there he stood, six and a half feet of very real Viking.

So, she amended hesitantly, almost with bated breath, 'Okay, how would you manage that?'

'With Blooddrinker's Curse in my hand.'

'The sword? Are you telling me this is yet another power it has, that it allows you to actually travel through time?'

'Aye.'

'How?'

'I need only envision a place I have been to, and there I will go.'

At that point, her excitement returned. 'Then I could do the same thing?'

'Nay, the sword is bound to me. It lacks power unless I am present.'

She sighed again, much louder this time. There was the catch, and she really should have seen it coming. She was beginning to think he'd do or say anything to get that sword in his hands again – including spinning a tale like this one just for her benefit.

But for the moment, she played along with him, asking, 'In other words, I have to lend you my sword and trust that you *and* it won't disappear on me?'

'It will not work unless you go with me.'

Why did that sound familiar to her? Ah, he'd said it once before. Well, at least he was being consistent in these tall tales.

'All right, let's suppose I do give you the sword, and we'll even suppose that I agree to go with you. What happens then?'

'The control of it will be mine. I will be able to go wherever I have previously been.'

'That's rather limited in choices, isn't it? Or have you been summoned so often over the years that you have a great many times to choose from?'

'The number of my summonings matters not,' he explained. 'Because the time need not be the same. It wouldst depend on what I envision. If naught has changed in a place from the way I remember it, then the time can be advanced forward or backward from when I was previously there. The time need not be only when I was there.'

'How much time leeway are you talking about?'

He shrugged. 'A week, a year, a hundred years. Again, it wouldst be determined by what I envision. A beach or an uninhabited countryside would be less likely to change over the years than a city street.'

'And if you tried to go back to a time you hadn't been to, say a year after you'd last been somewhere, and the place *was* changed, then what would happen?'

'I would appear in the place at somewhere in between the two times, when the place was last as I remembered it.'

'What about going forward, say a week from now, or a month?'

'Nay, the sword will not go beyond its present time. It will only journey to its past. Yet will it always return to its present, no matter any changes that might have occurred.'

A fail-safe clause that would get them back home no matter what? That was nice to know. And Roseleen wasn't really interested in traveling forward anyway, so hearing that she couldn't was no disappointment. It was the past that fascinated her, and she got back to that subject.

'So if nothing has changed in the past, then you can pick an exact date to go back to?'

'Aye, and anywhere I have previously been.' And then he grinned at her. 'Also, I can fight in whatever war I have witnessed. Odin has assured me all this is possible.'

Odin? She groaned inwardly. Oh, sure, take a Viking god's word for it, when she didn't believe in Viking gods? She should have put a stop to this particular tale when he'd started it, instead of humoring him. But then it clicked, *exactly* what he'd just told her.

'Wait a minute,' she said. 'Are you saying you haven't tried it yet?'

'Nay, I have been denied that chance. As I have stated, the female possessor of my sword must accompany me, yet have none thus far agreed to do so.'

'So you don't even know for sure if it works?'

'Odin has—'

'Yes, yes, he assured you,' she cut in, barely managing to keep to herself how little that counted in her book. Insulting his god wouldn't go over very well, and she did still want to keep the peace with him – even if he was trying to con her out of her sword.

'Okay, just for the sake of clarity,' she continued, 'you're saying that right now, right this minute, if you had my sword in your hand, we could go and visit King William?'

'King William? You mean Duke William—'

'Whatever you called him. Could we?'

'Aye.'

'Or even some other king in a different century?'

'Aye – or any war I have fought in.'

Roseleen frowned. He was repeating himself, and if it were any other subject, she might not have noticed, but war? She knew how much he loved fighting, and his expression clearly told her how delighted he was right now, that they were having this conversation. Was it possible that he really believed he could travel through time, that what he was telling her wasn't just a ruse to get his sword back?

Again she experienced a leap of excitement. If she let herself believe, even for a minute, that everything Thorn had just told her was true – the resulting possibilities would be astounding. To be able to travel through time, to have the opportunity to meet the very people who had changed the course of history. With that at stake, how could she not give him a chance to prove it to her?

But that meant giving him her sword, or rather *lending* it to him. How could she take that risk? Then again, how could she not? If there was even the smallest likelihood that she could visit the past, actually see history in the making, gather her research firsthand . . .

'Wait here and I'll get the sword,' she said before she could change her mind.

He didn't, of course. She didn't know what made her think he would. He was right on her heels as she left the library. It seemed he was even closer than that as she mounted the stairs, though it was only her awareness of him that gave her that feeling. But that feeling kept her from hesitating when she entered her room – at least until she had the heavy sword in her hands.

At that point, she was assailed again by indecision. Having a sword that was capable of slicing through time was just too much for her logical, want-to-see-the-proof mind to accept. Her first conclusion was more than likely the right one. And she didn't want to lose her sword, she really didn't . . .

'Give it to me, Roseleen.'

She closed her eyes. She almost groaned. It wasn't the sword that came to mind with those husky words. But *he* was talking about the sword.

She turned around to face him. He wasn't as close as she'd thought. And he was holding out his hand, silently demanding that she place the sword in it.

It worked. She did. In fact, she practically shoved the weapon at him. And she was so anxious, she almost missed seeing the transformation in Blooddrinker's Curse as Thorn's fingers curled reverently around its hilt. She did think she was imagining it, the filling in of those two small chips on the double-edged blade, the age-blackened metal slowly changing to a shining silver. And the amber gems not covered by his large hand were no longer murky, they sparkled with crystal clarity in the overhead light.

She *had* to be imagining it, a trick of the light, her own anxiety in thinking her sword *and* her Viking were about to vanish from her life. And yet there was still that small, budding hope that if she closed her eyes, she'd open them and be in another century, that somehow, miraculously, everything he'd told her was true.

She did close her eyes now, to give him the chance to prove it to her. Of course, nothing happened. She could still hear the soft tick of her bedroom clock, still feel the fragrant summer breeze coming in from her open—

'We cannot depart,' Thorn said. 'Not until I hear your words of agreement, that you wouldst go where I go – of your own free will.'

Her eyes snapped open. They *were* still in her

bedroom – well, of course they were, he'd just said they couldn't leave yet. And he was standing there, Blooddrinker's Curse still gripped tightly in his hand, and looking somewhat . . . disgruntled. Because of her silence? Could he really not leave without her cooperation?

Her anxiety lessened quite a bit with that thought. She even considered asking for her sword back to relieve the rest of it. But she didn't want to see disappointment in his expression again, or at least she didn't want to be the cause of it. And as the logical part of her mind reasserted itself, she reminded herself she didn't want to be disappointed either.

She was going to trust that Thorn really did think time hopping was possible. But he was going to feel disappointed soon anyway, when he found out for himself that his Odin had been pulling his leg. But he had to hear her agreement first.

She was torn now about giving it, because she really *didn't* want to see him downcast again. But she knew neither one of them would ever be sure unless she did.

So she was going to say what he wanted to hear, but first she said, for her own peace of mind, 'Just so there's no misunderstanding here, I'm only *lending* you my sword, Thorn. I do want that clear between us. And you will give it back when I ask for it, right?'

His answer was a long time in coming, and it wasn't verbal. All she got was a curt nod that he was obviously reluctant to give. That was good enough for her, though. But there was one more point she wanted him to confirm.

'And I want your promise that you'll return us here when I say so.'

This answer came a little more easily but not much. 'You have it.'

'Very well,' she continued, and even gave him a half smile, for what it was worth. 'You have my agreement to go with you wherever you like, and I'm giving it willingly.'

His smile was immediate, and incredibly beautiful in the delight that prompted it. And Roseleen didn't need to close her eyes again. Suddenly, there was nothing but blackness in front of them, and a sensation of floating in air. But seconds later, there was a lot more, the clang of metal striking metal, horses screaming, and what appeared to be thousands of mail-clad warriors trying to kill one another.

17

Finding herself in the middle of a raging battle was cause for her to panic, but shock came first. Roseleen was held immobile by it. All she could do was stand there and stare, while her mind searched desperately for excuses – logical acceptable excuses – to account for the medieval army that surrounded her. Immediately, she thought of drug-induced hallucinations and holographic imaging, then a simple dream – was she back to dreams?

To explain Thorn, no. But this? Definitely, and instant relief came with that notion. She thanked God that you couldn't get hurt in dreams, because that eager-for-battle Viking of hers had jumped right into this one.

She found the details of this dream incredible though. She could actually smell the stench of blood and horse manure – there were just too many horses around for a dreamer *not* to expect that kind of stink, she supposed. And all that sword clanging was giving her a mean headache.

Thorn, however, seemed to be having the time of his life. In fact, Blooddrinker's Curse had not been still from the first moment this dream had commenced. It flashed in the sunlight, it sliced, it . . . severed.

Roseleen closed her eyes, wincing at the screams she was hearing, of man and horse alike. The blood splatters on her clothes she was going to ignore. They wouldn't be there when she woke up. But she was definitely going to have to reclassify this dream as one of her worst nightmares. She couldn't ever remember having such vivid, horrid details . . .

A horse bumped into her shoulder, pushing her closer to Thorn. When she regained her balance, she turned to see a meaty arm swinging in a downward arc, and in its hand, a bloody sword moving in the direction of her neck. She didn't move. She wasn't even scared. It wasn't real, after all, and dying in her dream was almost guaranteed to wake her up, which she really wanted to do at the moment.

But death wasn't to be hers, not yet anyway. Another sword clashed with the one that was about to strike her, knocking it aside, then sinking swiftly into her assailant's chest. More blood splattered down on her. She'd be getting annoyed by now if this were for real. Who was she kidding? She'd be scared out of her mind if this were for real.

Thorn, of course, had saved her – from getting out of this dream. She decided she ought to tell him how grateful she was that he was prolonging it for her, but he didn't wait around to listen to her. Three men-at-arms nearby were surrounding a knight who had apparently been unseated from his mount, and Thorn jumped in to even the odds for the fellow.

Roseleen sighed. She had a couple of choices at this point. She could get in the way of another deadly weapon, or she could get Thorn's attention long enough to insist they leave. In fact, by choosing the latter, she would probably accomplish the former as well, since Thorn had already made mincemeat of the three men-at-arms, and was now fending off two mounted knights.

As dreams went, this was becoming a long one anyway. She'd just as soon they switch to something more agreeable. Actually, *anything* would be preferable, even a different nightmare. She'd had enough of watching Blooddrinker's Curse prove just how sharp its double blades were.

So she marched the few feet to reach him – he hadn't ventured too far from her for any of the fights he was participating in – and pushed aside another foot soldier who had been sneaking up behind Thorn, so she could grab his nonactive arm and pull him around.

It didn't work. In ordinary circumstances,

budging him was next to impossible. Now, when he was *busy*, it was definitely impossible. But he did acknowledge her attempt.

She had no idea how he guessed that it was she pulling on him, since he didn't bother to glance behind him to see who was, but he said to her in a surprisingly calm tone, 'Not now, Roseleen.'

It was probably that calmness that tipped the scales on her annoyance. For all his exertion, the man wasn't even out of breath. And that soldier she'd pushed had regained his balance and was dividing his attention between Thorn's back and her belly, probably trying to ascertain whether his long spear could take on both targets in one stroke.

Her anger had narrowed down her own choices. To hell with dying – at least she didn't want to now, until after she'd made her displeasure felt. To that end, she doubled both fists and slammed them into Thorn's back. It was infuriating to realize that he probably didn't feel it.

So she shouted to be heard above the din, 'Yes, now! I'm leaving this nightmare, with or without you. This might be your idea of fun, but it's not mine – and your back is about to be ventilated!'

As if he'd had his eyes on the spear wielder all along, instead of on the one remaining knight he was hacking away at, Blooddrinker's Curse came about. That foot soldier who'd made his choice, the wrong choice, slowly sank to the ground, minus his—

At that point, Roseleen said with a heaping dollop of disgust, 'Oh, sure, cut off a few heads, why don't you? What do I care? I'll just stand here and twiddle my thumbs until you've had enough of this gory stuff. But the next time you drag me into one of your dreams, how about making it a nice one, maybe with candlelight, soft music—'

His blue eyes were on her now. 'And a bed?'

How quickly she blushed these days, she thought, as she felt her cheeks grow warm. 'As long as it's only a dream—'

She stopped, incredulous that she'd actually said that . . . to him. She might as well have sent him an engraved invitation. And he was grinning, that wickedly sensual grin of his that proclaimed his thoughts so clearly.

Fortunately, at least for the sake of her embarrassment, he still had one knight to finish off, so his attention didn't remain on her. Unfortunately, it took him only a few seconds to dispatch that one, and even one more who came charging up to take the fallen one's place. And then he was mounting one of the many now-riderless horses and dragging her up behind him.

His finally getting her out of there took the edge off her anger, tempering it to mere annoyance with him. That he had to stop every few moments to fend off more spears and swords that tried to prevent their leaving kept her annoyance uppermost in her mind. But when he stopped at a tree near the edge of the battle, pulled her around him into his arms, and actually *tossed* her up to the lowest branch of the tree, she was infuriated.

'Just what do you think you're—!'

'You will be safe there for the nonce,' he told her, then had the audacity to grin in the face of the potent glare she was giving him. 'Remain inconspicuous, Roseleen, and silent. I wouldst not be pleased with you, do you draw attention to yourself.'

'Is that so?' she huffed.

But that was all she got out before he was turning his mount about, ignoring her, and trotting off. He didn't go far, though. She could have shouted at him. He probably would have heard her too, but only because he'd be listening for just such shouting. Otherwise he wouldn't, because the noise was just as loud here on the edges of the battle as it had been in the center of it.

She didn't bother to make herself heard. She knew damn well he wouldn't come back, no matter what she yelled at him. He'd found himself a war and was going to take full advantage of it.

From her new vantage point, she was able to see that there weren't all that many combatants out there, certainly not the thousands she had first thought. Of the two groups that were barely distinguishable in their motley assortment of armor, there were maybe forty on the one side, fifty on the other. If she had used her head to begin with, she would have recalled that the average medieval clash of arms consisted of about this number, or even fewer – unless a king was involved, which apparently wasn't the case here.

Of course, there weren't all that many warriors out there now who were still alive to fight. There were a few wounded loudly bemoaning their fate, but most of the bodies scattered on the ground were quite dead, or so their utter stillness and gaping wounds proclaimed.

Roseleen stared at the scene before her and shuddered. This was the fantasy stuff of macho males. Modern-day women just didn't dream of being caught up in medieval battles. And this nightmare really was taking too long to come to its conclusion, or switch to something else.

She frowned as something else occurred to her. When had she ever before had control of her thoughts in a dream? Of course, most dreams weren't remembered. You could have them all night long, yet only recall whichever one you were having at the time of waking, and even that was usually gone from your memory within seconds if you didn't think about it immediately. So she supposed it was possible to have thoughts, even in-depth, coherent, logical ones, and she'd merely never had any before in the dreams she remembered.

On the other hand, Thorn was being awfully consistent for a dream. So was she, for that matter. How often did anyone ever behave in a normal, true-to-their-character manner in a dream, much less a nightmare? Not very, at least not completely, without a few deviations.

Roseleen knew exactly what she was doing now. She was talking herself out of a nightmare and into reality, and some very alarming dread was quickly creeping up on her. Her little talk with Thorn about time traveling could have been the dream that led into this one, then again, it could have happened, and . . .

She wondered whether she'd feel pain or wake up if she jumped out of this tree and broke something. For half a minute, she actually stared at the ground about six feet below her, but finally gave up on that idea. There was an easier, less dangerous way to find out what would happen if she experienced pain. She bit her finger, hard, until tears came to her eyes. Dread filled the rest of her.

Oh, God, she thought, she wasn't dreaming, was she? Thorn had actually swept them both into the distant past, just as he'd said he could. And he might have killed someone out there who would have otherwise survived this battle. He could be changing history as she knew it, even as she sat there, doing nothing to stop him.

She remembered a time-travel movie she'd once watched in which images disappeared from photographs as history was altered. So it wasn't surprising that the panic that should have hit her earlier caught up with her now.

She started shouting Thorn's name. If he heard her, he was too busy to pay her any attention. He wasn't actively seeking fights. He didn't have to; they came readily enough to him, and mostly in pairs.

She supposed his size accounted for that. No one wanted to take him on singlehandedly. Yet she wasn't worried that he might get hurt with those uneven odds. He'd assured her he couldn't die except by the hand of one of his so-called gods, or by that fellow Wolfstan who bore him an apparently everlasting grudge.

She gave up shouting when her throat started to feel raw. She had to calm herself. Amazingly, everything he'd told her was true. She couldn't explain it, but it was nevertheless happening to her. They'd landed in the middle of a battle, probably because she'd foolishly said 'wherever you like' to Thorn when she'd agreed to go with him. He'd been looking for one ever since she'd first summoned him. And she'd thoughtlessly given him the power to find as many battles as he liked, anywhere he liked.

She was going to have to disabuse him of that notion. If he thought she was going to tag along every time he felt like spilling a little blood in any old battle he cared to lend his sword to, he had another think coming.

Carefully, she climbed down the tree he had left her in. There were about twenty-five combatants still going at it, though with less enthusiasm than previously. Due to exhaustion, she supposed. Eight of them were mounted knights, and one of those was presently crossing swords with Thorn, who was also still on his borrowed mount.

Destriers they had been called in their day – this day – and they were much larger than the average horse. Big and mean, they were bred specifically for war, and were certainly not the kind of animal she'd care to get near, yet she really had no choice.

Between her and Thorn there were four bodies she had to step around and one war-horse, minus his knight, that for some reason chose to follow her after she cautiously walked around it. Having something like that behind her made her move a little faster. And then she was near enough to the warring pair to get trampled – or caught by an overswing from one of their swords.

Once more, she shouted Thorn's name. He heard her, he couldn't help but hear her when she was standing so close – he just didn't take his eyes off his opponent's blade. Nor did he spare her even a few words.

Although she knew it was smart of him to avoid any distraction that might cost him his head, Roseleen was still furious that he was ignoring her because she was terrified that he was killing men who weren't supposed to die here in this battle, thereby preventing whole generations from being born, maybe even one of her own ancestors for all she knew.

She had to stop him at any cost, so in desperation, she turned to the only thing that had a chance of separating Thorn from the man he was fighting, long enough to get him to listen to her. She turned to mount the war-horse that was breathing down her neck.

There was a stirrup, but it was so high off the ground, she guessed the knight who'd owned this destrier had to have been much shorter than she was. She couldn't reach it. Making a running jump for the saddle was going to be her best bet, if she could only get the animal to stand still instead of following her again.

But before she even turned away to attempt it, she was lifted up from behind and set down across Thorn's thighs, and one of his thick, steellike arms went around her waist to keep her there.

'What in Odin's name do you think you are

doing, woman?' he demanded sharply. 'Know you how easily that beast could kill you?'

She ignored the angry glare of his eyes and retorted, 'I was quite aware of that fact, thank you, but since you – never mind that. I'm ready to leave, Thorn, pronto, this second. And if you don't get us the hell out of here, *now*, then – then I'll take my sword back and stand by cheerfully watching while these knights make a pincushion out of you.'

Considering how angry he seemed to be, she probably should have phrased that in the form of a request. But this was no time for niceties, and she wasn't about to be shuttled to the sidelines again. She didn't look behind him to see if his last opponent was down and out for the count; she simply didn't want there to *be* any more opponents.

And he must have taken her threat seriously. He didn't answer her. He didn't have to. As quickly as they had arrived, he got them out of there.

18

'Do you have any idea of how dangerous it is to tamper with history? One of those men you killed today could have been the ancestor of someone important, someone who made an impact on his own time. If you ended the man's line, before he had a chance to bear children—'

Roseleen was pacing back and forth in her bedroom, where Thorn had returned them. He was standing in the middle of the room with his arms crossed over his chest, simply watching her.

She'd done some swearing when they'd arrived, and scowling in his direction, because what she'd really felt like doing was hitting him for the anxiety he'd caused her. And it was frustrating to know that he'd probably be no more than amused if she'd tried it.

But she'd finally calmed down enough to explain to him what he'd done wrong, only to have him cut in now with 'You worry over trifles.'

Trifles? her mind shrieked. When the whole pattern of history could have been changed?

Her eyes narrowed on him as she demanded, 'Just what battle was that anyway? Has it been documented?'

' 'Twas no more than a minor skirmish between neighbors, of little import.'

There was an indifference in his tone that really irritated her. To Vikings, battle was glorified, a highly integral part of their lives. They lived for it. They gave no thought to who fell under their blades. Even if a battle was worthy of retelling, there was no remorse or pity for the side that lost, just pride and satisfaction that the winner was skilled enough to be the one to tell about it.

'You're missing the point here, Thorn. That battle took place hundreds of years ago. It was a done deal, with set results, and time went on to reflect those results. But if someone like you, who wasn't in the original battle, shows up to alter events, killing someone who should otherwise have survived—'

Again he interrupted her, but this time with something of an explanation. 'Odin did caution me against taking lives not destined to perish, also to avoid myself in the times I wouldst visit.'

'To avoid yourself?' she repeated, surprised by what she hadn't considered. But the rest of what he'd said was too pertinent for her to wait for an answer. 'So why didn't you take your god's advice?'

'I did,' he said. 'The two sides involved in that battle had long been at war with each other. There were few survivors from their clash that day. There was yet a third neighbor who hated both the other two and took full advantage, coming upon the battle near the end, and dispatching those who might have survived. All died in that battle, Roseleen, so what difference if some died by my hand, or by another's?'

He had her there. '*Why* couldn't you have said so sooner? And how do you know?'

For the first time, he sounded disgusted. 'I rode with the third factor that day. They were the retainers of the possessor of my sword, and a vicious lot they were. They toyed with their victims ere they put them out of their misery.'

'*You* participated in that?'

'Nay,' he replied. 'But I watched it done, unable to prevent it. At least some died more nobly and quickly by my hand this time.'

How could anything noble come out of killing? she wondered. While she was trying to digest that, his voice took on an angry edge as he added, 'You will not disobey me again, Roseleen. My life was not in danger, yet your life is not cursed as mine is. That war-horse you approached could have crushed you in seconds.'

She grinned, hoping to offset his anger. 'Actually, the beast kind of liked me.'

174

It didn't work. With a low growl, he said, '*Now* who is missing relevant points?'

'Oh, I got yours,' she remarked dryly. 'You stick me up in a tree – and I didn't appreciate that one little bit – without telling me that that battlefield was *supposed* to end up as buzzard fodder.' Then with a heavy dose of sarcasm in her voice, she added, 'Had you mentioned that sooner, I might have been able to sit back and enjoy the show, even if there wasn't any popcorn to be had.'

Only briefly did an expression of curiosity cross his face when she said 'popcorn,' so intent was he on expressing his anger. 'Had you done as you were told—'

'Guess again, Viking,' she interrupted. 'I know this is going to be a shock to your medieval system, but women today don't jump when the master says jump. We think for ourselves, do for ourselves, and we don't *obey* – God, I hate that word – arbitrary males who have no business bossing us around in the first place.'

'When your life depends on it, you will.'

He was back to sounding calm. She really wished he had yelled that command instead. But his calmness said he *knew* he was right, and if she weren't still so annoyed with him, she might have agreed.

'All you had to do was take a few moments to

explain things to me, Thorn, then I wouldn't have panicked, thinking you were out there killing the forebears of kings and presidents, changing the whole fabric of society as I know it. You don't think I'd risk my life for just any old reason, do you?'

'Presidents?'

'Different countries—' she started to explain, then waved her hand dismissively. 'Never mind, democracy wasn't around when you last were. But if we're going to travel back in time again' – she paused, hardly able to believe she was really saying this, before continuing – 'and the operative word is *if*, then I would appreciate knowing beforehand what's going on. And what happened to meeting William the Bastard? I could have sworn that was the inducement you used to get me to agree to accompany you.'

Now he was grinning at her. 'Lord William does not like it when I challenge his supporters, yet would I have done so, did I not first see to my need for battle. We may now safely visit him.'

'Oh, we may, may we?' she said, annoyed. 'Well, I'm afraid I'm not up to two emotional upheavals in one day, thank you. The renowned conqueror of England will have to wait until tomorrow. Right now, I'm going to bed to recuperate from your killing spree.'

'Bed does indeed sound pleasant, yet would I experience your "shower" first.'

She remembered that he'd been eager to get into one earlier – had it only been hours ago? – and he most definitely needed a shower, as well as a change of clothes. She did too, for that matter. She'd forgotten that her clothes were splattered with blood, that what should have been a nightmare had been very, very real instead.

'You can use the room down the hall. My brother usually leaves some clothes in it – and just remember to get the water to the temperature you want before you step into the shower.'

'You may see to the water for me, Roseleen, since I will be sharing your shower, as well as your bed this night.'

19

The images flashed across Roseleen's mind before she could stop them, of Thorn and her standing in her steamy shower, her soapy hands running across his broad chest, then of him sprawled across her bed, his body still damp, her body straddling his, her hands exploring every inch of him.

Her breath caught. Her eyes closed as heat spiraled deep into her belly. The sudden weakness in her knees had her swaying. She needed to sit down. She needed to get those images out of her mind. She needed . . . God, she needed him.

She opened her eyes to find him right in front of her. And he knew what she was feeling. If he hadn't seen the effect his words had on her, she might have stood a chance of convincing him that she wanted no part of what he had planned for the night. But he wasn't blind. And she was too drained emotionally to fight it anymore.

When he picked her up in his arms, she gave not a single protest, merely wrapped her arms around his neck while he carried her into the bathroom to set her down right in the shower. He removed only his leather scabbard, boots, and dagger before he stepped into the stall with her. But it wasn't the water he was interested in starting.

His hands came to her cheeks, lifting her mouth to receive his. Of its own volition, her body moved closer to meld against his. And they stood there, she had no idea how long, tasting each other, sensually exploring each other with their tongues and lips and roaming hands.

Roseleen was growing hotter, weaker, by the second. Thorn seemed unaffected, yet the hard bulge pressing against her belly told her otherwise. He'd probably gone from bloodlust to sexual lust, a natural transition, except – he wasn't behaving very lustfully. He was calm, in perfect control, just absolutely determined. His seduction was simply methodical, leaving nothing to chance. He guided, he set the pace, he controlled.

And now that he'd made mush of her with his kissing, he told her, 'You may attend to the shower now, Roseleen, and see to the matter of the thing called "temperatures." '

She could? she thought dizzily. But she did, without objection. She was too dazed to do other than follow his exact directions. And it didn't even dawn on her that they were both fully clothed, until the water started streaming down on them.

Showering together usually came after love-making, not before, or so she'd read. Of course, a Viking wouldn't do things in the usual way. And this Viking was still reeking of the battlefield.

He threw back his head to receive the full blast of the spray on his face. She turned away from him, her shyness intruding, at least until his arms came around her shoulders, wrapping over her chest.

His lips grazed her ear as he said, 'I have a very great need to rip these clothes from your body again, yet do I recall your dislike of simple methods of expediency, so I will restrain myself this time. In fairness, however, do I offer you the same opportunity.'

'You're suggesting I rip your clothes off?' she asked with nearly bated breath.

'If you feel the need to.'

If? She could think of nothing she'd like better at the moment – no, no, this was insane, she told herself. He was corrupting her with his barbaric ways, or trying to. They could both take their own clothes off, or each other's off, without ruining their clothes.

She turned around to tell him so, but confronted with his tunic which was now plastered to his chest, she asked instead, 'You're sure you won't mind?'

His answer was a grin. She grinned right back at

him, her shyness forgotten, the need for ripping and tearing that he'd mentioned just as strong in her. But after a minute of trying to rip his tunic apart, she gave up and started laughing. And that wasn't like her. Usually when she couldn't do something that she was attempting to do, she got quite frustrated with herself.

'Do you require help?' he offered.

She glanced up at him and saw that he wasn't teasing her, he was serious. 'No, no – actually, the urge for ruining perfectly good clothes has passed.'

'The clothing can be easily repaired.'

'Are *you* going to wield the needle and thread?' she asked with a grin.

'Nay, you wouldst—'

'Oh, no, I *wouldst* not,' she assured him. 'Not when there are numerous clothing stores in every town. It's only the rare few who still make their own clothes these days, Thorn. The rest of us buy ours. And although most of us might sew up an unraveling seam to get a little more use out of a piece of clothing, we sort of draw the line at big rips and jagged tears. Anything that damaged usually ends up in the rag—'

He was kissing her again, probably to put an end to her nervous jabbering. Whatever the reason, she certainly didn't mind. But she *was* experiencing some nervousness. He literally towered over her, after all, and the water had showed her all the hard planes of his body, such a big body, and she knew exactly what he was going to be doing with it as soon as they finished in the shower . . .

'Remove it, then, if you cannot rip it,' he said against her lips.

Yes, of course she would, just as soon as he told her – what? But then he dropped to one knee before her, and she dragged her mind out of the bedroom where it had just gone, to realize he was still talking about his tunic, and now making it easy for her to take it off him.

She reached down to tug on the garment. His lips grazed her neck as she did, then her cheek. She felt his hands at her hips, and suddenly her wet skirt was sliding down her legs. Her fingers were starting to tremble as it occurred to her that they might not make it to the bed, that his idea of a shower and hers might be quite different.

Not that she minded, with the way she was feeling. The sooner the better, actually. But if given a choice, she would prefer a bed for her first experience of lovemaking, to feel his weight on her again. She nearly groaned at the memory of lying beneath him.

She decided to hurry this shower along, and drag him to her bed if she had to. To that end, she lifted his tunic with a yank, forcing him away from her to get it over his head and arms. No sooner did it hit the floor than she was reaching for the soap and making full use of it across his shoulders and chest. The earlier image she'd had of doing so flitted through her mind again, but reality was so much nicer than anything she could imagine.

' 'Tis very soft – your soap.'

He had moved his hands up under her blouse, his wrists gradually lifting the material up, but he had stopped over her breasts when he'd said that. Roscleen's breath suspended, her own hands stilled. When she chanced to see his expression, she saw that he was grinning at her. For some reason, she burst out laughing, and it felt wonderful.

She'd actually never expected to have fun with a man like this. She didn't know why, but she'd never related lovemaking with fun, yet it was the most natural thing in the world to want to laugh when you were feeling good, and right now, she was feeling really, really good.

With a smile, she turned him around so she could wash his back. In the process, she discovered that he was ticklish, very ticklish, actually, but he was quick to discover the same about her. They did a lot more laughing, and she some squealing, before they got the rest of their clothes off. Roseleen didn't experience any more shyness after that.

Much later, Thorn picked her up again to take her out of the shower stall, but he didn't set her down. She started to mention the benefit of towels as he headed straight for the bedroom, but then thought better of it. He was going to do things his way no matter what she said. She'd already figured that out. And besides, she was starting to like his way.

He was very careful in laying her down in the center of her bed. He was careful also in laying himself down on top of her. And his expression was one of deep satisfaction, that he finally had her where he wanted her.

She didn't begrudge him whatever feelings of gloating he was experiencing. She felt like gloating herself, for how easily she'd overcome those annoying old-fashioned scruples of hers. She might wonder about that later, at just *how* easily she'd overcome them with him and why, but now she was simply glad that she had.

Right now, with his wet hair dripping on her, she smiled at him and remarked, 'You know we're getting this bed all wet, don't you?'

'The bed will dry.'

So it would, she thought, before he added, 'And I will dry you.'

He proceeded to do so with his tongue, licking the moisture from her, leaving more drops behind him. It was a strangely sensual feeling that was somewhat ticklish, but very erotic, especially when he reached her sensitive areas. But he had her laughing and shrieking at one point, when he raised his head and shook it, sending a shower of cold drops down on her so that he could start all over again.

By the time his licking turned into kissing, Roseleen was a squirming mass of sensitized nerves that reacted to Thorn's slightest touch. And her perception of medieval man was changed forever.

All of her historical research and studies had led her to believe that in those days, sex had been a tiresome, though necessary duty governed by the Church. And duty had been tended to quickly and efficently. Also, medieval attitudes had held women as valueless unless they owned property. Both of those facts supported the conclusion that women wouldn't have been given much care or tenderness by men, and certainly not the kind of stimulating foreplay Roseleen had just been so generously treated to.

And Thorn wasn't done. He might come from a pagan era that preceded Church intervention in the bedroom, but Vikings had an even worse reputation with women. Rapers and pillagers just didn't call to mind pictures of gentle, sensitive sexual partners, yet her Viking was being just that.

Whereas his tongue had been stimulating, his kisses were incredibly hot. Or maybe it was her skin that was hot. She felt feverish. She'd never felt so hot – on the inside. And she knew the cause of that heat. Desire, the likes of which she never could have imagined.

It was consuming her, a deep, primitive need to join with him, and it grew stronger as he drew her nipples, then the whole of her breasts into his mouth, and stronger still when his lips came to her neck, then her ear. Simultaneously, his tongue pushed slowly into that small opening as his hand slipped between her legs and he drove one finger into her.

She climaxed instantly. It was unexpected and explosive, the release of that coiled tension. She cried out, unaware of it. She nearly choked him, her arms squeezed so tight around his neck, and she was unaware of that too.

He wasn't. It took every ounce of his will to keep from driving into her now and pummeling her with the strength of his passion. He was nearly mindless with his need, having contained it too long. Yet he refused to inflict on her the savage side of his nature, which she herself brought out in him.

It seemed to take eons for her to release her death grip on him, and for her heartbeat to slow. Yet she was still breathless when she told him, 'I should warn you, before you get surprised by it. I've never done this before.'

His urge to laugh at that eased some of his own tension. 'I know,' he said.

She raised a brow at his smug tone. 'Oh? And how do you know?'

Now he couldn't resist chuckling. 'Think you I cannot tell the difference? You call no man yours, nor are you a whore, since you have made no attempt to solicit coin from me. Thus are you virginal.'

'I see,' she said, nodding her head. 'That's a very logical deduction, but it doesn't apply to women of this century. Today's women aren't—'

He kissed her again, a most effective way to end one of her long-winded discourses on the differences between their respective times.

She scolded him more than any woman he had ever come across, though usually he minded it not. Verily, 'twas singularly unique and amusing, he thought, since no female had ever dared chastise him before, not even those who had held power over him through his sword. But now was not the time for such things. And she must have agreed, for she was kissing him back, her arms wrapping around his neck again, her body arching into his in a most provocative way.

It really was more than he could bear at that point. She was so soft, and having attained her pleasure, so yielding, that he couldn't wait another moment to claim her as his. He entered her slowly, yet was the path slick with her essence, and with only the slightest thrust, he was able to push aside the barrier of her innocence to sheathe himself fully.

She made no sound. And when he glanced at her to see how badly she was hurt, he saw only that her passion had returned instead, and that drove him over the edge. He pummeled her after all, yet with a restraint he'd never shown another woman, and when he felt her climax around him again, his own bliss was there to join with hers.

She was his now. The possessor of his sword had finally become the possessed.

20

Roseleen stretched luxuriously as she awakened. She felt inordinately refreshed, as if she'd slept for several days. She also felt . . . good, incredibly good. In fact, she couldn't remember ever feeling quite so wonderful upon waking, and she was determined to savor the feeling for a while, in no hurry to get up and face the day.

She heard horses, a few nickers, some blowing, the jingle of tack. There was a stuffy smell she couldn't quite identify, almost like mildew, but it didn't really intrude on what she was feeling. Neither did the slight scratchiness of the bedding, that for some reason reminded her of wool army blankets rather than her soft linen . . .

Horses?

Her eyes flew open, but she had to blink them several times, and even then, she still doubted what she was seeing. Not her own bedroom, not even close. She was in some kind of tent. The mildew smell was coming from the mattress and pillows, the scratchiness from the coarsest-looking sheets she'd ever encountered. The mattress, if it could even be called that, was lying on the floor, minus a bedframe, and wasn't even as big as a twin bed.

The same canvas that the tent was made of covered the ground. A single fur hide was set on it to resemble a rug. Against one of the walls was a very large, ancient-looking trunk with a huge key padlock on it, presently unlocked and sitting open. Two smaller chests were on either side of it. They, too, had fat iron padlocks on them, but these were locked tight, one even wrapped with rusty chain. An iron pot, or, more exactly, a cauldron, was set up on some kind of thin pole contraption, with charred wood beneath it.

This couldn't be . . . ? No, Thorn wouldn't, not without telling her. He'd probably just had an aversion to sleeping indoors and so had moved them outdoors at some time during the night. So where had he found a tent?

Roseleen threw off the sheets and left the bed to search for her clothes. Her complete nakedness gave her pause, and then the memories of last night came rushing at her, and she stood still. She even grinned. Okay, so maybe she wouldn't kill him when she found him. Maybe she'd just mention, casually, that it would be nice if he informed her beforehand, the next time he wanted to go camping. And where *had* he found a tent in the middle of the night?

She started looking about for her clothes again. She was on the way to that big open trunk when the tent flap moved and a boy of about fourteen or fifteen stepped inside.

'Good morrow, my lady,' he said cheerfully upon noticing her standing there.

Roseleen didn't answer him as he might have expected. She shrieked instead and dived for the bed to bury herself under the sheets. She really was going to murder Thorn. The kid's dress or partial dress, bare legs under a long tunic that fell to his knees, with a sword dangling from the belt strapped around it, told her clearly that Thorn hadn't moved them into her backyard, but into another century.

When she got up the nerve to stick her head out from under the sheets, she found the boy still there. And he didn't seem the least bit embarrassed about having caught her in her birthday suit. He was merely looking at her inquiringly.

She recalled then how little importance nakedness had been given in medieval times. Most everyone slept without any kind of clothing to restrict them, and it was not uncommon for dozens of people to sleep in a room together. The ladies and female servants of households helped to give perfect strangers baths as a sign of courtesy and welcome. A half-dozen servants could be present when the lord and lady of the castle dressed, and in the kitchens, workers thought little of stripping down to nothing when the heat became unbearable.

Embarrassment, at least over one's body, had yet to be realized back then. It was only in the latter centuries that man had tacked shame to what was one of nature's finer creations, the human body.

Unfortunately, Roseleen was a product of her day, not theirs, and she, at least, was suffering acute embarrassment. She tried to get it into her mind that she shouldn't be, but it didn't work. Even the fact that she had a real live medieval youngster on hand to interrogate, who apparently spoke the Norman French that she was familiar with, didn't help to get her tongue moving.

She'd prefer he just go away so her embarrassment could go with him. But he wasn't leaving, was just standing there waiting for she couldn't imagine what. She finally noticed that garments of some kind, possibly a woman's dress, were draped over his arm. For her? She certainly hoped so.

But since he wasn't offering the garments to her, or doing anything else, for that matter, she was forced to say something. And getting herself clothed might be uppermost in her mind, but finding out her Viking's whereabouts at the moment took precedence.

'Thorn Blooddrinker, do you know who he is?'

'Certainly. He is my lord.'

Roseleen frowned at that answer, and asked suspiciously, 'Of the noble kind, or the deity kind?'

'My lady?'

That she was confusing him told her what she wanted to know, but just to be sure, she asked, 'How is he your lord?'

'My sister, Blythe, gave me into his keeping,' he said, and his chest puffed out a bit as he added, 'I am to be his squire once I am sufficiently trained.'

She and Thorn had only just arrived here. How the devil could all this have taken place? Unless this Blythe was one of the women who had come into possession of Blooddrinker's Curse. And that could mean that Thorn might be in danger of running into himself in this time he had brought them to.

'How long has Thorn been your lord?'

'Nigh two years now.'

She was definitely starting to get worried. Thorn hadn't explained what would happen if he came upon himself in the past, just that his Odin had said he should avoid it. She needed to talk to him, and quick.

'Where is Thorn right now, do you know?'

'Aye, 'tis early, just dawn, but he has gone to the docks to confer with Duke William.'

So he had brought her to meet William the

Bastard this time. Her excitement rose along with her annoyance, because he'd left her behind in this tent. He could have woken her. They could have gone together to meet the first Norman king of England.

'Lord Thorn bid me find you some raiments,' the boy continued, 'and assist you in the donning of them, since you are without maid.'

Oh, he did, did he? she thought with mounting anger. But she wasn't going to take her anger out on the boy. She had a much bigger target in mind.

'What is your name, anyway?' she asked him. 'Mine is Roseleen, by the way.'

'I am Guy of Anjou.'

'Well, I thank you, Guy, for the clothes, but assistance I don't need. If you'll just lay them down, I'll manage fine on my own.'

'Nay, I was told to assist you, and I always do exactly as Lord Thorn bids me.'

The mulish expression he was suddenly wearing told her she was in for an argument, but she still tried again, albeit more sternly. 'If I *need* assistance, I'll call you. In the meantime, you can wait outside, if you please.'

At that point, he grinned. 'You will need me, my lady. There are nigh a hundred ties on this chemise.'

'A hundred?' she asked doubtfully. 'Show me.'

He separated two garments and held them up

for her inspection. The yellow bliaut had no ties at all that she could see, but the dark blue chemise had quite a few, twenty maybe, certainly not a hundred, but every one of them was at the back. Splendid. She was going to need some help, but she wasn't going to be dressed by a teenager.

'All right, I'll concede that I might need some help, but what I need first is some water to wash with. Would it be too much trouble for you to fetch me some?'

'Nay, 'twill only take a minute.' He beamed, now that she was cooperating with him.

'You can leave those here,' she called out, when he started to walk out with her clothes still in hand.

'Certainly, my lady,' he said, and came the rest of the way into the tent to lay the garments on the bed beside her, then rushed out.

She hurried to get into the chemise before he returned with the water. It was tight going. The sleeves were long and fit like a second skin, obviously made for someone with smaller hands than she possessed, since they had no ties themselves. But that was the worst of it. The rest would conform to her curves once it was laced, then the sleeveless bliaut, which was slit up the sides of the skirt, would fit over it, showing off a lot of the under chemise.

She recognized the style. It was indeed from the

tenth or eleventh century. And if King William was still being called Duke William, then Thorn had brought them to a time that preceded the Norman conquest. That was all right with her. She didn't care when she met the man, just as long as she did.

Guy came back into the tent carrying a bucket of water. There was no point in upbraiding him about not knocking before entering, much as she wanted to, when there was no door to knock on. And it finally occurred to her to wonder why she was in a tent, anyway.

'Tell me, Guy, how far from here is this dock that Thorn went to?'

'Not far, my lady. Just a short ride.'

How long would people whose only speedy transportation was horses consider a short ride? One hour or two, when it took them days to get from town to town?

'Were there no' – she tried to remember what inns had been called in the eleventh century, then added – 'hostelries near the docks?'

He chuckled a bit before he enlightened her. 'Aye, but not enough for an army six thousand strong.'

An army? Camped near docks? God, was it possible? Had Thorn brought her here to witness one of the most famous battles in history? Were the Normans about to cross the Channel to Pevensey Bay?

She was dying to ask Guy what the date was, but that would sound too strange, and she was probably already sounding strange enough to him with her rusty Norman French. Thorn was the one she needed to ask, and she couldn't do that until she located him – which she was going to do as soon as she was properly dressed.

To that end, she ignored the blush she felt warming her cheeks, lifted her hair out of the way, and turned her bare back to Guy. 'How about taking care of these laces you were so eager to get your hands on?'

'My lady?'

She rolled her eyes and rephrased her request. 'Fasten the ties for me, Guy, if you please. I need to find Thorn.'

Just as she felt the chemise being pulled closed, it gaped open again as he released it, saying, 'Nay, I am to keep you safe here until his return.'

She started to argue with that, but had a feeling she wouldn't get the chemise laced if she did. So she said, 'Is that what he told you to do?'

'Aye.'

'How . . . wise . . . of him.'

That must have worked to put his mind at ease on the subject, because his hands came back to start the lacing, and after about ten *long* minutes, he managed the last tie and said, 'There,' with something of a sigh.

She immediately tossed the bliaut over her head and smoothed it into place over the chemise. Definitely too long. Some heels would have helped, but they weren't the fashion of the day. A belt would have to do, and so she looked inquiringly at Guy again.

'Did you think to bring me some shoes and a . . . girdle?' she asked.

'Aye.' He beamed.

He reached inside his tunic, where he had stored the smaller items, letting them catch against his own belt. He came out with a pair of cloth boots with no more than hide soles on them, and a long strip of embroidery that was the belt, or as it was then called, the girdle.

'Excellent,' she praised him and dropped down on the mattress to work the pointy-toed boots on.

Amazingly, everything fit rather well, considering she was probably a bit bigger than the average medieval female. Maybe a little too well, she decided, when the form-fitting waist refused to gather under the girdle without looking ridiculous. She gave up trying. She was simply going to have to lift the front of her skirts to walk, and let the back trail on the ground as it was designed to do.

'The water, my lady?' Guy reminded her.

'I'll get to that,' she told him. 'But first . . .'

Without finishing, she rushed out of the tent

before he thought to stop her. He called her name, shouted it actually, and sounded pretty worried, but she wasn't stopping. How hard could it be to find the docks if they were close by? The smell of the sea would lead her in that direction, or the sight of ships – it had been documented that there had been over seven hundred of them. So even though she was walking so fast she was practically running, she managed to glance in all directions looking for some tall masts. But all she saw was tents, everywhere, hundreds and hundreds of them. She was beginning to think that the short ride Guy had referred to was definitely of the several-hour kind.

There were so many men, literally thousands of them, standing around talking, sitting, gambling, cooking their morning meals over campfires, practicing arms, cleaning arms. There were some women about too, but not very many of them, and all of a certain class known as camp followers; at least their ragged dress and coarse behavior suggested they were.

Clothing really did hold great importance in medieval times, in that it distinguished the different social classes on sight, for only the rich nobles could afford fine raiments. The clothes obtained for Roseleen were of a good quality, but she had a feeling that that wouldn't offer her much protection in the midst of an army, not when an army was composed of men from every level of the social ladder. Nobles and peasants alike filled the ranks, and probably a number of criminals, for there was always easy pickings when this many people were gathered in one place.

She had already turned around to return to Thorn's tent, deciding she could wait, after all, for him to find her. Unfortunately, she had no idea what the tent looked like on the outside, having avoided looking back in her hurry to elude Guy. Her only hope was that the boy had followed her and would soon catch up.

But she hadn't gone far in retracing her steps when an arm came around her shoulders to steer her in another direction. Her first reaction was to shrug off the arm, but the fellow had a firm grip on her, so that didn't work. She then glanced at him and groaned inwardly. A common soldier no taller than she was, but quite hefty. He was young, but his grin still showed a great many missing teeth, and his full beard sported the remains of several meals and probably some well-fed lice.

And then she saw three more just like him – and he was leading her toward them.

21

It occurred to Roseleen, albeit a bit too late, that although she was wearing the clothes of a lady, her hair was an absolute disaster after she had slept on it wet. She hadn't given it a thought before she'd rushed out of the tent. And medieval ladies rarely went out in public with such untidy hair, let alone uncovered hair.

So unfortunately, anyone who happened to see her might assume that she had just come from bed. And her walking through an army camp without an escort would lead to the worst conclusion, that she'd probably had a secret rendezvous last night with one of the soldiers, and if she could consort with one of them, why not a few more?

She hoped that the men now gathering around her hadn't drawn that particular conclusion, but from all the grins coming her way, she was afraid it was a slim hope. And these weren't twentieth century men who might back off with an apology, once she explained their mistake.

These were coarse, rustic peasants, who had been pulled from their homes to further their duke's ambitions, men greedy for whatever few pleasures came their way in their otherwise dismal lives. And these particular men had to know they would soon be facing death. The Normans might have won the Battle of Hastings, but not without losses.

She would have felt sorry for them if they weren't planning on making her one of those few pleasures they got out of life. And their expressions told her that was exactly what they were planning. In broad daylight no less, with others all about. This bunch had to be pretty desperate – or just uncaring of any consequences.

She should have started yelling her head off, come what may, instead of trying for a calm approach and merely warning them, 'I shall scream, gentlemen, and draw you quite an audience, if you do not immediately desist and let me be on my way.'

One of them laughed at that threat. Another one reached for a lock of her long hair and began rubbing it between his dirty fingers. The one with his arm still around her shoulders squeezed her to his side. The stench of his unwashed body nearly made her gag.

But the words of the one who plastered his hand to her breast turned her blood cold. 'If ye want more'n just us riding ye, wench, then commence yer screaming. We mind not the sharing of ye.'

Raped by the masses? Roseleen thought, horrified. No, thank you, and he was probably right. She hadn't noticed enough nobles around to hope for some heroic interference, and odds were that any lords who were around could be just as crude as their underlings, and would simply take their turn with the rest of the men.

After all, Vikings didn't have a monopoly on raping and pillaging at the end of a well-fought battle. These men were preparing for war, and rape was an anticipated part of medieval warfare, a sort of bonus for the winners, a further blow to the losers.

It was to Duke William's credit, as well as an indication of his deep coffers, that for all the months that he had maintained this army, waiting to cross the Channel, he had kept them from pillaging the surrounding neighborhood. But pillage and rape his army did once it reached England.

The fellow still holding her knocked the other man's hand away from her breast before she got a chance to try it. Thanks weren't called for, however, since he wasn't helping her, merely asserting the pecking order.

'I found her,' he growled at his friend. 'I taste her first.'

She really wished the friend would have objected. A fight between them might have given her an opportunity to slip away. But the friend simply laughed and shrugged. He hadn't been kidding about his not minding sharing her.

She realized it was time for her to lie and drop some names, and pray that they weren't so ignorant that they didn't know who the top dogs were around here. 'I am a guest of Duke William's, here to meet with him. His half-brother, Odo, the Bishop of Bayeaux, was escorting me, but we became separated. If one of you would be good enough to take me to the duke, I'll see that you are rewarded.'

'I will take ye wherever ye like, wench – after I have my reward,' said the man who was holding her. He turned her toward him, his mouth moving in to start claiming his reward.

She was going to puke if he kissed her, she knew she was, and thank God for that, because she couldn't think of anything else that might stop him. Violence wasn't a feasible option. Not because she'd never inflicted any on anyone in her life, but because fighting them would just draw more of their kind to participate in their assault on her, and she was already outnumbered.

Nonetheless, the moment the man's wet mouth covered her clamped-together lips, she went for his groin with her knee. She missed, but something else didn't. Something else knocked the man off his feet, and she nearly fell with him, or would have, if someone hadn't grabbed her arm, nearly wrenching it from its socket, and pulled her back.

Roseleen's would-be rapist was groaning and thrashing about on the ground, his hand pressed against his ear, which was bleeding so badly the blood seeped through his fingers. He'd been clouted with a mail-gauntleted fist. She saw that fist now as she turned, and the fresh blood that was on it. But she saw also that it belonged to a quite splendid knight in steel armor, the chain links so shiny in the morning sunlight that she longed for a pair of sunglasses.

He was tall and broad of chest, his blond hair cut short in the Norman fashion. Emerald green eyes were fixed on her, rather than on her attacker, who was now trying to crawl away unnoticed, and not very successfully, since she noticed. The fellow's friends had already disappeared, having scattered in different directions, leaving her standing there alone with the knight – and Guy of Anjou.

It took her a moment to even see the boy behind the broad-shouldered knight. When she did, and she noted the anxious expression on his face, she realized that he'd undoubtedly brought the knight to her rescue, since he would have had no better luck at dispersing those burly soldiers than she had. He'd been closer behind her than she'd figured, had apparently seen what was happening, and had taken care of it the only way he could, by fetching someone who *could* rescue her.

She was immensely grateful. She was also pretty shaken, or else she might have noticed sooner the admiring way the tall knight was staring at her. She did notice now, and also that he was damn good-looking, his shining armor adding to his overall magnificence.

She almost laughed, but that would have been so inappropriate, she managed to contain the urge. It wasn't easy though. An actual *real* knight in shining armor to the rescue, and a handsome one at that?

This was an age-old fantasy, but one that twentieth-century women didn't have a hope of ever realizing outside of their dreams – unless, of course, they were transported to the past as Roseleen had been. And she didn't imagine there was all that much time traveling going on for that to happen, not unless there were others out there like Thorn, with supernaturally cursed swords.

She should ask him about that. She had also been meaning to ask him what he'd done to get himself cursed by Gunnhilda the witch in the first place. But right now he wasn't here, and she wanted to express her gratitude. She started with the knight.

'Thank you,' she told him, even managing a smile to add to her sincerity. 'Your intervention was most timely and very much appreciated. And thank you also, Guy, if you're responsible for this good knight's presence.'

'Aye, but an unnecessary doing,' the boy grumbled. 'Had you stayed where you were—'

'I know, I know,' she interrupted, before he started chastising her. 'And believe me, I won't make such a mistake again. I just hadn't realized there were so many common soldiers here . . .'

Roseleen let that trail away, so they wouldn't think she was a complete dolt, but also wouldn't suspect she wasn't from their century. Women *did* know their limitations in this time period, and rarely bucked the system. And one of the things they all probably took for granted was what would happen if they walked about unescorted in an army camp.

'They are a churlish lot, yet do they know better than to accost a lady,' the knight said.

She could have remarked, and quite dryly, *Oh sure, that bunch knew exactly what they weren't supposed to be doing. I can vouch for that.* However, under normal circumstances, what he'd said was probably quite true. But how long had these men been waiting here without their wives handy to satisfy their basic urges, and without coin in their pockets to pay for a little time with the camp followers? A lady, of course, wouldn't mention such things, so she didn't either.

He had, however, practically dismissed any real harm from the situation with his confident remark, so she replied, 'Whatever they were up to, I'm just glad you interrupted it when you did.'

' 'Twas my pleasure, demoiselle,' he offered gallantly. 'If you need further assistance—'

'She is under Thorn Blooddrinker's protection,' Guy cut in at that point.

'Verily, she needs no more protection than that,' the knight said, a sigh in his tone when he added, 'A pity.'

For some reason, Roseleen blushed. The knight's eyes were assessing her too frankly now, as if he had just changed his opinion of her and was contemplating taking over where those soldiers had left off. But she reminded herself that he couldn't be thinking that. Knights to the rescue didn't cause damsels to need further rescuing.

But Guy possibly sensed a problem brewing, because he quickly came around to take her arm, probably hoping he could get her out of there without further incident. And in fact, he started pulling her back around the knight, who stood in their path.

'My thanks, my lord,' was all he said in parting.

Roseleen felt like clouting the boy for his rudeness. She didn't, but she did resist the pull on her arm, long enough to say, 'Farewell, sir knight, and again, thank you. Perhaps someday I can return the favor.'

He threw back his head and laughed at that, causing her to blush all the more.

22

'What did he find so amusing in my parting remark?' Roseleen asked Guy as he hurried her along the narrow path between the tents.

He didn't pause as he replied, 'You as much as hoped some women would attack him so that you could chase them off.'

'I did no such thing,' she said indignantly.

'Aye, you did,' he insisted. 'How else could you return the favor he had done you, unless—?'

He didn't finish, and when she saw that he was blushing, she realized that his 'unless' would have been of the unsavory sort, and then she was blushing right alongside him. At least the knight hadn't thought of 'unless' – or had he? Was *that* why he'd laughed?

She went from pink to scarlet in seconds, feeling annoyed that she was blushing at all. She was a sophisticated woman, after all, thoroughly experienced in *all* aspects of life, now that Thorn had disposed of her virginity. Actually, considering the time period she was in, she was probably the most well-educated person in the entire world right now.

What an incredibly satisfying thought that was, after all the long hours of studying and sacrificing of her social life she'd done year after year, to get those above-average grades. It was also amusing. What, after all, could she do with that fine education here?

But the thought served to temper her annoyance at the moment, as well as her embarrassment, enough so she could inquire of her young escort, 'Who was that knight you fetched? Anyone important?'

'Important?' he repeated, his tone now thoroughly condescending. 'Anyone who has the duke's ear is important, my lady, and Reinard de Morville is a very good friend of Robert of Mortain.'

That Guy didn't elaborate on who Robert of Mortain was, told her that he was someone everyone should know, and in fact she did know who he was. He was another of Duke William's half-brothers, who was as deeply involved in this campaign as Odo was.

If Sir Reinard was a good friend of Robert, then he was certainly on his way up in the world. If he wasn't important in his own right yet, he definitely would be when England was carved up and distributed to William's supporters – unless he died in one of the upcoming battles.

That thought wasn't a pleasant one. She wished she recognized his name, so she would know already what had happened to him. But she didn't, and actually, so many of William's barons had changed their names after they'd settled in England, that their original names hadn't been documented.

Finally, they reached the tent, but Guy didn't let go of her arm until she was inside it. 'You will stay here now until our lord returns.'

Our lord? Thorn wasn't *her* lord. Now she wondered just who Guy thought she was, in relation to Thorn, or what he'd been told about her. She wasn't going to ask him, however. She might not like the answer, and she'd undergone enough embarrassment for one day.

But his commanding tone did raise her hackles, if for no other reason than he was a fourteen-year-old boy taking it upon himself to order about a woman of twenty-nine. Teenage boys might carry more weight than adult women here, but *she* wasn't going to abide by that social convention too, on top of all the other restrictions that were apparently going to be imposed on her during her short time here.

So she told him in a tone that she assumed would brook no contradiction, 'I'll stay here, Guy, but only because I choose to now. But I don't need a babysitter, so why don't you run along and try to get Thorn back here pronto – that is, at the soonest.'

His cheeks flushed with color again, but he looked angry now. The tone she had taken with him had probably reminded him of his mother, and it was a sure bet that no other woman besides that lady had ever before dared to tell him what to do. Medieval boys were under their father's governance, and those of rank like this one were fostered off to other households at young ages to be trained by other knights.

He didn't reply to her own directive; he merely turned on his heel and departed. Roseleen sighed. She supposed that it hadn't been very smart of her to alienate one of the few people she was acquainted with here. That incident with the soldiers must have upset her more than she'd realized, for her to be so touchy. Still, she had no business getting all bent out of shape just because a teenager was acting *normal* – for his time. After all, as a teacher, she'd been trained to handle young people.

Annoyed with herself now as much as with Thorn and Guy, she paced while she waited for her Viking to appear. It wasn't easy with her long skirts, as she continually had to kick them out of the way.

An hour passed, then another. She was beginning to suspect that Guy hadn't gone to fetch Thorn as she'd suggested. In his anger, he might have decided to let her stew all morning. *Bake* was more apropos, with the sun slowly turning the tent into an airless oven.

She was sweating profusely by midday, and her stomach was assuring her that she was starving. And the two discomforts combined soured her mood further, which was probably why she blasted Thorn the second he joined her.

She didn't even give him a chance to straighten up fully after he ducked to get inside through the tent flap, before she was snapping at him with a fulsome glare, 'It's about damn time! How dare you bring me here and then desert me? If I didn't know my history so well, I could have gotten into serious trouble this morn—'

He was lifting her off the ground by her upper arms, which was why she abruptly stopped her tirade in mid-sentence. The several hard shakes he proceeded to give her made her forget entirely what she'd been upbraiding him about. But he was quick to remind her.

'How dare you leave this tent when you were expressly told not to, woman? Have you no care for your own safety? Can you not imagine what would have happened—?'

'You can hold it right there,' she cut in. 'I know exactly what would have happened if that nice Sir Reinard hadn't come along when he did. But I wouldn't have been caught in an unpleasant situation like that if you had been here when I woke up this morning. We're here together, Thorn, remember? We're not here so you can go off and do your own thing while I sit around twiddling my thumbs. And that little twerp squealed on me, didn't he?'

'Twerp?'

'The boy. Guy.' And then she said even more dryly, 'You didn't *really* expect me to follow the dictates of a teenager, did you?'

He gave her another shake at that point, probably because she wasn't sounding very contrite after the first ones. Still dangling off the ground, she responded by frowning darkly right into his face. He was actually making her feel like a kid, because he was so much bigger than she was and people – at least the people of her time – just didn't treat an adult woman the way he was treating her.

Although *teenager* wasn't a word he knew, he must have assumed she was still talking about Guy.

'I expected you to have the sense to do just that,' he informed her. 'Guy was given explicit directions concerning your welfare. Did he not warn you to remain in this tent?'

'Actually, he only said something about keeping me safe here until your return.'

His dark frown was much more effective than hers had been, making her feel distinctly uneasy, making her wish she hadn't used the excuse that she'd translated the kid's warning too literally.

They both knew she had understood she wasn't to leave the tent, but had done so anyway.

He didn't even bother to point that out, saying simply but emphatically, 'You will never again go against my express orders, no matter *who* informs you of them. Because of your willfulness, I am now indebted to a man I had no wish to be indebted to.'

Was that why he was so angry, rather than because she had nearly gotten seriously injured? Roseleen wondered. The thought hurt, and she said derisively, 'Well, isn't that too bad.'

That got her yet another hard shake. She realized then she ought to wait until he put her down before she laid on the sarcasm quite so thickly. And it definitely was time for him to put her down. She was about to say so, but he wasn't finished with his chastisement.

'Aye, it will be too bad, for you, when he finds out you are my leman rather than my lady.'

She knew the word well enough, the medieval equivalent of *mistress*, a kind of woman who had been treated with no more respect in the past than she was in the twentieth century. Which was why she screeched, 'What?! How dare—!'

'He may now be bold enough to ask for payment in the form of . . . you.'

'He – he wouldn't – dare!' she sputtered, outraged, but in the next breath added, 'And I suppose you would just give me to him if he does?'

216

'Nay. Does he ask, I will kill him.'

That upset her even more. 'Oh, sure, the man does a good deed and you lop off his head for it. What kind of thanks is that, when a simple no-you-can't-have-her would suffice?'

'The insult will have been given—'

'I don't want to hear any of that macho male garbage, Thorn. Why the hell did you say I was your leman in the first place?'

' 'Tis what I was forced to tell Lord William, in order for you to be presented to him, since he had previously asked and had been told, that I have no lady.'

'Why didn't you tell him I'm a damsel in distress that you just happened upon? Or a sister who's come to visit? Or simply a friend—'

'When he will see the way I look at you?'

She made a loud sound of exasperation and struggled to get her feet back on the ground. It was a vain attempt that had her snapping, 'Put me down!'

He did, with a sigh and the complaint, 'What am I to do with you?'

That really rubbed her the wrong way, as if she were a bothersome chore he had to deal with. 'Not a damn thing,' she informed him. 'I'm not your responsibility.'

'Here you are just that, or have you so little knowledge of this time that you are not aware that women are under the care and direction of either their father, their husband, or their liege lord? They are never left to their own devices. Those without a man's protection do not survive long.'

She did know that, and it infuriated her that she could say nothing to contradict it. That's the way it was, no matter that it was rotten, chauvinistic, and unfair. And that equality of the sexes hadn't come about until her lifetime showed just how long that medieval system had survived. They called it protecting. She called it a nice name for slavery.

Unable to refute his last statement, she attacked on another front instead, one she had a legitimate grievance over. 'The next time you decide to sweep us back in time, Thorn, kindly inform me about it beforehand. Waking up in strange places has a way of putting me in a really rotten mood.'

'So I have noticed.'

'No you haven't,' she corrected him. 'You didn't get to see that mood, because you weren't here when I woke up. The mood you're seeing now is a result of your not having been here to see the other. "He is conferring with the duke," I was told. Why the hell couldn't you have waited for me?'

'Because 'twas not even dawn when I left, and you needed your rest – after last night.'

She gave him another glare, because he'd

managed to make her blush with that pointed reminder of what had passed between them last night. What a rotten tactic, she thought, to stir up soft, mellow, sensual memories in the middle of an argument. She wasn't going to let it work, and pushed those warm feelings away, telling her awakening body to *cut it out*. Quickly, she turned around to march away from Thorn.

Unfortunately, she forgot to kick her long skirts out of the way. Stepping on them sent her toppling to the floor, facedown, in a heap of skirts and acute embarrassment. How *could* she be so clumsy when she'd been doing so well at getting her complaints on record? She wasn't going to move, ever – at least not until he left.

Thorn had other ideas. With one hand, he turned her over. His other hand took hers and was about to pull her up when he must have changed his mind. His knees hit the floor beside her. His chest was suddenly pressing against hers. And his mouth, well, his mouth was reminding her that she really did love the way he kissed.

So much for complaints and high tempers, she thought. That easily, he made her forget what they'd been scolding each other about. And it was quite some time before Roseleen was capable of any coherent thoughts. By then, she really didn't care.

23

'You do that very well,' Roseleen said, her fingers drawing circles around the hard nub of Thorn's nipple.

She didn't need to be more explicit. He knew she was referring to his lovemaking. That the remark produced a blush in him made her smile. He wouldn't be used to twentieth-century frankness. She wasn't used to it either, for that matter, but for some reason, she felt she could say just about anything to him.

'It's true, you know,' she continued. 'Not that I've had much experience at this sort of thing, mind you' – that with a grin. 'But when you manage to bring me to climax twice in a matter of minutes, well, I can guarantee you the average Joe can't boast of such a rare accomplishment – at least not truthfully anyway.'

' 'Tis unseemly, of what you speak,' he grumbled.

Was his blush a little darker? She almost laughed. It really was amusing to see this big, fearless, battle-hardened Viking getting embarrassed by her talking about sex.

So she asked him, 'How can anything that was that beautiful be unseemly?'

' 'Tis for doing, not discussing.'

'Why?'

He started to get up, his way of avoiding the subject. They were still lying on the floor where that beautiful experience had taken place. She leaned over him to keep him there. He let her have her way, but his expression was quite disgruntled now.

She did laugh this time, unable to help it. 'Go ahead, call me brazen. I know you're dying to.'

'Aye, you are that.' He snorted.

'You still haven't told me why.'

'Such loose talk is for prostitutes and . . .'

He thought better of finishing. Wise of him, but too late, since it was easy enough for her to complete the statement for him. 'Lemans?' she said, and was amazed that she felt no anger as she said the word this time. She was even able to ask, 'What we just did, doesn't that make me your leman – to your way of thinking?'

'It makes you my woman.'

'There's a difference?'

'Aye.'

That had her brow shooting up at a skeptical slant. 'Oh, and what would that be?'

'A man does not take his leman to wed.'

Roseleen became very still upon hearing that. A sort of panic set in, but with it, and contradicting it, was a warm feeling similar to joy – which she had to be mistaken about. Marry Thorn Blooddrinker? Of course she couldn't. He was a thousand years old. He could disappear on her at will. And she was probably certifiably crazy, and imagining this whole experience *and* him.

Yet nothing in the world would have kept her from asking, 'You're saying you would wed me?'

'Aye.'

And then hesitantly, with bated breath, 'Are you asking me to wed?'

'When 'tis time for asking, you will not be in doubt, Roseleen.'

Her expression turned abruptly to chagrin at that point. 'So you aren't asking?'

'There needs be some taming done, ere you will make a good wife,' he informed her matter-of-factly.

She reared up until she was kneeling beside him. Her chocolate-brown eyes sparked with rancor. 'Taming? *Taming!* I'm not a damn animal that you can snap your fingers at. I thought I'd made that perfectly clear in previous discussions. And I wouldn't marry you if you were—!'

She didn't get a chance to finish telling him the facts of liberated life. In no more time than it would have taken to snap her own fingers, she was flat on her back again with his body half covering hers. It was a sensual way for him to remind her that they were both still naked.

But more lovemaking wasn't on his mind, complaining was, and he didn't hesitate one little bit. 'You do need taming, wench. You are a veritable shrew.'

She gasped. 'I am not!'

'Are you not?' he countered. 'Do you not yell at the least provocation? Do you not rail at me for what only you perceive as faults? Verily, you are more oft in a temper than not.'

Roseleen just passed from simmering to boiling, but managed somehow to say in a moderately level tone, 'Get off me, you jerk.'

At which point the big jerk grinned down at her. 'Nay, I am most comfortable at present. Such close proximity allows for swift quieting, do you think to yell again.'

He was talking about kissing her to shut her up. It had worked for him before. He probably thought it would work every time. He was in for a rude awakening if he tried it now. But she wanted up and away from him, pronto. She was fairly choking on the insults she had just received. However, she found that getting that big, heavy body to move was an impossible task unless he cooperated with her, and at the moment, it didn't look as if he would.

'All right, what's it going to take to get you to back off?'

His finger brushed her cheek as he said, 'Is this what you really want?'

'Right now? Damn right.'

He moved, but not to let her up. He covered her completely instead, and let his weight settle slowly against her. His head came to rest against her breast. For some unfathomable reason known only to him, he hadn't believed her. Either that, or the man was going to have *his* way regardless of her feelings on the matter, and she sincerely hoped he wasn't that high-handed.

'Did I make mention, Roseleen, of how fetching you looked in these clothes you wore?'

She knew he was changing the subject in an attempt to defuse her anger. And it even worked for a moment, the mention of clothes reminding her that Thorn had been wearing new ones himself, not those that had been left in her shower last night. And he certainly hadn't borrowed his long brown tunic and cross-gartered leggings from her brother's closet.

'Did you go to Valhalla for a change of clothes?' she asked without thinking.

He leaned up to show her that he was still amused, his grin proving it. 'How, then, could I have returned here, without your summoning me?'

She really hated stupid questions, especially when they were hers. 'All right, so where did you get such perfect-fitting clothes on such short notice? You're not exactly an average medieval size, easy to accommodate.'

'The clothes are mine from my previous time here. There are more in yonder trunk.'

She recalled then what she had suspected earlier, and all the questions she had wanted to ask him. She wasn't exactly in an information-gathering mood, but some of those questions were too pertinent to put aside until she was, particularly . . .

'You aren't in danger of running into yourself here, are you?'

'Nay.'

'But the boy Guy spoke as if he's known you for a long time.'

'So he has.'

'Okay, let's say my mind isn't functioning with a full load today, because I don't understand.'

He recognized the sarcasm in her tone, but he had some definite trouble with the content of that sarcasm. 'Neither do I understand your meaning.'

She sighed and tried to clarify. 'If I were thinking properly, I could probably figure this out for myself, but since I'm not, why don't you explain it to me. You were here previously. Guy knows you. So why aren't you going to run into yourself?'

'Because I had already departed from this time. I have brought you and me here to the very day that the possessor of my sword ceased to exist, thus was I released from your world's time and returned to mine on that day.'

'Ceased to exist? You mean she died?'

'So I assumed. That has always been the means that allowed my release from this world ere you received Blooddrinker's Curse. You are the only one of all the possessors who has seen fit to send me away. The others readily accepted the power of the sword and kept me in their times. Nor would they part with the sword, giving or selling it to another, which could have released me if that other were not a woman. Thus was I bound to them until each of them ceased to exist.'

'But you don't really know for certain if the woman here died. You didn't see it happen, right?'

'Nay, she resided in Anjou.'

She remembered what the boy had said, about being given to Thorn for training. 'It was Guy's sister, wasn't it?' she asked. 'Blythe?'

'He made mention of her?'

'Yes, this morning.'

Thorn nodded. 'Aye. She and her brother are both wards of Lord William. Her loyalty to her liege lord was admirable. I was here at her bidding, to guard William's back and support his cause.'

'Why did you agree to that? It certainly wasn't your cause – no, don't answer that,' she said with mild disgust. 'Dumb question. Any upcoming battle is exactly where you'd want to be.'

His grin turned into an outright laugh. 'Think you, you know me so well, do you?'

'When it comes to fighting?' she snorted. 'Yes, I've got you pegged squarely.' His confused frown had her correcting before he asked, 'That is, I know your sentiments on the subject exactly.'

'Mayhap,' he allowed. 'Yet in this instance, the cause was a good one. William is the rightful king of England. The English will be made to regret the choosing of the usurper, Harold Godwineson, in his stead.'

Hearing that, she felt like laughing. Offhand, she could name a dozen scholarly sources who disagreed with the Norman's right to the English crown. William the Bastard was simply an ambitious man of his times. Yet history was history and couldn't be refuted. The man did become the first Norman king of England and tied up that country in a pretty ribbon for his descendants. And yes, the English had been made to regret resisting his rule.

She wasn't going to argue with Thorn about it, though. She knew the facts that supported both sides of the argument, whereas he didn't, so she had an unfair advantage over him on that score.

227

Besides, the subject reminded her that she wanted to know how much time they had before the Normans set sail for England.

So she asked, 'What day is this?'

'A day for celebration.' He grinned. 'The fleet that has been gathering all summer is finally large enough to accommodate the entire army in one crossing. All is in readiness now, and we have news that Harold Godwineson has abandoned his vigil of the southern coast. We sail on the morrow.'

'You mean William actually found out that Harold was forced to disband his army due to lack of provisions?' she questioned excitedly. 'This is incredible! It was documented, of course, that Harold had to disband because the bulk of his army, which was composed of peasants, couldn't be contained once harvest time approached. But nowhere is it written that William was aware of this.'

Thorn shrugged. 'It matters not.'

'Of course it matters. This is the kind of unknown information I had hoped I would learn in coming here.' And then she grinned, glad that he hadn't done what she was about to point out. 'But you know, you could have just answered my first question and told me the date, and I would have known exactly what is going on. So how did William learn about Harold's return to London?'

'That news came from an English spy during his interrogation.'

She winced, imagining the degree of torture the poor fellow had to have undergone, to divulge something that important to his enemies. 'Amazing. And of course, that would explain why William was so impatient and frustrated with that north wind that prevented him from sailing from Saint-Valery for a whole two weeks.'

'Saint-Valery? We sail from the mouth of the Dives, where the fleet has assembled.'

'Yes, I know,' she said, her knowledge of what was going to happen making her tone slightly condescending. 'But the fleet moves to Saint-Valery on the Somme in order to be within closer striking distance.'

'Nay, why would you think so? For what reason would we not sail directly for the southern coast of England when we know it is presently unprotected?'

'Because on a shorter crossing there will be less chance of encountering the English fleet . . . Wait a minute!' She frowned. 'If William knows that Harold returned to London, does he also know that the English fleet dispersed? Is that why he would sail directly to – no, it doesn't matter. It's on record that he moves his fleet to Saint-Valery on the twelfth of September, regardless of whatever he found out about the English armies' movements.'

'Best you change that record,' Thorn told her, 'because this day is the first of September, and the fleet *will* sail on the morrow – for England.'

Roseleen paled. 'But it can't. That isn't the way it happened.'

24

Before Roseleen panicked for no reason, she wanted to verify the facts. 'You could be mistaken about the date, couldn't you?' she demanded of Thorn. 'You could have brought us here to the wrong day, and that means that your other self is still running around here somewhere and could walk in on us at any moment.'

'Nay, the day is correct.'

'But it can't be,' she said, panic creeping up on her despite her resolve. 'Did you ask someone around here? Did someone tell you specifically that today is September first?'

'Lord William made mention of it himself,' he answered, 'when he informed his barons that we would depart with the morning tide.'

She shook her head, searching desperately for a way to contradict that alarming statement, and it came to her after several agonizing moments. 'A false start! Of course, that has to be it. Maybe the duke did intend to sail for England tomorrow, but something will happen to prevent it. And none of this was ever documented. He'll sail on the twelfth as he's supposed to, and – don't shake your head at me. That is what's going to happen.'

'What could prevent our sailing, when the time is ripe to attack, and the ships are stocked and ready?'

'Another north wind, for one thing,' she told him. 'That's what stops the fleet from sailing from Saint-Valery on the twelfth, and—'

She didn't finish. That couldn't be right. If one north wind was documented, why not the other? It would have been just as important. And so was that spy. There had been mention of another spy who had been captured and sent back to King Harold with William's boasting message that if he didn't get to England within a year's time, then Harold could stop worrying about him. So why was there no mention of this one, whose confession nearly—?

'Wait a minute,' she said, frowning. 'If this is only the first of September, the information obtained from that spy can't be true. Harold Godwineson doesn't abandon the south of England until the eighth of September. If you sail tomorrow, you'd be sailing into an ambush that could cost William the crown of England.'

'The spy—'

'Could have been sent here purposely to get caught and convey that false information.'

'And to die?'

She winced, but she should have known that would have been the spy's fate. 'Don't sound so skeptical. Such sacrifices have been made many times before, for any number of reasons. Sometimes a man will volunteer out of simple loyalty, but more likely it's a man who's going to die anyway, either for his crimes or because of some disease, a man who has family and is promised by the powers-that-be that his loved ones will be taken care of.'

'You know this for certain?'

She sighed. 'No, of course not, but I do know for certain that Harold would just love for the Normans to arrive now, while he still has all his resources handy, including a much bigger army than William's, because he hasn't yet been called north to fight his brother, Tostig, and the Norwegian threat.'

'The Norwegian threat? Harold Hardrada of Norway finally attacks?'

It surprised her for a moment that he didn't know that, when that battle had been the last great Viking attack, and the last great triumph of an Old English army. But she was forgetting that Thorn had left this time today, on the first of September, and that battle took place later in the month, just days before William finally sailed for England. In fact most scholars agreed that if the Viking king, at Tostig's urging, hadn't attacked England at that time, Duke William wouldn't have won at Hastings.

Apparently, at Thorn's subsequent summonings, he'd never bothered to read any history books to find out the outcome of those battles. And she really didn't feel like getting into an in-depth history lesson just now. She still hadn't gotten Thorn to move off her, and now that her panic had subsided with the realization that nothing had been done yet that couldn't be undone by having a little chat with William before morning, she was becoming too aware again of the weight of his naked body, which was settled so comfortably on her.

So she told him, briefly, 'Yes, Hardrada attacked and lost. But Harold Godwineson exhausted his army in racing up north to deal with the Norwegian king, and some say that only half of those men he summoned when he learned of the Normans' landing had arrived back in London when he rushed south to deal with William, so he wasn't at full strength. And the host he did have with him was certainly weary from that hurried dash south, while William's army, though it might have been smaller, was in better shape to fight. However, that all happened many weeks from now. As long as William doesn't sail tomorrow—'

'I still ask you, why would he not?'

'Because we're going to tell him that that spy lied, that King Harold is still guarding the southern coast of England with far superior numbers than William has available.'

'And what proof do we offer?'

Roseleen groaned. Informing William of the trap had seemed so simple, but she hadn't considered how it would sound to him. If she tried to claim she knew the future, his future in particular, William of Normandy would undoubtedly label her a witch and toss her in the nearest dungeon to await burning by the Church. That certainly wouldn't stop the Norman fleet from sailing off to England tomorrow morning.

'All right, so we stay out of it,' she corrected. 'Telling someone here what's going to happen to them in advance of its happening is tampering with history, anyway, and we don't dare do that. But *something* is going to happen to keep this war on its proper timetable. We'll just have to wait and see what it is, I suppose.'

'And if naught—?'

'Don't even think it,' she cut in. 'History has *not* changed here, it just failed to document this unexpected development, and undoubtedly because nothing came of it. Now would you please get off me? I'd like to get dressed and meet the great man. That is why we're here, remember?'

He still made no effort to move, merely replied,

'Meeting Lord William will have to wait, Roseleen. This day he will be much too busy with preparations for the departure.'

She didn't try to hide her disappointment. 'And tomorrow I suppose he'll be too busy canceling all those preparations.'

'If he does not sail instead.'

He said that with a grin, which she found most annoying. Of course, any change in history wouldn't affect him, so why wouldn't he find this amusing? He didn't live in her world on a regular basis, merely for a few years here and there whenever he happened to be summoned.

He'd been born before this time. But she hadn't. A change in the history of the eleventh century could affect her and everything she knew. She might even cease to exist, and that would free Thorn to return to Valhalla, wouldn't it? No wonder he was grinning. He was probably hoping the Normans would sail tomorrow.

If they did sail – no, she didn't even want to think about it. They wouldn't, and on the bright side, that spy, and whatever was going to happen to keep the Normans from acting on his confession, was going to make great material for her book. But having to wait to find out what happened was going to drive her up a wall. She liked a good mystery, but not when she was personally involved in it.

'Since we have the rest of the day to kill, how about showing me around the docks?' she suggested. 'I'd love to see the *Mora*, the ship that William's wife gave him for this campaign.'

'First, you needs tell me how it is possible to kill a day.'

'That's just a figure of – never mind,' she said. 'I merely meant that since we have time to waste today, with nothing better to do—'

'You will have time enough to view the docks, Roseleen. I have something better in mind that will keep you busy for the rest of this day.'

Since he was already in a position to demonstrate what he had in mind, it didn't take her any time at all to find out what was going to keep her busy. He was, and he did.

25

Roseleen found it difficult to be angry with Thorn. A man who inexhaustibly doled out pleasure all day and all night was a treasure to be hoarded. She had been in seventh heaven, having Thorn's magnificent body accessible, even eager, for a full exploration. And she'd lost count of the climaxes he'd brought her to. She barely remembered being fed at some point during the evening.

It had been quite an experience, one she'd certainly never forget. This morning, she didn't even feel overused or exhausted, despite their excesses. He'd been too gentle with her for anything but pleasant memories to prevail.

But she ought to be angry with him. She suspected that he'd made love to her all day and night to take her mind off what was going to happen this morning – or what wasn't going to happen. She should have spent the time analyzing the situation and coming up with all possible outcomes, instead of wallowing in sensual indulgences.

And now, with dawn less than an hour away, and with her having had only a few brief snatches of sleep to enable her mind to function, it finally became apparent that the camp was breaking, and probably had been all night. A quick glance outside the tent confirmed it. There was barely anyone left in the area. William's army had marched to the ships. They were going to sail.

She didn't panic – yet. But she did rush Thorn out of the tent. Guy had the unpleasant task of taking it down and packing all of Thorn's possessions in a baggage wain he'd obtained, though he'd hired several peasants to help. He'd be following behind them, already appraised of which ship they were to sail on.

She tried to tell the boy not to bother, that they'd be back, just as everyone else would, but Thorn cut her off, reminding her only after they were galloping toward the coast that they needed to play this out as if they weren't aware of other possible outcomes. At least he said something to that effect. She missed a few words because they were traveling so fast, but he was right.

Once again she'd forgotten to stick to their plan of action, but she had an excuse this time: Her mind was sluggish due to lack of sleep. She reminded herself though that no excuses of any kind could be tolerated because time traveling was serious business. One little mistake on their parts could alter millions of lives, and a major mistake could obliterate millions more – *herself included*.

The sun still hadn't quite made it over the horizon when they reached the still-crowded docks. Roseleen hoped that the hundreds of ships out in the mouth of the river were waiting to come in and load, but it was a slim hope. If anything, all the ships presently berthed were probably the last to be loaded with men and horses, the other vessels simply waiting for the tide to send them on their way.

Obviously, nothing had happened yet to end this premature departure of William's army. And if they actually sailed . . .

No, there were still a number of possibilities that could occur to send the army back to their campground. A sudden storm at sea would do it. Another fateful wind could blow down from the north. Or maybe one of the duke's spies would show up at the last minute with the real facts about the position of King Harold's army.

But nothing did occur, at least not before the last ship departed. That Roseleen happened to be on that ship was due to the stubbornness of her Viking. Thorn had refused to stay behind with a battle in the offing, even though she'd assured him – she was still positive that something would yet occur – that there wouldn't be a battle for another month.

Roseleen had never sailed on a modern ship, much less an ancient vessel like the one she was on. Seasickness didn't bother her, but then it wasn't one of her worries. She kept watching the sky for some dark clouds, and the sails to determine which way the wind blew. Unfortunately, they couldn't have asked for a nicer day for sailing. And the winds continued at a steady pace in the wrong direction – wrong in her opinion.

She didn't give up hope, however, which was why she almost fell into a state of shock when they sighted the shores of England. Simultaneously, English ships swooped down from the north to attack their flanks, ships that wouldn't have been there if history had been following its correct course. But it wasn't, and as soon as they had landed, the Normans would find out that the English, at full strength, would be too formidable to defeat.

Maybe not. Maybe some miracle would still occur. Maybe only the timetable had been altered, not the final results. But Roseleen had no intention of being there to find out firsthand. She had been taken unawares into one battle with Thorn. She would pass on this one, thank you, especially since she only had to open a history book to find out the results of it. But she had to get to that history book first.

So she turned to Thorn, who'd never been far

from her side during the crossing, and told him, 'Take me home.'

She supposed it was natural for him to look back in the direction they'd sailed from. When his eyes came back to her with a frown, she added, 'Not to Normandy. To my home, in my time.'

'You wouldst leave before the battle?'

'Most definitely,' she assured him, despite his amazed tone, then quickly said, 'Look, I'm sorry. I know you'd love to be in on this battle, but we can't. History is changing even as we speak. There was never a sea battle here, yet those ships yonder are engaged. And Duke William really doesn't stand a chance of winning at this point in time. Circumstances helped to give him an advantage next month. Right now, King Harold has all the advantages.'

'If one thing has changed, could not other things have changed also?'

Roseleen knew he was right. Anything was possible now, with history rewriting itself.

So she said, 'Yes, and we'll know in a few minutes, as soon as I get to my research books. With them, I can find out what went wrong here, what changed things. So take me back now, Thorn.'

He stared now at the English shore in front of them, as if he were actually undecided, as if the choice were his to make whether they left or stayed for the battle. She reminded him that it wasn't.

'You promised, Thorn, that you'd return us when I ask. So let's go, and pronto.'

'What does this "pronto" mean, that you keep—'

'It means *now*,' she fairly snapped, no patience left. 'As in yesterday, as in . . . just do it.'

He did. With a sigh to let her know how much he objected, he drew his sword. The next moment, they were both back in modern-day England, but not in her bedroom in Cavenaugh Cottage, or any other room in the lovely old home that had been bequeathed to her.

They stood in open country, with a high wind blowing. There were only a few trees to break the monotony of the dismal landscape. Not a house or a barn was in sight, or any roads, or utility poles. No signs of life at all. Dark gray clouds moved swiftly overhead, threatening rain at any moment.

In horror, Roseleen whispered, 'Where have you brought us, Thorn? And please tell me it's a mistake.'

But he said exactly what she didn't want to hear. 'I have returned us to your house, in your time, as I did before – yet it is not here.'

26

Thorn had put it rather simply, for such an alarming statement. No, Cavenaugh Cottage certainly wasn't there. But why wasn't it? Roseleen wondered. Had it been destroyed somehow, or had it never been built in the first place? And this was only one change, she realized. How many other things would be different now?

The world as she knew it had been altered, but the question was, how drastically? Obviously, her own ancestors had survived, because she still existed. And she assumed she looked the same, since Thorn wasn't staring at her strangely. But had her grandparents moved to America as they'd originally done? Was she English now, or still American? Was there even an America, or was it a country by a different name now?

The possibilities and questions were endless, and pointless. She wasn't going to get any answers until she could find a phone. She'd call David or Gail. They'd think she was crazy, when she posed the questions she was going to ask them, but she had no choice.

As for what changes had occurred in the history of the world – obviously, her research books weren't going to be available to supply those answers. If she had lodgings anywhere around here, she had no idea where to find them. And maybe she didn't have any research books in this different world. She might not even be a professor here, might not have attended college, might not . . .

She *had* to get to a phone. She also had to find a library. And she had to fight down her feelings of dread and her fear that there would be nothing she could do to get things back to the way they should be.

'What has occurred here, Roseleen?'

Thorn sounded merely curious, while she was approaching the red section on the panic scale. 'Just what I warned you would happen. Everything's different, because that battle wasn't supposed to take place at that time. But it did, and the rest of history went on to reflect it, a chain reaction of changes in every century thereafter, leaving us with . . . I don't know what. The people I know and work with might not even exist now – oh, God, I can't believe this has actually happened, and just because of one little spy's false confession.'

His arms were suddenly around her, gathering her close, and his wide chest was there for her to cry on. But she didn't cry. His simple action had reminded her that she wasn't alone. Without a doubt, she knew that her Viking wouldn't let anything or anyone hurt her, and that made her feel safe and protected, tamping down those other negative feelings that had been getting out of hand.

She drew from his strength, and he had a lot to give. With a sigh, she said, 'I need to get to a phone to call my brother, but it doesn't look like we'll find one around here. Are you sure you've got us back to the right century?' she added hopefully. 'You couldn't be a few hundred years off the mark, maybe?'

'Nay, as I told you, the sword will return to its own present, no matter if that present is altered.'

'Okay, so you've got this time-hopping thing down pat.' She sighed again. 'It looks like we've got a long walk ahead of us, to find someone who can help or point us toward the nearest phone or library – if such things even exist.'

Before that thought could cause her further panic, another occurred to her that brightened her expression with excitement. 'Wait a minute!' she said. 'Maybe things have only gone drastically different in this country. You said you could travel back to anyplace you have been before, didn't you, Thorn? And it doesn't even matter what country you're in when you do it, because we ended up in France on that last jump.'

'Aye.'

'Then take us back to my classroom, to the night I first summoned you. If my college still exists, they'll have all the history books we need.'

'To take you there, Roseleen, would be to have you meet yourself,' he pointed out.

She groaned again, very loudly. 'Did your Odin ever say exactly what would happen if that occurred?'

'Nay, he did merely stress that it must not occur.'

'Then could you maybe advance the time a bit, to the day after I first summoned you, but still get us to my classroom? I wasn't there the next day, and neither were you.'

'Certainly,' he replied. 'Did I not say such was possible?'

He expected her to remember every little thing he'd told her about time traveling, when they were in the middle of a crisis? But before she could say something to that effect, they were already on their way – and in for another surprise.

The classroom was there, it just wasn't Roseleen's classroom – or rather, it was smaller than it should be. The view out the windows was the same though, the grounds lit up even on a

Saturday night. At least, she assumed it was Saturday night, the night after she'd first met Thorn.

And there was electricity, certainly enough light from outside to see the light switch by the door, which she flipped on immediately. Thank heavens for small advancements. No Age of Invention was just one of the possibilities that could have occurred in this altered world.

'Okay, this is at least familiar ground,' she told Thorn with a great deal of relief. 'Obviously, the founder of Westerley College still founded it.'

'Yet is it not the same,' he remarked.

'I noticed,' she said as she headed for what she hoped was her desk. 'And thank goodness this change is only a minor technicality that was due to probably nothing more than a shortage of funds this time around, which would have cut down the size of each classroom—'

'Speak so that I may understand you, Roseleen.'

She stopped abruptly, turning back around to him. That had been pure testiness in his tone. *Now* he was getting upset about something? When she saw that he was staring at the walls where the medieval posters should have been, but weren't now, she guessed what was bothering him. He even confirmed it before she could ask.

'I am beginning to realize that Lord William did not achieve his goal,' he said.

'I already told you the odds were against it if the Normans attacked at that time. You didn't believe me?'

'We had strength in numbers.'

'Harold Godwineson had greater strength in numbers,' she reminded him.

'William's cause was just.'

'There are those who disagree—'

'*Why* did this happen, Roseleen?' he demanded impatiently. 'You said he became king.'

'Yes, in the proper order of things he did, but that proper order must have been changed by that premature attack we were witnessing. And since that attack was a direct result of that English spy and his false confession, I can only assume that something went wrong there.'

'Where?'

'With that spy. Maybe he wasn't caught originally. Or if he was, maybe he thought better about lying, or somehow William found out he was lying, or . . . There I go speculating again, when there *has* to be a history book around here. I kept the first and second semester volumes from the course I taught in the bottom drawer of my desk. We're due for a little luck . . .'

She yanked open the bottom drawer, and there were two books. But they weren't hers. They were different in size and the authors were different, though the subject was still medieval history. And they were engraved as she'd had hers engraved with her name. The name on these . . .

'I don't believe it!' she fairly shrieked. 'Roseleen Horton? Roseleen *Horton*! I married that lying, cheating, conniving bastard?'

'Who?'

'Barry Horton,' she lamented in disgust. 'You remember? *Blueberry*.'

'The one whose likeness you destroyed?'

'Exactly. I despise the man. He stole from me. How could I possibly be so stupid in this revised version of the world as to marry him?'

'You are married?'

There was a sharp edge to his tone that she failed to notice in her agitation. 'Not for long,' she assured him. 'There has to be a way to correct whatever went wrong and get things back to normal here, because I'd go nuts if I thought I had to live with Barry as my husband. We just have to figure out what needs to be corrected, and I'll get started on that right now. Pull up a chair, Thorn. This may take a while.'

It would have taken much less time if the authors weren't so detailed in their chapter summaries, or such overall good writers. Roseleen's fascination was caught in discovering all the differences in the two histories, and what things didn't change. And included in the back of the second volume was a brief accounting of the centuries after the Middle Ages, right up to modern times, at least these new modern times, listing all the major events of importance.

It was a good two hours later before she closed the second book, and she'd merely been skimming through the summaries in both books, not the whole chapters. Thorn had sat there silently all the while, mostly just watching her read. That took quite a bit of patience on his part, which the average man just didn't have. Of course, there was nothing average about Thorn. She'd discovered that right from the start.

And now she had to tell him the bad news, that his hero, his liege lord, had died far sooner than he should have. But she didn't have to go into detail about that, and she could keep him from dwelling on it by mentioning all the other incredible events she'd just read about.

So she told him, 'It's what I suspected would have happened, Thorn. What had previously been Duke William's advantage, that Harold God-wineson had come straight from battle with another army, became Harold Hardrada's advantage instead. The Norwegian king was able to defeat the English and become their new king.

'His house ruled England for a little more than a century, then what they call the Great Scandinavian Wars broke out. Instead of England's becoming more powerful from the infusion of strength it received through William's Norman line, it became just a minor country that supplied soldiers for the wars up north, which lasted several centuries.

'America was discovered much later than it should have been, and given some ridiculous-sounding name I refuse to repeat,' she said in disgust. 'It was still a melting pot of nationalities from tyrant countries, and still became independent, but not until the eighteen twenties.

'Europe has regressed to feudal states, under what is very similar to the feudal system of old that you're familiar with. The new "America" finally went democratic, though more than a hundred years late. Of course, better late than not at all, I suppose. With all the extra wars, little and big, and so many that I lost count, it's no wonder the Age of Invention got passed by, with only a few of the wonders of my day making an appearance in this new time. At this rate, it will be another hundred years before this world catches up to where it should be in the way of technology.'

She took a deep breath after that long recital and waited for Thorn's reaction. And waited. She was annoyed that he just continued to stare at her, making no comment after all that.

She let another few seconds pass before she finally demanded, 'Well, say something.'

He obliged her, but first he glanced again at that

empty wall that should have held the medieval posters. 'Do those books make mention of that English spy?'

Roseleen sighed. So much for getting him a little distracted from William of Normandy's premature demise. 'Yes, it's documented this time around, and that spy's confession, verified as false, by the way, gets full credit for the Normans' defeat. Up to that point, history is as I know it, every other occurrence exactly as it should be.'

'As it should be,' he repeated thoughtfully. 'And as it should be, there was no spy, correct?'

'Yes, at least, it was never documented. He *could* have been part of the original scenario, but not have been important enough to be mentioned.' Then she suddenly frowned. 'You know, it occurs to me that this undocumented incident might not have occurred at all if you and I hadn't been there, but I can't see how we could have changed anything that concerns that spy. I certainly didn't meet the fellow. Did you, when you went to see William yesterday morning?'

'Nay, he had already been disposed of.'

'Then it was a done deal before we even got there – wait a minute! What about your other Thorn?'

'Other Thorn?'

'I mean you,' she said impatiently. 'When you were first summoned to the eleventh century through the sword. You weren't really supposed to be there that time either, you were there only by unnatural means, because of the sword's curse. But when you were there then, did you have anything to do with that spy? Were you the one who captured him, or interrogated him?'

'Nay, I did not even know of him, until Sir John du Priel made mention of him.'

'Sir John?'

'He was present when the spy made his confession. He liked not the handling of the interrogation, and intended to question the man once more the next morn, but I challenged him to a bout of drinking that eventide, and he lost. He still slept the next morn, I believe.'

Roseleen's eyes flared wide. 'And that morning was when we were there yesterday, right? When the duke made his decision to sail?'

'Aye.'

'So the spy was disposed of before Sir John could speak to him again. That's it, Thorn! This Sir John fellow would probably have gotten the truth out of the man, and everything else would then have continued as it should have, with the two Harolds fighting first, and William not sailing to England until the end of September.'

'Yet how can that be changed?' he questioned. 'I have no control over what was previously done when I was first there, Roseleen.'

'Yes, you do,' she said with a grin.

'How?'

'We just have to go back a day sooner, before you were whisked back to Valhalla, and prevent your other self from challenging Sir John to that drinking match.'

He looked at her as if she'd asked him to chop off his own head. 'I cannot confront myself. This you were told. The very heavens would shake—'

'Don't exaggerate Viking style,' she chided him. 'And I'm not asking you to meet up with your other self. I can take care of that. You can just make sure that Sir John gets to bed early that night.'

He stood up, slapped his hands down flat on her desk, and leaned halfway across it. His blue eyes had narrowed so much, she actually drew back, somewhat intimidated. And she couldn't imagine what brought this on, but her Viking was most definitely angry about something. He didn't keep her in suspense for very long.

'How, exactly, wouldst you take care of it, Roseleen?'

The question came out in too slow and accusatory a manner for her not to grasp that he was thinking the worst, and that stirred her own ire. 'Just what have you tried and convicted me of here, Thorn? Do you honestly think I would do you – or rather, your other self, bodily harm, just to . . . keep . . .'

Her words trailed away because he was now

looking so startled by what she was saying, she knew she was mistaken in the conclusion she'd drawn. He confirmed it.

'That did not occur to me.'

'Then what—?'

She didn't finish – again. She started laughing as the only other reason that could provoke that kind of reaction in him came to mind. He was jealous, and of himself no less. It was absurd. It was also kind of thrilling. She'd never had anyone be jealous over her before.

' 'Tis not amusing,' he growled now.

'No, of course not,' she agreed with him, though she was still grinning widely. 'But the only thing I had in mind doing was distracting your other Thorn, and only long enough for you to put Sir John to bed.'

'But how will you distract him?'

'Have you never heard of conversation?'

'He had only two interests, and neither was for conversation.'

'Fighting and – women?' she guessed, and almost laughed again, recalling one of their earlier conversations about his needs. 'And in all these centuries, you've only added one interest to those two – food.'

He was getting annoyed with her amusement, enough to say, 'Nay, there is one other interest I now have – the proper training of my woman.'

It was a deliberate provocation. She knew that, and still it caught her squarely. She rose up along with her temper, to lean forward across her desk just as he was doing, glaring at him nose to nose.

'You are borderlining it, big guy, using the word *training* in a context other than job-related. When is it going to sink in that women today stand on an equal footing with men?'

'If there is aught equal between men and women, I would you show it to me now,' he countered.

'I'm not talking brawn and size, and I believe you know that.'

'Nay, what you speak of is having the last say in all things. Wherein is that equal?'

That gave her pause. Had she been coming off with a superior-than-thou attitude without realizing it? Had she let the fact that he knew next to nothing about her world fool her into thinking he wasn't intelligent? He was merely barbaric in certain aspects of his thinking – where women were concerned – and that was perfectly normal, all things considered, particularly since it had been more than two hundred years since he'd last been summoned. Equality between men and women certainly hadn't existed in the seventeen hundreds.

She owed him an apology, she supposed, and a broad one, since she'd probably tweaked his pride in more areas than just one, albeit unintentionally. But she wasn't looking forward to it at the moment, when she was still simmering over that 'training' crack. So the interruption just then would have been welcome – if it were anyone other than who it was: her nemesis, Barry Horton.

27

'What are you doing here, Rosie? Didn't I tell you to stay home today?'

Even though Roseleen had read the name engraved on the books, it was still disconcerting to realize that she had actually married this man in this altered world. And he was vastly changed from the Barry she knew. His gray eyes were the same, of course, but his light blond hair was long and unkempt, his clothes casual and sloppy, rather than in their usual pristine condition, not exactly the sophisticated academic look he'd always strived for.

And to be confronted with questions that she wasn't sure how to answer? How nice. He couldn't just say 'I see you're busy so I'll talk to you later.' No, good old Barry, rude to the last drop, and in a tone guaranteed to annoy her.

'Did you?' Roseleen replied stiffly. 'I don't recall.' And then she couldn't resist adding, 'And even if you had, Barry, you don't really think I—'

'Do you need another lesson in obedience?' he cut in as he walked toward her.

His expression, not to mention his tone, had turned downright threatening. And what he'd said implied that she'd been taught lessons before. Unbelievable. Barry Horton had turned into a wife beater? And apparently he didn't care who knew it, if he could say something like that in front of Thorn.

But then, he hadn't even spared a glance at Thorn, was treating him as if he weren't even there. And their medieval garb hadn't drawn a single comment from him, though her own yellow gown, elaborate as it was, was a little less out of the ordinary than Thorn's cross-gartered leggings and sword. But still you'd think Barry, as derisive as he could be, would have made some remark . . .

Treating him as if he weren't there?

Roseleen looked sharply in Thorn's direction. She'd wondered once before if anyone else in her time could see him. Mrs Humes might have served dinner for two that night at the Cottage, but Roseleen didn't actually recall the woman looking at Thorn or speaking to him. She'd been told there would be two for dinner and she'd served two settings, but she wasn't the type who would mention the fact that no one was sitting in the other chair. An American housekeeper wouldn't hesitate to ask, 'You do realize, don't you, that you're eating alone?' But the reserved Mrs Humes would put it down to American eccentricity and might discuss it with her husband later, but she wouldn't remark on it to her employer.

Only in the past had she actually seen people talk to Thorn.

On the other hand, Thorn Blooddrinker was a very intimidating man, especially with that sword on his hip. Any contemporary man with any sense at all wouldn't want to draw his notice, might even go to extremes to avoid it, and ignoring him as if he weren't there could be one of those extremes.

She decided to settle the matter and ask Barry outright if he could see Thorn, but when she glanced back at him to do so, she found him raising a fist to her. She gasped, but there was simply no time to avoid the blow he intended to deliver. There was barely enough time for her to cringe and close her eyes.

But nothing happened. He obviously had thought better of it, or decided to wait until they were in the privacy of their own home, wherever that was. Or maybe just the threat of impending violence had worked on her in the past. Was she supposed to be properly subdued and submissive now? Fat chance of that. What she was was angry, furious actually, at the scare she'd just been given.

But she opened her eyes to find that she was wrong on all counts. Barry hadn't changed his mind about hitting her, he'd had it changed for him. Thorn had hold of his fist, and although Barry was straining mightily to break that hold, he couldn't quite manage it. Thorn, on the other hand, wasn't straining at all. When Barry finally noticed that – he *could* see Thorn, obviously – he gave up.

With an impotent glare in her direction, Barry ordered, 'Call off this cretin, Rosie, or you'll regret—'

'I wouldn't be making any threats right now if I were you,' she said as she crossed her arms over her chest. It was all she could do to keep from grinning. 'My friend here might not like it.'

'I don't care what—' he started to bluster, but she was pleased to cut that off too.

'Also, I'd apologize for calling him a cretin. Vikings take exception to being likened to idiots, and although I'm sure you didn't mean it in that context, that you were more or less only making reference to his considerable size, albeit in a derogatory way, he wouldn't see it that way.'

To give him credit, Barry did pale somewhat, though it just wasn't in his character to back down, especially since Thorn hadn't actually done him any harm, and it didn't really look as if any was forthcoming. That in itself annoyed Roseleen quite a bit. Thorn could have at least looked a little angry, considering Barry's intention had been to do *her* harm. But his expression was inscrutable, giving away nothing of his thoughts or feelings.

Barry must have taken courage from that, because his tone didn't change at all as he accused her, 'You've taken leave of your senses, right?'

'Yes, apparently, or I wouldn't still be talking to you. So state your business here, Barry, then get out. Or is your business stealing again? After all, you assumed I wouldn't be here, didn't you?'

He actually looked uneasy now. Had she hit it on the nose with her taunting dig?

'I don't know what you're talking about,' he insisted, though his voice lacked the strength that that statement demanded.

'Sure you don't. I wouldn't happen to keep my research notes here, would I? Haven't you gotten around to stealing them yet, this time around?'

'This time? I've never—'

'Oh, shut up, Barry,' she interrupted him again. 'I'm not going to get into how I've been through this before. But it was wise of you to wait until after you married me this time. Sort of gives me a second chance to stop you if I was willing to take it, but I'm not. I'd much prefer getting back to where I *didn't* marry you.'

Of course, he really had no idea what she was talking about now. How she wished it were the Barry *she* knew standing there instead, rather than this wife-beating double. Ironic, that both Barrys were apparently real jerks.

'Divorce?' Barry concluded from what she'd

said. 'If you think I'll grant you one—'

'Divorce won't be necessary,' she told him with a tight little smile. 'I have a much quicker way of getting you out of my life.'

And to get on to it, she turned to Thorn. 'We can go now, back to the date we decided on. I've got everything I need here.'

His nod of agreement was typically curt. And there was one glorious moment of watching Barry blanch as Thorn let go of him to draw Blood-drinker's Curse. Apparently, Barry thought killing him was her 'quicker way.' But the moment was a brief one, because Thorn extended his hand, and she took it. However, it was replaced by an even briefer moment that was priceless – the expression on Barry's face as they disappeared right in front of him.

28

It took Roseleen a few moments to realize where she and Thorn were, back in the eleventh century. They were standing outside a hostelry, with sounds of rowdiness coming from inside, and the smell of the docks intruding from close by. But then she was still savoring Barry's incredulous expression, and thinking that it was too bad that she would never see that particular Barry again so that she could get in a little gloating over it. But putting world history back on the right track was more important, a lot more.

Still, she was grinning when she glanced at Thorn and said, 'If we had to shock someone with our disappearing act, I'm glad it was him.'

He grunted. 'Your Blueberry husband is a man not to my liking.'

She recalled that inscrutable expression he'd worn and remarked, 'Well, you could have fooled me. You seemed not to mind him one way or the other. And he won't be my husband anymore, at least he won't be as soon as we correct things here.

"Ex-fiancé" has a much nicer ring to it where that jerk is concerned.'

'I minded, Roseleen,' Thorn said with an edge to his tone. 'Did I do as I would have preferred, Blooddrinker's Curse would have feasted—'

She cut in with a tsking admonishment. 'Killing wasn't called for, Thorn.'

He sighed. 'Verily, did I know you wouldst say some womanish thing as that.'

She realized he wasn't asking a question, but stating a fact. So he'd refrained for her sake?

That produced another grin from her and the comment, 'But I wouldn't have minded if you had socked him.'

'Socked him?'

'Hit him a little bit.'

He looked down at his hands. 'There is no little bit involved when I hit. Ask my brother, Thor. I am the only one who can—'

'Are you bragging again, Thorn?'

He shrugged before replying, 'Vikings brag – but only with the truth.'

She laughed at that, feeling inordinately pleased with him all of a sudden. So he'd merely contained his anger? And he'd come to her defense, rescued her in his own fashion. He might not be wearing armor, but he was definitely a shining knight in her eyes.

'Well, I guess it's time for me to meet your other

Viking. But I hope you aren't going to tell me he's already inside that drinking establishment we've arrived at. Or are ladies allowed in—?'

'Nay, 'tis a place not for *ladies*, but for—'

'You don't have to elaborate,' she cut in. 'I catch your drift.'

'And I wouldst not allow you to enter such a place,' he added.

'Thank you – I think. Then I take it your other self hasn't arrived yet?'

'Nay, but Sir John was already here when I came that night. I will speed him on his way to bed now, so you needs not deal with my other self.'

'Wait a minute,' she said in surprise. 'I was looking forward to meeting you – the other you, that is.'

'You do *not* want to meet him, Roseleen. He would know you not, and he—'

'Yes, yes, I know, he had only two things always on his mind. But are you sure he isn't going to show up while you're busy in there? What if Sir John doesn't want to leave right away? And remember, he has to be hale and hearty in the morning, not suffering any wounds that you might inflict if he gives you a hard time.'

He frowned, probably realizing that he didn't have too many options for getting Sir John out of there. 'Aye, he had a woman chosen for the night, the prettiest to be had. 'Twas why I challenged him to the drinking bout, as I recall. I wanted her for myself.'

Jealousy came up out of nowhere to poke its green horns at Roseleen. And it was absurd. It wasn't this Thorn who wanted that other woman, at least not now, but the other one, and . . . and that didn't seem to matter where these particular emotions were concerned.

'Just make sure you don't get tempted this time,' she grumbled.

He grinned at her tone, and suddenly she found herself pressed up against him, his arms tight around her, while his mouth played havoc with hers. Within seconds, he had her turned on, so it was rather frustrating when he ended that stirring kiss and let go of her.

It took her a few moments just to remember where they were and what they were supposed to be doing. But when she did, she decided she'd have to get even with him for making her want him that much, when he had no intention of actually making love to her.

'Verily,' he said softly, 'there is only one female capable of tempting me now.'

That had her blushing, and fighting to keep from grinning like an idiot – and forgetting about getting even. 'Well, in that case, you better get busy. And I suppose it wouldn't hurt if Sir John continues on as he had intended. Maybe if you slip a coin or two to the female, she'll hurry him out of there for you.'

'An excellent suggestion,' he replied.

'I'll just hide around the corner here, just in case you take too long and I need to do some distracting.'

He stopped long enough to say, 'There is a back door to this place. Await me there. There will be no need for you to do any distracting.'

'All right, all right, just go.'

He did, but she didn't.

Roseleen moved just around the corner of the building, where there were plenty of shadows to conceal her, and leaned against the wall there to wait. Thorn would realize where she was when he finished and would call her to join him. She had no doubt of that, and she'd worry later about his annoyance with her for not doing what he'd told her to do.

In the meantime, she wasn't going to take the chance on having his other self show up too soon and walk into the hostelry while he was still in there. She couldn't imagine what would happen if they ended up facing each other, but she didn't want to find out.

But as luck would have it, time passed, and she heard footsteps approaching before she heard any call from the back of the building.

29

Roseleen peeked around the corner of the building, her breath held tight, her eyes straining. There he was – the other Thorn! He hadn't reached the light cast by the torches outside the hostelry yet. When he finally did, her eyes widened.

He seemed bigger than life. Of course, it had to be only her nervousness that made him seem so. He was still Thorn, just not the Thorn she had come to know.

This one's light brown hair was maybe a little longer, a little bit shaggier. Not for him the Norman fashion of short locks. He wouldn't conform any more than the other Thorn would – what was she thinking? They were the same man, just at two different times in their lives.

And this one didn't know her.

Her nervousness took a big leap toward apprehension. Why had Thorn been so insistent about her not meeting this other self of his? Was this one really so different from him? And then it hit her.

Of course he was. Think of how many centuries separated the two selves. The Thorn she knew had lived so much longer, had undoubtedly mellowed, matured, learned to control his emotions . . .

She was going to talk herself right out of doing what she knew she had to do, if she didn't stop it. And he had almost reached the door. Short of rushing over to stand in front of it so he couldn't pass her, and appearing quite deranged in the process, she wasn't sure what she could do to keep him out of that tavern. Of course, she didn't have to delay him for very long – she hoped.

With that firmly in mind, she called out, 'Excuse me, I could use a little help.'

When he glanced around, but after a moment, still reached for the door of the hostelry, she realized he couldn't see her. She quickly stepped out from the shadowed corner of the building to correct that.

The light caught her yellow gown and drew his eyes to her. His hand returned to his side. She apparently had his full attention – for the moment.

Her nervousness took another leap, especially since she still hadn't figured out what to say to keep him there. An easy time-consumer in her day would be to ask for directions to someplace and play dumb in confirming them, so she'd get a number of repeats and a very frustrated good Samaritan. But considering that ladies didn't go traipsing around towns in medieval England at night, at least not alone, she had to scratch that idea. Hadn't she already been reamed out for going around alone, even during the day?

His blue eyes were moving over her for a complete, leisurely inspection, the kind that bordered on insulting in her day. But men probably got away with it regularly in this time period. Come to think of it, he'd done the same thing to her before – rather her Thorn had. But this wasn't her Thorn. She had to keep that uppermost in her mind. This one didn't know her, was seeing her for the first time, and his inspection brought color to her cheeks that, fortunately, the torchlight wouldn't detect.

When his eyes finally came back up to settle on hers, it wasn't to ask what kind of help she needed. 'Where are your attendants, lady?'

She sighed in relief. He'd just given her her delaying excuse, and if she weren't so addled by this encounter, she would have thought of it herself.

'I've lost them,' she told him, and tried to sound suitably bewildered.

'Lost them?'

'My escort. We became separated. I have been wandering around looking for them for hours now. But I'm afraid to go any farther alone. I don't know this area, and it seems most – unsavory.'

'Where is it you should be?'

'I was to join the duke's party.'

He nodded, quite curtly. So he'd always had that habit? she thought, trying hard not to smile.

'There are bound to be some of Lord William's men in the hostelry. I will fetch several to escort you where you needs go.'

'No, don't do that,' she said quickly, and wracked her brain for a reason. All that came to her was, 'The duke's soldiers are notorious gossipers, and I can't have this getting around, that I was found lost and alone down by the docks. My reputation would be ruined. Just now, only you know – and of course my previous escort. But they will be too ashamed of losing me to speak of it.'

He seemed satisfied with that excuse, but still wasn't inclined to help her. 'I have not the time—'

'You have an engagement?'

'Nay, but—'

'Ah, you're just in a hurry to get to your . . . amusements. I understand, Thorn, but this really is an emergency. And the duke will be most apprecia—'

He interrupted with a frown, 'How do you know my name, lady?'

Roseleen groaned inwardly. That had been a real blunder, one she certainly hadn't intended. But this quibbling with him had been so familiar, she'd forgotten for a moment which Thorn she was dealing with. And unable to come up with any acceptable excuse for her blunder, she was forced to improvise again, this time with a little mystery that she hoped would hold his attention for a bit longer.

So she said, 'I know many things about you.'

'How so?' he asked. 'You are not one I would forget, had we met.'

That remark, complimentary as it was, was doing unexpected things to her, most critically making her forget again that he wasn't her Thorn. She found herself staring at his lips, for so long that he had to repeat his question.

'How do you know me, lady?'

Her eyes came back to his with a jolt, and she sighed. She really wished her Thorn hadn't kissed her so thoroughly just moments ago, leaving her wanting and . . . and here stood his double, with the same looks she found so handsome, the same war-hardened body, the same lips that knew so well how to devastate her senses . . . He was damn lucky she wasn't crawling all over him already.

'Let us say your reputation has grown far and wide,' she said, unable to keep the grouchiness out of her tone at that moment. Sexual frustration sure was a bitch she hadn't counted on ever experiencing firsthand.

It was her tone that raised his brow, and after a

moment, had him chuckling. It was an easy guess which reputation he'd decided she was referring to, and it wasn't his prowess on the battlefield.

After his humor wound down, she got another one of his curt nods, albeit with a grin, and the remark, 'I cannot guarantee your safety, do I take you to Lord William.'

She all but snorted. 'Nonsense. Look at you. You're more than capable of dealing with any—'

'From myself, lady.'

She blinked. 'Excuse me?'

He didn't bother to elaborate. He simply cornered her against the wall of the hostelry, with one arm braced on either side of her, and leaned forward to prove just how unsafe she would be with him.

He kissed just like Thorn – well, why wouldn't he? But that made it that much more difficult to keep her senses intact, with his mouth working on hers in that sensual way she found so thrilling. And he brought his body into play, carefully pressing against her so that she could experience all of him – as if she weren't already familiar with that body.

She'd been warned. She'd been told not to deal with this Thorn. She really should have listened, because it appeared he wasn't going to stop proving his point, and soon she wouldn't want him to.

She strained to hear the call that would release her from this dilemma, but she heard nothing beyond her own rapid breathing and his. Apparently her Thorn was having trouble in getting Sir John off to his bed, which meant she still had to keep this Thorn occupied, but she hoped, not in the way he seemed to have in mind.

Again, her choices were limited. She could appear to accept his attentions, which she seemed to have no trouble whatsoever in doing, or she could pretend to be outraged and insulted.

Which would keep him longer? Acceptance most likely, and besides, it would be pretty hard to play the outrage scenario convincingly considering how long she'd been standing there, letting him kiss her. But she had to throw in a little objecting. After all, the goal was to stall, not to find herself in the alley with her skirts tossed up.

She managed to free her mouth and push him away a little. She even managed to get back to the subject that had prompted his demonstration. That her voice sounded breathless and husky was entirely his fault. Just like his other self, he'd managed to stir her passions, with barely any effort on his part.

'I see you do manage to live up to your reputation, don't you? But in this case, couldn't you just *try* to restrain yourself for once?' she asked him. 'At least long enough to escort me to William.'

One more torrid look down her length and back. 'Nay, I think not.'

She realized she would have been disappointed had he answered otherwise, and yet, damnit, this wasn't *her* Thorn. She didn't really want to be kissing him anymore; she just had to make him think she did.

'I would know your name, lady.'

For some unaccountable reason, Delilah came to mind. She said it, then had to bite her tongue to keep from laughing at how apt it was. The classic sexual deceiver, which was exactly what she was about to be.

To that end, she gave him what she hoped was a come-hither smile to keep him interested, but since she'd never had any practice at sending such smiles, she didn't know if she was doing it right. By the curious look she got from him, however, she had to assume her smile was probably more on the sickly side, so she gave that up with a sigh.

'You are impatient, Thorn Blooddrinker. In some ways, that isn't such a bad thing, but in others . . .' She glanced around at the immediate area. 'This is hardly the place for us to become better acquainted.'

At that provocative remark, he took her arm and started her off down the street so fast, she went into minor shock. She'd just blown it. The idea was just to keep him occupied, not get herself dragged off where she'd have the devil's own time finding her Thorn again – if she could manage to get away from this one.

'Wait!'

He did stop, but by his expression, it didn't look as if it would be for long, so in desperation she said, 'Since it is quite possible now that I won't be joining the duke's entourage tonight, there is no longer any hurry, is there? And just now . . .' She paused to gather her courage to say the rest. 'I have a powerful urge to taste you again.'

She never would have been so bold if she hadn't panicked, but that boldness was going to get her exactly what she'd asked for. He pulled her close, his hands cupped her cheeks, his mouth started to descend . . .

And she heard her name called at last from down that dark alley.

Her decision was swift and final, and made with only a little regret. Just as his lips grazed hers, she slipped her foot behind his and pushed with all her might. He tumbled to the ground. She ran like hell, down the alley and smack into a very hard chest.

'Get us out of here quick! I may be followed by you-know-who!'

'Aye, you will be followed' was Thorn's terse reply as he grabbed her hand, a tad too tightly, bringing a slight wince to her brow. 'I have the memory of it now, and verily, did I search long for you, Roseleen.'

Her mouth dropped open. Fortunately, she was in another place and time, and so away from the dire threat of the two Thorns meeting, before she got to close it. She wished she could have left her shock and embarrassment behind as well, but wouldn't you know, that managed to travel right along with her.

30

Roseleen was mortified. In fact, she didn't think she'd ever been quite this embarrassed before. All she wanted to do was find a deep dark hole and bury herself in it. She wouldn't look at Thorn. He was still holding her hand, but she kept her back to him, concealing the furious color in her cheeks as long as possible.

I have the memory of it now.

Why hadn't that occurred to her? It stood to reason that whatever happened to the younger Thorn in the past, or was added to the past by unnatural means as in the case of his meeting her, this Thorn would gain the memory of. And that was just what had happened.

Thorn probably had a clear memory of everything she'd said and done to the other. He probably even got those memories exactly as they were occurring, so they'd be as fresh to him now as they'd been to his other self – who was at this moment in the past searching for her.

She groaned inwardly. It was too much to hope

that that particular memory of his would rapidly fade, simply because nine hundred plus years had come and gone since the actual occurrence. She couldn't get that lucky, and Thorn was about to prove it.

He didn't let her ignore him for long. His hands came to rest on her shoulders, weighing against her guilt. And his tone was fraught with anger.

'You were warned—'

'Don't,' she cut in. 'I know I handled him – you – wrong, so you don't have to elaborate on it.'

But he was determined to do just that. 'He only had one thing on his mind, getting you into his bed, and you encouraged him.'

She swung around to face him, drawing on what little defense she had available. 'What else was I supposed to do, discuss cursed swords and un-natural summonings with him? That would have freaked him out. He probably would have thought I was a witch, and left me on the spot – to run right into you. I saved you from your dreaded global catastrophe, or whatever would have happened if you two had gotten close enough to say howdy, so why are you complaining?'

'You are a woman of intelligence, or so you keep reminding me,' he said in a low grumble. 'You could have easily distracted him with your incessant chattering. You do that well enough with me.'

A double blush, scoring on both counts. Was Thorn right? Had she let her curiosity about his other self convince her that she had no other recourse than to provoke his sexual interest in her?

It was easy to come up with other ideas when she wasn't directly facing the crisis. She could have simply claimed an injury, a twisted ankle perhaps. She could have told him someone had already gone for help, and merely asked him to stay with her until that help arrived. He wouldn't have been so uncharitable as to refuse a lady in distress. Then again, maybe he would have, considering he had only two main interests, and she would have been keeping him from one of them.

'Is there a little wounded pride getting in the way here, because I managed to dupe you and get away from you – I mean him? Is that why you're so angry?'

'Nay, I am angry because you let him touch you!' he growled.

She blinked. And then she started to laugh. She simply couldn't help it.

'You're jealous of yourself? Oh, come on, Thorn, isn't that a little bit ridiculous? I mean, think about it. He was still you – at least to me he was. Even the fact that so many centuries separate your ages didn't matter, because he looked exactly as you—'

'Only a few years separate our ages, yet is there a very great difference between us that you cannot deny. I have full knowledge of you, Roseleen. He had none. Though he was eager to do so, he had never tasted the pleasures of your body. Wherein, then, were we the same?'

He had her blushing again. 'All right, I'm sorry I didn't slap him for kissing me. I thought about it, but I was afraid he'd leave me if I did and go right off to run into you. And anyway, it's your damn fault that I let him kiss me,' she said, and pushed him back for good measure.

That a couch happened to be behind him and he went tumbling back over the armrest on it was all to the good in her opinion, since it gave her the opportunity to climb on top of him, which she quickly took. 'Next time you kiss me like you did, Viking,' she continued, 'make sure you stick around long enough to put out the fire.'

To demonstrate what she was talking about, she started kissing him in a very passionate manner, with more aggression than she'd ever attempted before, and apparently his anger wasn't strong enough anymore for him even to try to play not interested. Before long, his large hands were gripping her backside to press her firmly against the seat she had chosen, and she was trailing small bites and kisses along his neck and as far down the opening of his tunic as she could get.

It was the most inappropriate time to be interrupted, but that didn't stop David from entering the room and clearing his throat rather loudly to make his presence known. Roseleen's head came up, swung in his direction, and after a few seconds of bemusement – how long it took to gather her scattered thoughts back together – she was filled with delight.

'David!' she exclaimed, and immediately swung back to Thorn to exclaim again, 'We're back to normal!'

'I beg to differ,' David said rather dryly. 'You, sister dear, aren't doing anything *you* normally do.'

She blushed mildly over that remark, because she was too thrilled that their attempt to correct history had worked. And she'd been so distracted by Thorn's remark when they'd arrived that she hadn't even noticed they were back in the very familiar surroundings of Cavenaugh Cottage.

But David was still staring at her with a somewhat disapproving expression, which surprised her a bit. Hadn't he always pestered her in a brotherly fashion about making an effort to find the right man and settle down?

Just now, her blush got a little brighter as she climbed off Thorn to allow him to sit up, and gathered her nerve for the introductions. Explaining who Thorn was was *not* going to be easy by any means, and at the moment, her brother didn't look as if he'd be receptive to the incredible tale she had to relate.

So she began by simply saying, 'Thorn, this is my brother David, if you haven't guessed that by now. And, David, meet Thorn Blooddrinker.'

She waited for some wise-ass remark like, 'Bringing ghosts home for dinner now, are we?', but none was forthcoming. In fact, all David did was give Thorn a brief nod, as if he'd never heard that name before.

She was surprised, again. He obviously wasn't making the connection, or recalling what she'd told him about her dreams – or rather, what she'd thought had been dreams.

She decided to give his memory a chance to jog itself, and asked instead, 'When did you return from France?'

'France?'

'Yes, and did you bring Lydia with you this time for a visit?'

He was frowning at her now. 'What's wrong with you, Rose? I haven't been to France since we went together last summer. And who, might I ask, is Lydia?'

All she could do was stare at him as her body turned cold with dread. He never called her Rose. And they hadn't gone to France together last summer. The last time she had been to France, not counting her recent visit with Thorn, had been for David's wedding, which had taken place in one of Lydia's mansions on the southern coast. But he didn't even know who Lydia was, had obviously not met her as he should have, let alone married her, and . . .

She threw her arms around Thorn's neck, nearly choking him as she said in a frantic whisper by his ear, 'That's not my brother. I mean, it is, but, like the Barry you met, he's not acting right. I'm afraid it didn't work, Thorn. We may have gotten the cottage back, but something still needs to be corrected in the past, because this still isn't the way my present should be.'

He peeled her arms away so he could look at her. 'You are certain?'

She nodded, but it was the fact that she was close to tears that had him wrapping his arms around her now. Behind them, David made a sound of disgust.

'Do you mind saving that for when you are alone?' David asked in a disapproving tone.

Roseleen stiffened and turned to frown at him. 'Oh, stuff it, David. We were alone until you showed up. But don't bother leaving. We will.'

She grabbed Thorn's hand and pulled him off the couch and out of the room. This David was obviously a prude and one she had to wonder if she even liked. She certainly wasn't going to waste her breath explaining to him what had happened to her. But she was hopeful that the next time she saw her brother, he'd be the brother she knew, not that puritanical imitation they'd just left shaking his head at them.

Only how was she going to accomplish getting her David back? She'd run out of ideas, couldn't possibly imagine what else had gone wrong in the past to account for these new changes in the present. And she was exhausted. Last night, she'd barely slept at all in the tent. The last good sleep she'd had had found her waking for the first time in Thorn's tent in Normandy. But it felt as if weeks had passed since then, with everything that had happened to her in the last two days.

Having reached her room, she closed the door and leaned back against it, giving Thorn a lack-luster smile. 'I don't even want to discuss it. In the morning, I'll figure out what we did wrong, or what someone else did wrong, but right now I just want to get some sleep, so let's go to bed.'

He made a flourish with his arm toward the bed, but he didn't look all that happy. 'I will join you there,' he said. 'I will even make an effort to forget what you were doing ere your brother made his appearance.'

She had to grin at his subtle reminder that she'd deliberately provoked his passions. And come to think of it, she wasn't *that* exhausted.

'That's very sweet of you, Thorn, but you don't need to forget about it,' she said as she came away from the door. 'I don't believe I need to go . . . right to sleep.'

She heard his chuckle just before he swept her up into his arms. And a few moments later when he laid her carefully on the bed, she was chuckling as well.

'It doesn't take much to encourage you – or that other you, does it?'

'When you are the prize, Roseleen? Nay, it takes no encouragement at all.'

She wondered how glib that remark was, or if he really meant it. In either case, the words still thrilled her, and she reached an arm around his neck to draw him down for a thank-you kiss. But he wasn't interested in any tepid pecks. His tongue slipped between her teeth and started the magic that was uniquely his. Within moments, she had no thoughts to spare except those of pleasure.

He kissed her for a long, long time while his hands made forays to her most sensitive areas. And she had so many that she had never known about until she knew him. Actually, anywhere he touched her produced splendid results. It was as if her body were fine-tuned to his, and he knew every way possible to make it sing.

She was ready for him long before he was

willing to end his sensual explorations, so that when he did finally cover her and enter her, sinking deep into her depths and holding there for long, exquisite moments, it was the most glorious feeling, nigh equal to the climax she knew would soon come. She gasped. He did it again, thrusting slow and so deep, and she felt vibrations of pleasure, as if her blood were humming.

And still he didn't hurry, savoring his own pleasure even as he increased hers. Only when he drove her over the edge and she was clinging to him for dear life as she rode the crest of her climax, did he increase his tempo to join her in that splendid pinnacle of completion.

And even then, as that blissful languor urged her toward slumber, he was kissing her, caressing her, showing her in the tenderest way that she was special to him. That, more than anything else, pulled at her heartstrings.

31

Roseleen was still in the cottage upon waking, and Thorn was still lying beside her, one arm draped over his eyes to block the morning light. She smiled at him and leaned over to place a gentle kiss on his chest. He didn't stir. He had to have been as exhausted as she was last night, and yet he didn't skimp when it came to giving pleasure.

She sighed, wishing she could just curl up next to him and go back to sleep, instead of confronting the same dilemma she had faced yesterday. But it wasn't something that she could postpone, now that she was wide-awake. She might have her cottage back, but something was still changed in the past, because David was definitely not the David she knew.

And if his life had changed drastically, she had to wonder about her own again and if her career was still the same. If it wasn't, then she wouldn't have the research books here that she needed, would instead have to go out and hunt down the answers to what else had gone wrong. The trouble was, she didn't have the slightest clue this time to lead her to what she needed to look for.

She sat up in bed, then had to smile as she noticed the spread of clothes that littered the floor in front of her. As difficult as that yellow gown had been to get into, Thorn had had no trouble getting her out of it. She didn't even recall his doing it . . .

' 'Tis hoped that smile is for me,' Thorn said from behind her.

Before she could answer or even glance back at him, his arm slipped around her waist to prevent her going anywhere, and his lips began pressing against her bare back, producing a stream of shivers that broadened her smile.

'Well, if it wasn't,' she said with a chuckle as she turned and leaned across his chest for a good-morning kiss, 'it is now.'

He hugged her close. 'You are pleased this morn?'

She arched a brow, teasing, 'Are you fishing to hear what a great lover you are?'

'Nay, a wench named Delilah once told me how widespread was my reputation – umph!' he ended on a grunt when she poked him in the ribs, but he was quick to retaliate.

Suddenly, she was on her back and shrieking as he began tickling her. A while later, out of breath, holding his head to her chest, she shook her head at his playfulness. The man was definitely wooing her bit by bit out of the disciplined shell she had encased herself in so long ago. And she decided that wasn't such a bad thing.

It was with regret that she broached the subject that had to be faced. 'We have to talk, Thorn.'

'Aye.'

He sighed and rolled until he was sitting on the edge of the bed. He searched through the clothes on the floor to find his braes, then stood to work his way into them. With him standing there in that tight underwear, his chest bare – she blushed when she finally noticed a hickey above his left nipple – his hair tousled about his shoulders, it was damn hard to concentrate on what needed to be discussed. At the moment, she would prefer he come back to bed.

But she forced herself to sit up, wrapping her arms around her knees, and began, asking him, 'Your other self didn't do anything different, did he, after meeting me? Please tell me that meeting didn't change anything, because I really don't want to have to go through meeting him again.'

'Nay, he searched for you, he asked William about you, but otherwise, he did naught else different. There was no time, Roseleen, for him to cause further mischief. He still returned to Valhalla the next day.'

'But he must have done something different

that night, because previously, he got Sir John drunk and then entertained that tavern girl that Sir John was supposed to have for the night. But if you got Sir John out of there, did you – he – still get the girl, or did he choose another?'

'When I could not find you, I returned to camp instead. I was in no mood by then to entertain another female.'

She blinked. 'Really?'

That got her a scowl that had her grinning for a moment. 'All right, so the only thing different is that you *didn't* spend the night with that girl—' Now she was scowling as she realized, 'If that's what has to be corrected, I'll keep this altered present, thank you, even if I have to put up with a stick-in-the-mud brother.'

He chuckled. 'You forget that originally, Sir John was to have the girl, not I. That has been corrected now, so wouldst not need changing again.'

'Good, because I don't really want to be stuck with that new David. But if we didn't change anything else . . . I guess it's time to dig into the books. Why don't you go down to the kitchen and find us something to eat while I head for the library, where I hope to find my research books.'

He nodded and left the room. She rummaged through her closet and quickly discovered that her taste in clothes had not improved in this new present, had gone from plain to gaudy, in

293

ridiculously bright colors. With nothing there that she cared to put on, even temporarily, she grabbed a robe that was at least a simple white, and headed for the door.

David was standing there as she opened it, about to knock, and before she managed even to get out a gasp of surprise, he was saying in a tone that reeked with censure, 'That man you wallowed in sin with all night long is now destroying your kitchen. You'll be lucky if you don't lose your housekeeper when she sees the mess.'

'Mrs Humes wouldn't—'

'Who?'

Damn, she groaned inwardly as she rushed down the hall. No Mrs Humes here? And *why* had she sent Thorn to the kitchen, of all places?

She arrived to find an electric blender shattered on the countertop; three cans of vegetables hacked right down their centers, their contents splattered everywhere, a battery-operated carving knife spinning in circles on the floor; the top chopped off of a juice carton now sitting in a puddle of spilled juice. There was also a large dent the size of Thorn's foot in the refrigerator, which unfortunately had latch handles he probably hadn't been able to open. And Thorn was standing there now, his sword in hand, glaring at more cans in a cupboard because he couldn't figure out how to open them without destroying their contents.

She shook her head at the mess. All the modern wonders were there, and some she didn't even recognize. And apparently Thorn had pressed some buttons, turned some things on, then hacked them to pieces with his sword when they started doing things he figured they shouldn't.

'I don't think you'll ever make it as a cook,' she said, tongue in cheek.

He swung around to complain, 'There is no food to be had here, Roseleen.'

'Yes, there is.' She grinned as she walked to the refrigerator. 'You just have to know how to get at it, like so.' She twisted the handles on the doors and swung them open. 'Voila, lots of goodies. So why don't I cook you some breakfast, an omelet maybe, some bacon and sausage, toast and jam – how does that sound? You have to be as hungry as I am. The books can wait a bit more.'

Cooking breakfast for Thorn was one of the more satisfying things she'd ever done. It was also amusing to watch him examining everything she set before him. Toast didn't come so thin and smoothly cut the last time he'd been summoned, bacon hadn't come precut in a package, jellies had never been so clear before, and butter certainly hadn't come out of a box two hundred years ago. But he was willing to try anything and everything, and he put away a mountain of food before he was done.

They managed to get to the library without running into David again. And Roseleen's luck was holding. She had research books there. Not all of them were familiar, but it was reassuring to find that some were. However, she was in for another unpleasant surprise.

Having curled up in a reading chair, she merely skimmed over one of the history books, so it wasn't all that long before she glanced over at Thorn, who'd settled in one of the other chairs, and was able to relate, 'It's worse than I'd thought, not just a small change this time, but another major one. The Norwegians lost in the north as they did originally, and the Normans sailed on the correct dates. Everything seems the same, and yet the Normans lost again. This time, incredibly, England won both wars.

'Harold Godwineson even went on to rule England for twenty-four years. From his lines there were two kings who did great things for their country, a couple tyrants, one of which was murdered by his queen, and the rest were mediocre, doing little more than enjoying their power.'

Thorn sighed. 'So Lord William died again ere he should have?'

'No, not this time. But he went home in defeat and never made another bid for England. Some of his descendants started a war with France a few centuries later and lost, making France the major power in Europe for a while. England prospered and started its Industrial Age sooner. It still warred frequently, but closer to home, with the Scots and the Welsh, which is nothing new.

'But there is a major change later on, and this one is widespread and can certainly account for that moralistic prude I have here for a brother. The Puritan sect that formed in the sixteen hundreds didn't just migrate to America, they gained such power in England that they have retained it to this day. And because it was so strong, America never found a need to go independent. Incredibly, England still owns and governs it.'

That subject held no interest whatsoever for Thorn. As before, he was concerned with only one thing, and he asked now, 'But why did William lose this time if, as you said previously, the English came exhausted to the battle, after fighting the Vikings in the north?'

Roseleen shook her head. 'I don't know. It all reads the same here as it originally happened. The north wind that kept William landlocked for an extra two weeks is mentioned, as is his sailing on the evening of September twenty-seventh, even how his ship, the *Mora*, got separated from the others late in the night. The landing is the same, early the next morning at Pevensey Bay, with

Harold still far in the north. Immediate construction was started on fortified strongholds, but Pevensey was still too exposed, so the Normans moved eastward, clinging to the coast, to capture the port of Hastings.

'Harold was still in the north at this time, having dispersed his army, so he didn't actually arrive back in the south until October fourteenth. He took a strong defensive position on a high ridge and stayed there, forcing the Normans to attack, and they had no luck breaking through Harold's tightly held ranks.'

Roseleen sighed before she continued, 'Even the retreats are the same, the first one real, because the Normans became demoralized at their lack of success. The English, though exhausted, gave chase and were slaughtered when the Normans turned again to fight. The Normans retreated twice more, but these retreats were feigned, not real, in order to draw the English away from their solid defensive, and both of these worked for them as well, cutting down large chunks of Harold's army. But the last charge they made, the one with their cavalry, the one that originally gave them their victory – it didn't work here. Harold remained tightly guarded; his housecarles rallied to fend off the Norman cavalry and finish them off when they started a fourth retreat.

'*That* is where this history begins to change.

The original account has the Norman cavalry victorious on that last charge, with Harold dying under the blade of a mounted knight, already wounded from an arrow that struck his – wait a minute!' Roseleen gasped. 'It's not mentioned here.'

'What?'

'William's unprecedented order to his archers, to fire their arrows up into the air. That order has been termed famous because it brought about the turning point of the battle, the arrows falling into the English ranks killing enough of them that the Norman cavalry that then charged was able to break through their gridlocked shields and finish them off. And one of those arrows caught Harold in the eye. The accounts vary on whether the arrow killed him outright, or merely wounded him enough that one of the mounted knights easily killed him, but all accounts say he took that arrow in the eye.'

'Except this one,' Thorn said, nodding toward the book in her lap.

'No, this one doesn't mention it,' she said, bent over the book again to double-check, her finger skimming down the page. 'There is no mention of the famous order to the Norman archers, no mention of Harold's being wounded at all.' She looked up to finish. 'That order wasn't given this time, and because it wasn't, the English won instead of the Normans.'

Thorn shrugged with apparent unconcern. 'Then that is what needs be corrected.'

'But how?' she cried. 'When we don't know why the order wasn't given. We would actually have to be there with William at that moment in time to find out what went wrong.'

At that, he began a slow grin. 'Verily, I find that an excellent suggestion.'

She glared at his eagerness to get into another battle. 'This isn't a battle where you know everyone is going to die anyway. There were survivors on both sides, so you don't dare kill anyone. And you can't just pop us into that battle, because you weren't in it to begin with, so you can't envision it to get us there. We'd have to return to the last time that you can envision, when the ships were finally about to sail, and that means we'll be stuck for weeks on the English coast, waiting for that battle to finally take place.'

'Do you see any other alternative?' he said.

She slumped back in her chair before she mumbled, 'No, damnit, I don't.'

32

Roseleen shook her head at the yellow gown she held up before her. 'Since it's a good guess that I won't find a washing label anywhere on it, I'd be afraid to run this through the washer.'

'You mean "to," ' Thorn corrected as he finished dressing himself.

'To what?'

'Run it *to* the washer.'

She looked over at him and grinned. 'No, my washer is a machine, not a person – never mind. I suppose it won't kill me to wear it again as is, wrinkles and all. But for the next three weeks? No way. Will Guy be able to scrounge up something else for me to wear, or should I hunt down a costume shop while we're still here?'

'Scrounge?'

'Acquire, as he did this gown.'

'Ah,' he said, nodding his understanding. 'The lad is an excellent scrounger, so worry not.'

'If you say so,' she replied, and began working her way back into the medieval outfit. 'But since

Guy isn't here at the moment, you get to tie me back into these "raiments." ' '

Thorn chuckled as he came over to assist her. 'I much prefer—'

'Yes, I know,' she was quick to cut in, her tone exceedingly dry. 'Removing clothes is more your specialty, which you do very well. But that will have to wait until we're back in your nice, barbaric camp tent. And since this is going to be an extended stay, I'll just gather a few of what I call essentials to take along this time.'

She moved off to grab a handful of underwear out of the bureau and stuffed them into a pillow-case. One of her suitcases just wouldn't go over well in 1066. Then she headed for the bathroom, dropping in things as she noticed them, her toothbrush and toothpaste, deodorant, perfume, brush, razor, her small travel kit of first aid items, and a bar of soap – she hadn't been looking forward to trying the medieval kind that would undoubtedly take off several layers of skin – that she wrapped in a washcloth.

Coming back into the bedroom, she said, 'Don't let me leave this behind.' She held up the sack so he knew what she was talking about. 'A rusted aerosal can showing up in some nineteenth-century excavation would send shock waves around the world – and would be something else we'd have to go back to correct. And I think we've messed up enough history to prove that time hopping is something that shouldn't be tampered with.'

He nodded curtly, looking unhappy about her last remark, so she added, 'Cheer up, Thorn, you can still participate in your fights in Valhalla whenever you feel the urge. You don't need to hunt down fights in the past.'

'I will not be returning to Valhalla' was all he said to that.

She blinked. 'Why not?'

He gave her a look that said, 'Stupid question,' and his own question explained it. 'Once we marry and you give me children, why wouldst I leave you?'

'Now hold on—'

'But you still needs be trained first.'

She clamped her mouth shut. His grin suggested that he might be only teasing her. He *knew* what she thought about his 'training.' But she wasn't going to get into that subject again, in either case. She wasn't even sure yet that she'd be able to get back to her own present, so she was certainly in no position to think about settling down with anyone.

But the mention of Valhalla had made her remember a few unusual things that he had said in passing, that she'd never had the chance to question him about. When he'd been telling her

303

about Guy's sister apparently dying, to explain why he wouldn't be running into himself, he'd said he'd been 'released from your world's time and returned to mine.' And last night, when she'd pointed out to him that so many centuries separated his age from that of the other Thorn, he had replied that only a *few* years separated them.

She couldn't believe she'd let that one pass, but she got back to it now. 'What did you mean last night when you said only a few years separated you from your other self? Have you lived so long that you consider centuries only a few years? And before, you spoke of your time and my time as being different. How is it different?'

He raised a brow at her. 'Am I to assume we are not ready to depart?'

'Don't even think about avoiding those questions, Viking. I'm not budging from this spot until—'

His chuckle cut her off. 'You do not tease well this morn, Roseleen. And 'tis no secret that time moves differently in Valhalla.'

'But how is it different?'

'One day there can equal a full stretch of years here in your time.'

'Full stretch?'

'What you call a century.'

She was incredulous. 'Are you saying you aren't a thousand years old?'

He laughed. 'Nay, at the last date of my birth, I reached only a score and ten.'

'Twenty and – you're saying you're only *thirty* years old?' She gasped.

'Think you I look older?'

He was grinning widely. She felt utterly foolish herself. Of course he didn't look any older than thirty. She had just assumed, because he had been born a thousand years ago, that logically, he had to be that old and thus, immortal. She hadn't considered that time practically stood still in his Viking heaven.

'How old were you when you were cursed?'

'Less than a score in years.'

'So you aren't really immortal, are you? You're actually aging – just at a different rate of time.'

Typically, his nod was curt. And she was having a hard time accepting this unexpected news, when she had thought him so *old* – too old for her anyway. Now – he was barely a year older than she was. Apparently, he only aged whenever he was summoned. He could actually grow old with her . . .

She had to tamp down that thrilling thought. This was no time for it, and there was still one other thing she'd never gotten around to asking him, which she got to now.

'Why did that witch, Gunnhilda, curse you in the first place? Was she just having fun, flexing her magic muscles, and you happened to get in the way? Or did you do something to warrant getting cursed?'

He snorted at that. 'All I did was refuse to marry her daughter.'

Roseleen blinked in surprise. 'Her daughter wanted to marry you?'

He shook his head. 'Nay, she liked me not. 'Twas Gunnhilda who coveted an alliance with my family. But she had not the nerve to approach Thor, so 'twas me she came to, suggesting the match.'

'And you refused?'

'Her daughter was a hag in appearance, Roseleen, twice my age. Gunnhilda was mad even to suggest it. But my mistake was to laugh at her offer. That enraged her, and she cursed me and my sword on the spot. Yet that was still not enough for her. She also killed my enemy, Wolfstan the Mad, just so he would bedevil me for eternity.'

'I haven't seen much of that bedeviling,' she said carefully, now expecting a ghost to pop in on them at any moment.

Thorn chuckled. 'Wolfstan, he had not too much up here to begin with,' he explained, tapping his head. 'So he has much difficulty in finding me each time I am summoned. The few times he has managed to make an appearance, I merely dispatched him back from whence he came. 'Tis a shame, though, that he does not have better luck, for he is a skilled fighter and offers me good sport.'

Good sport as in the only time his life is actually in danger, she thought. She could have hit him for that remark. And good old good sport Wolfstan could stay the hell away as long as she was around. If she had to watch Thorn in a fight where he might actually die . . . She wished she'd kept her questions to herself.

In a grumble, she said, 'Okay, wc've wasted enough time. Let's get this correcting stuff over with so I can get back to my real life.' And, she added to herself, figuring out what she was going to do with a Viking who intended to stick around.

33

It was a shock to appear right on the deck of a ship, with dozens of people all about. Roseleen was so shocked that she had to be yanked out of the way of a sailor with a large barrel hefted on his shoulder, who hadn't seen her in his path, because she was suddenly *in* his path, when she hadn't been before.

Thorn did the yanking. And he was chuckling at her expression, wide-eyed and openmouthed – until she rammed an elbow into his stomach.

'This *isn't* funny,' she told him in a furious whisper. 'Do you realize that any one of these people could have seen us just appear out of the thin air? I'm amazed that someone isn't screaming and pointing fingers at us right now, or calling for a stake and kindling.'

He wrapped his arms around her tightly, more as a protective measure against her elbows than anything else, and whispered back at her, 'Be easy, Roseleen. Someone wouldst merely wonder had they seen this space empty, then so quickly filled. And 'tis highly unlikely we would actually be seen appearing, when these men are so busy preparing the ship for departure. Even were it so, they would be more apt to think they were mistaken in what they see, than to try and explain it to themselves or anyone else.'

He'd brushed aside her worry very nicely, he must be thinking, and since no one *was* pointing fingers or screaming, she had to allow he'd summed up human nature pretty well. And she'd gotten so used to that crack of thunder and flash of lightning whenever he showed up anywhere, even when she was with him, that she didn't even notice it anymore. But anyone else around would notice, and immediately be looking toward the sky for signs of a storm.

That made it even less likely that their sudden arrival would be seen by anyone. But that didn't alleviate all of her annoyance with him at the shock she'd experienced, just some of it.

So she grumbled in a low voice, 'Remind me to introduce you to television when we get back to my time. Or better yet, I'll take you for a ride on one of those big birds you saw in the sky that night.'

He heard her, of course. He was too close not to. And she could actually feel his sudden excitement.

' 'Tis possible to ride those giant birds?'

She rolled her eyes at his eager question. She

should have known a prospect like that would appeal to him, that she couldn't shock him in retaliation with something that wasn't actually here for him to goggle over firsthand. She could have pointed out that those 'birds' were like automobiles, but she didn't bother. Having her revenge backfire on her took the fun out of it.

'Forget I mentioned it, Thorn. They're rideable, yes, but not the way you think. Now, where are we, aside from being on a ship, and what's the date?'

He shrugged. 'I know not the date. I merely envisioned the *Mora* as I last saw her with you, when she was ready to sail to England.'

'Okay, since everything here is back to normal up until the day of the big battle, I hope that makes this the twenty-seventh of September when the fleet did sail for England, rather than the twelfth of September, when they only sailed to Saint-Valery for a better position, and ended up getting stuck there due to that north wind.' And then she sighed. 'Either way, we've got a long wait ahead of us. If your squire is going to find me another outfit or two to wear, he'll have more luck here than in England. Any idea where he is?'

He frowned thoughtfully. 'Nay, I needs find him. But I cannot leave you alone here whilst I do—' He broke off and was suddenly grinning as he noticed something beyond her shoulder, and then he spoke to that something. 'Lord William, may I make known to you the Lady Roseleen.'

Roseleen twisted around in Thorn's arms. Her mouth was still hanging open in surprise, though she didn't realize it. And she understood now why Thorn had assumed that medieval poster in her classroom was a picture of William the Bastard. The resemblance between that poster hunk and the actual man was uncanny. Someone in her day had come up with a real winner without even knowing it.

And now that she was finally meeting the great man himself, all she could think to do was nod her head and say reverently, 'Your Majesty.'

He laughed. 'Not yet, my lady – but soon.'

She blushed profusely over her blunder, though it was a natural mistake. He did end up as the King of England, after all, and so all the history books ended their accounts of him by calling him that.

'My lord, wouldst you lend the lady your protection whilst I locate my squire?'

'Certainly, Thorn, and bring the lad here when you find him. I would you sailed with me on the *Mora*, since you tend to disappear when I do not keep you close. Guy of Anjou brought his fears to me, that something dire had happened to you when he could not find you. You will have to tell us what you have been about.'

Thorn merely nodded to William, squeezed

Roseleen once before he let her go, and then abruptly walked away, leaving her in the duke's care. She had no idea what excuse he would give later for his absence these last weeks. He couldn't exactly say he'd returned to Valhalla where he resided between summonings, although a tale like that might be treated as if it were a tall tale for the amusement of all. But William was still going to want to hear something more reasonable, or he wouldn't have mentioned it.

However, Roseleen wasn't going to worry about that, when she couldn't believe the opportunity this presented for her. To have William of Normandy's attention for however long was just what she had hoped for when she had agreed to go time traveling with Thorn. The things that he could tell her about himself that had never been documented before, his hopes, his plans, those realized and those never fulfilled – this was the stuff that was going to make her own book unique. And she had him all to herself because his ever-present retainers and followers were otherwise occupied at the moment.

In terms of historical research, the time Roseleen spent with William was wasted, other than to learn that it was indeed September 27. She asked a few questions, but the minute he gave her a strange look, as if he wondered why she was so curious, she backed off. They'd done too much tampering with history for her to take any more chances, especially with someone who had had such an effect on history himself. All it would take was for something she said to occur to him at some later point, for him to remark on it to someone else, or whatever, and all kinds of possible changes might take place again.

It wasn't worth the risk, she decided. Just being here would have to suffice. After all, details were also important, and she would now be able to describe this period and the people in it with vivid detail, having experienced it all firsthand. That she wasn't going to obtain any otherwise unknown facts was a disappointment she'd just have to live with.

34

It was evening before Thorn returned to the *Mora*, with Guy of Anjou in tow. Roseleen had been glued to the railing, watching for him, since she had begun to worry as it neared the time of sailing. As it was, they arrived only fifteen minutes before the ship cast off, which didn't put her in a very receptive mood. Had he not returned in time, she would have been forced to leave the ship as well, with no idea of where to start looking for him.

Guy didn't appear to be a bit happy to see Roseleen again – they hadn't exactly hit it off on their first meeting – but her sentiments toward him had changed due to an abundance of sympathy, after she'd learned what had likely happened to his sister. If she had died as Thorn assumed, Guy didn't even know it yet, wouldn't know it for some time to come, because news traveled so slowly in these times, and whether that could be counted a blessing was subject to the individual and the circumstance.

So as soon as she had the chance to, she

apologized to Guy for her previous behavior, though it didn't seem to make any difference to the boy. His attitude was still I'm-a-man-therefore-more-important-than-you, which she was *never* going to agree with.

Thorn was amused by the exchange, though she couldn't tell it by his stoic expression. However, she knew him well enough by now to know he was chuckling on the inside, that slight twinkle in his blue eyes a dead giveaway, and she didn't appreciate that either.

She supposed her failed interview with Duke William was the major contributor to her now sour mood, though the worry she had undergone in thinking Thorn wasn't going to get back to the ship in time was the icing on the cake. So she was rather pleased to find that Sir Reinard de Morville would also be sailing on the *Mora*.

Since she had no desire to speak to Thorn anytime soon, or at least not until her annoyance with him lessened somewhat, she was relieved to discover that there was someone else on board with whom she was acquainted, however slightly. She was flattered that he came over to her the very second he noticed her. Sir Reinard was a very handsome man, after all, and it wouldn't hurt Thorn to see that men other than himself and his *other* self were interested in her.

But it didn't take long for her to discover that

Sir Reinard was a bit too interested. His opening remarks of 'What do you here, demoiselle? Nay, it matters not. I will not let you disappear so easily this time,' should have given her some warning.

But she was still too pleased at that point that the knight was there, and merely replied, 'I'm not going anywhere, at least not until we reach England, and even then, I will likely stay very close to the ship, if I'm even allowed off it. And it's good to see you again, Sir Reinard. Have you rescued any other damsels lately?'

She was merely teasing, but he took her seriously. 'Nay, and 'twould not be nearly as satisfying did I do so – unless you need rescuing again?'

His forming his reply as a question made her laugh. 'Do I appear to need rescuing?'

She was about to revise that answer when she noticed Thorn glowering at her, but she also missed Reinard's disappointed look. She heard his sigh, however, as he replied first, 'A pity. To have your gratitude again would be worth any hardship.'

It was at that point that she suspected the man wasn't just being gallant, and that he was somewhat smitten with her. It was the way he was looking at her now, with such soulful yearning in his eyes, all of which was very flattering, but she was in love with—

Oh, God, she'd just admitted it to herself, when she'd been trying so hard to avoid even thinking about it. She was in love with that Viking. Yet it was hopeless. Yes, he'd said he would stick around, but the fact was, he was from a realm that she couldn't begin to understand. He might not have aged much because of that realm, but he'd still been born more than a thousand years ago, still had a brother, living or ghostly, that the world knew as a mythical Viking god, and still had some kind of mystical control over the weather that defied reality as much as his very existence did.

And how would Thorn ever fit into her world on a permanent basis? It would take a full lifetime for him to grasp the intricacies of the late twentieth century and update his thinking and attitudes. And the truth was, she didn't want to change him. She'd fallen in love with who he was now, foolishly, and certainly not by choice.

And his profession and greatest pleasure was fighting. He would grow bored so very quickly without any wars for him to fight in, and any wars that he might find eventually wouldn't entail his kind of fighting.

It wouldn't be fair of her to ask him to stay with her permanently when he would do better to return to Valhalla, where at least others of his kind resided and entertained each other by testing their skills in the Viking tradition. He'd be happy there and would forget about her soon enough, she was sure. And she would . . .

She wasn't going to think about trying to survive without ever seeing him again. She was already so depressed in admitting her feelings for him that she suddenly felt like crying. And there he was across the deck, glowering at her because she was merely talking to another man.

'Will you share a trencher with me, demoiselle?' Reinard asked her.

'What?'

Roseleen brought her attention slowly back to her onetime rescuer and tried to offer him a smile, though it came out pretty weak.

'A trencher?' he repeated hopefully.

It took her a moment to concentrate and recall what a trencher was. Ah yes, what passed for the medieval dinner plate – a large scooped-out loaf of day-old bread. And men and women did frequently share them, the more gallant knights even feeding the ladies the choicest portions of whatever fare was served.

In her distraction, she hadn't even noticed that the evening meal was being served, but it certainly was, and in typical medieval fashion, in abundance. But then it was a well-known fact that Duke William had presided over a feast this night. Also well-known was what happened while the feast was in progress – at least, well-known to anyone who had studied this time period.

Roseleen couldn't mention to anyone that she knew the *Mora* had probably by now wandered off course to become completely separated from the rest of the fleet. Had the previous English king Edward the Confessor not dispensed with England's permanent fleet that patrolled the Channel because it became too costly, or had Harold Godwineson left some of his fleet behind when he'd disbanded his host on the eighth of September, instead of taking half of it back to London with him, and the rest dispersing on the way, then she would have had more to worry about. But she already knew that the *Mora* had encountered no difficulties while she sailed alone and unaided across the Channel, and that she rejoined the fleet before morning.

She could not discern in any way whether William was aware of the predicament of his ship. As all accounts of this incident stated, he kept his nerve and made merry at the lavish feast that was prepared. And it was a merry crowd, eager to get at the English now that they were finally en route, after months of waiting.

Roseleen would have preferred to leave that high-spirited group just then, when her own spirits were so low. But she had no place to go on a ship; she would be sleeping on the deck if she managed any sleep at all tonight, there being so few cabins to go around, and Sir Reinard was still standing there awaiting her answer.

So she tried to smile again, this time more successfully, and told him, 'I would be pleased to share—'

That was as far as she got before Thorn's voice interrupted her to give his opinion on the subject. 'It wouldst be healthier, de Morville, did you eat alone. The lady is in my care, and I am not mindful to share her company – or aught else she has to offer.'

35

Roseleen threw up her hands the moment she stepped into the tent and nearly shouted, 'I've never seen anything so absurdly macho, so unnecessary, so – so *possessive*. Do you realize that Sir Reinard could have taken offense and challenged you on the spot?'

The fact that she'd had to wait so long to get this off her chest had merely added to her frustration and anger, instead of lessening it. But she hadn't had a private moment with Thorn since the incident had occurred last night, or she would certainly have brought it up sooner.

It was now morning, the ships had sailed into Pevensey Bay without incident to land on the English shore, and the construction of an inner rampart inside the old Roman fort in order to fortify it had already begun. It was a wasted effort, as she could have told anyone who cared to listen, since it would soon be determined that Pevensey was too exposed and the ships would shortly be sailing again eastward to Hastings.

But since that order hadn't been given yet, tents were being erected, and she'd hurried Guy into erecting theirs even though she knew it wouldn't be up long, just so she could tell Thorn what she thought of his macho demonstration last night. It was beside the point that she wouldn't be so angry if that tense scene hadn't frightened her because she'd expected swords to clash during it.

'You as much as threatened him,' she continued to upbraid him, as she paced back and forth in front of him. 'You do realize that, don't you? I'm surprised he *didn't* challenge you.'

Thorn merely crossed his arms over his chest and replied in a tone that reeked with male confidence and certainty, 'I would that he had, so be more surprised that I did not do the challenging myself.'

'But why?' she cried in exasperation. 'All the man did was ask me to sit with him for the meal. You can't get much more harmless than that. So tell me why you blew it all out of proportion?'

At that point, he growled, 'Because I like it not that he is in love with you!'

That had her backing up and asking with a lot less heat, 'How do you know that?'

'Guy told me that de Morville came to him daily to ask of your whereabouts the whole while we have been absent from this time. That speaks for itself, Roseleen, yet did Guy make mention of the same suspicion. 'Twas necessary to show that lordling that you wouldst never be his.'

She had to allow he might be right in that respect. She wouldn't like thinking of Sir Reinard pining away for her here in his time, once she'd returned to her own time. He would be long dead, of course, but then he really wouldn't be, not with Blooddrinker's Curse making him accessible at anytime.

But regardless of whether he should have been discouraged, she didn't like the way Thorn had handled the situation, embarrassing both her and Sir Reinard. And that hadn't been the only way he'd embarrassed her last night.

'All right, forget Sir Reinard for the moment,' she said testily. 'Did you also *have* to tell the duke and everyone else within hearing that you'd been absent this last month because I was leading you on a merry chase around the neighboring country-side? You made it sound like a damn hunting expedition, with my being the hunted—'

'And caught—'

'Even worse!'

By now he was grinning and damn lucky there was nothing lying around the tent yet that she could hit him with. She recalled the duke had laughed. Sir Reinard had also heard the tale and looked utterly dejected. And she'd gone up in flames of embarrassment.

'Lord William required a reason for my absence,' he reminded her, still grinning. 'Verily, did I think that an excellent one, inasmuch as he would remember my other self asking him of you. And you *have* been caught, Roseleen, well and truly—'

'The devil I have. And that's not why you used me as an excuse. You did it solely for Sir Reinard's benefit, just to rub it in some more that he wouldn't stand a chance with me as long as you were around.'

'Nay, he understood that well enough already. That excuse was for your benefit.'

'Mine?' she gasped incredulously. 'How do you possibly figure that?'

'How do you not see it, when all others there saw it clearly? Even de Morville understood I was admitting my love for you.'

The hot steam just got knocked clean out of her. In fact, Roseleen suddenly felt like crying, hearing that. Instead, she threw her arms around his neck and kissed him for all she was worth. She wouldn't make a similar profession of love, no matter how much she ached to say the words. It would be too hard then to explain why she was going to send him away later. It would be infinitely better if he didn't think her heart had become involved.

But just now – just now she loved him so much, and the only way she could express it was this way.

And he didn't need much encouragement to respond in a like manner – no, not any at all. Within seconds, he had borne them both to the floor of the tent, his hands moving over her in a slightly rough manner, testament to the fire she'd ignited.

It was more passion than he'd ever released before, and she was more than receptive to it, too inflamed already to feel anything but the aching need to join with him immediately. And he was apparently of a like mind.

Their clothing probably suffered some rips in his impatience to get rid of it. She didn't hear or care. Each bit of his skin that was revealed to her, she kissed, caressed, or raked her teeth over. She made him groan. He made her tremble. And when he entered her . . .

It was over as quickly as it had begun, hard, fast, and incredibly explosive. Coming back to earth, Roseleen felt a bit like a tornado had just run over her. She almost laughed aloud. She had wondered once about Thorn's ability to keep his emotions under strict control. Well, she was kind of pleased to find he didn't *always* have that ability.

'Does this mean I am forgiven for whatever you think I did wrong?'

She opened her eyes to find him looking down at her, his expression full of male satisfaction and the knowledge that he'd curled her toes big time. So she perversely said, 'Not exactly. I'll get back to your weird way of telling me that you – well, what you said. This was simply because I really couldn't keep my hands off you any longer.'

He laughed. 'Then mayhap I should distract you a little longer.'

'Well . . .' She grinned back at him. 'You can give it your best shot, and we'll see what happens.'

He did, and it was a very long while before she thought about anything other than pleasure.

36

'I have noted, more often than not, that you like this time in your history.'

Thorn's offhand remark immediately caught Roseleen's attention. They had just finished eating a hastily prepared meal, and she was feeling well-sated in all respects. She'd even been thinking about a nap before the ships sailed again.

'Fascinated would more aptly describe how I feel about it,' she said, then joked, 'But let's face it, there is much to be said for modern plumbing.'

He smiled, though it was doubtful he caught her meaning. And she couldn't remember if she'd explained much about plumbing to him, or at least that toilets were a benefit of it. But now her curiosity was aroused by his remark, or rather, what had prompted it.

'Why do you mention it?' she asked him.

'Because we need not return to your time. We can stay in this time – if you like.'

The moment he said it, her heart leaped with excitement, and for a number of reasons. They really *could* stay in the Middle Ages. She hadn't even considered it before. But it was possible.

If they did, she could continue her research firsthand. They could even make a trip to, say, the eighteenth century, to get her book published once it was finished. But since women rarely got published before the nineteenth century, at least not if their work was of a serious nature, her book probably wouldn't come out under her own name, but nonetheless it would be published. And at least in an earlier century, she wouldn't have to worry about verifying the sources of the information she had gathered here. Books had simply been published in those days, without lawyers nitpicking over them.

Yes, it was possible, but what excited her even more was that she could then keep Thorn.

Here in this antiquated world, he could be happy. And she would be happy wherever he was. And what, actually, would she be giving up by staying here? She could still visit her friends thanks to the sword. Her career – well, that would be hard, yes. She'd worked most of her life to attain the position she had. And she would miss teaching. But when she weighed that against staying with Thorn for the rest of her life, well, he won hands down.

'We could build a fine home here,' Thorn added

when she made no response. 'There will be grants of land when William has secured England for his own.'

'Yes, I know, William was very generous to his supporters.' And then she laughed, her delight bubbling over. 'I'm amazed I didn't think of—'

She stopped and even groaned, as the one thing that threw a wrench in that wonderful idea suddenly occurred to her. Hadn't she already concluded that time traveling was too risky, because they could effect changes in the natural order of things without even realizing it?

Here they were, trying to right something that had gone wrong, and every day they remained here, something else could end up changing because of them. To stay here permanently would almost guarantee that they'd alter all kinds of things, and she couldn't take that responsibility upon herself, not even to keep Thorn.

'What is wrong?' he asked, his hand reaching across the space that separated them to caress her cheek.

She felt like crying, but she wouldn't put that burden on him. Instead, she took his fingers and kissed them, and somehow managed a smile for him.

'Nothing,' she lied. 'It was a nice idea, but of course, unrealistic. We'd end up changing more things, destroying more lives without even realizing it, and that's something my conscience couldn't bear up under.'

He sighed. 'Verily, did I know you wouldst say that. But have you considered that you are meant to stay here?'

She frowned. 'What do you mean?'

'Because of the sword, you are here. Who is to say that is not as it should be?'

She shook her head. 'I'm here by *unnatural* means, and that can't be as it should be. Besides, if I stayed, I'd have to go back often just to make sure I'm not changing things, and if I find that I am . . . I don't care to be fixing things like this the rest of my life.'

'But if you found nothing changed when you returned,' he pointed out, 'would you then agree that you are meant to stay in this time?'

Now she sighed. His persistence meant he really wanted this, yet how could she possibly agree?

'Let me give you an example of what you're suggesting. Say we stay here for a year and go back periodically to make sure we're not hurting anything by staying. We find everything okay and think we're safe to remain here. We check again the next year, and then the next, and still, everything's fine. But then ten years down the road, or even twenty, we suddenly find something really wrong.

'It would be almost impossible at that point to figure out what had happened to change things, when we're talking about a long stretch of years where the change could have occurred at any time during that period. And if we determine at that point that we can't stay here any longer, how can I go back to my time and resume my life there, when I will have aged ten or twenty years here? And you can't get us back to ten or twenty years later in my time, where I could maybe claim amnesia or something to account for being missing so long, because the sword can only return us to its present time. Do you get my point?'

'Aye, though I could wish it had not occurred to you,' he replied.

To be honest, she wished it hadn't either.

37

Shooting down such a nice idea sort of put a damper on their moods for the next few days. And then there was an encounter with Sir John du Priel that only reinforced Roseleen's conclusions that history shouldn't be revisited other than through normal means, in books or films.

They had assumed – or rather, Roseleen had concluded – that Thorn had effected the change that had caused the Vikings to defeat Harold Godwineson instead of William, because Thorn had gotten Sir John drunk enough that he missed his opportunity to get the truth out of the English spy the next morning before the spy was killed. That they had been able to fix that change supported her conclusion. Yet they were wrong. Thorn had had nothing to do with it. She kicked herself for not having realized that the other Thorn was a part of the original process of history that had created her time, the 1990s, and therefore could not have caused the discrepancy. This time traveling certainly was rattling her. She vowed to make a better effort to stay cool, calm, collected, and logical.

Sir John came aboard the *Mora* one day to confer with William, and as he was leaving, he noticed Thorn on the deck with Roseleen and came over to him to ask, 'You left ere the thieves showed up in the hostelry in Dives that morning, did you not? I recall seeing you there the evening before.'

'I must have,' Thorn replied carefully. 'There was a robbery?'

'Aye, though a botched one in my case. I dispatched both of the ruffians who thought to set upon me in my sleep. They were no match for a knight.'

Roseleen had to wonder if Thorn had also been attacked early that morning originally, when he had been in Sir John's place because he got him drunk, but had never mentioned it to her. She couldn't very well ask him in front of Sir John.

' 'Tis fortunate you did not overindulge the night before,' Roseleen remarked to Sir John, while she gave Thorn a see-didn't-I-warn-you look. 'You could have been seriously hurt by those thieves as well as robbed if you had been taken unawares in the common room.'

But Sir John disabused her of that notion quick enough. 'Nay, lady, 'tis to my fortune that I am well-trained to rouse at the first sound of armed combat, whether I am in a stupor or nay. Yet the common room was not disturbed that morning. Only those abiding upstairs were set upon and robbed. Though one of the two thieves who thought to do me ill revealed ere I dispatched him that it would have been otherwise.'

'Otherwise?' She frowned.

Sir John nodded. ' 'Twas mischief long in the planning apparently. The intent had been to rob the entire hostelry, common room as well as those sleeping above. Yet their leader was sore injured earlier that morning. Some knight had clouted him good when he and his cohorts attempted to molest some wench. But without the leader, the rest decided to avoid open combat in the common room, and just rob those few customers still asleep upstairs. Those in the common room were not disturbed by it.'

Roseleen groaned inwardly. In other words, Thorn hadn't changed things at all. Had that morning gone as it was supposed to, the common room would have been set upon as well, and Sir John would have been roused to defend himself, and probably sobered up enough afterward to make that morning interrogation as he was supposed to.

They had corrected the change by getting Sir John upstairs, yet the change hadn't been caused by Thorn, it had been caused by her. And the look Thorn was now giving her said so. *She* had caused the change when she'd left Thorn's tent, and run into those ruffian thieves who'd attempted to rape her. Because of her, their leader had been injured and so their plans had been altered, leaving Sir John sleeping blissfully unaware in his drunken stupor in the common room, well past noon, so that he had missed his chance to get the truth out of the English spy.

And they hadn't put the course of events back to exactly the way it had happened originally, but getting John back upstairs and preventing him from getting drunk had given them the same end result at least. Thank heavens for that.

Sir John and Thorn exchanged a few more words about the incident and thieves in general. But the moment the knight left them, Roseleen beat Thorn to any blame-casting.

'All right, so that altered history wasn't your fault, it was mine, but it doesn't change the fact that everything I've said is true,' she told him. 'Our presence here, mine in particular, obviously, changes things. So we need to leave here as *soon* as we find out how to fix this new change – if we can find out,' she amended with a sigh. 'I still can't imagine what went wrong this time, or why. But hopefully you'll be able to figure it out on the day of the battle.

'By the way, *were* you attacked that morning by those thieves – originally?' she asked him.

'Aye,' he replied. 'And likely by the same two that bedeviled Sir John.'

'Why didn't you mention something that important when we first discussed this?'

'Important? Nay, 'tis too common an occurrence in these times, to give it importance. I did not even recall the incident, until Sir John mentioned it.'

'I suppose you also dispatched both of the thieves that set upon you?'

'Certainly.' His look and tone said she needn't have asked.

She sighed. 'I guess it's just as well you didn't mention it, or I might have drawn still another conclusion that wouldn't have gotten things fixed quite so easily. That they *were* fixed is all that counts. And with a little luck, which we're due, this other matter with the arrows can be fixed too.'

38

It took two long weeks for October 14 to arrive. Roseleen spent most of that time aboard the *Mora*, usually by Thorn's order, but sometimes by choice, as when the smoke of burning huts was heavy in the air.

It didn't take long for the Normans to secure the port of Hastings and its immediate environs. *Devastate* would have been a more appropriate description. But then even the famous Bayeux Tapestry that depicted William's battle for the coveted English throne had one scene that showed him feasting at Hastings with his brothers Odo and Robert while a woman ran from a burning hut with her child.

This *was* war, after all, something that Roseleen had to keep reminding herself. That she knew the outcome and all the tactics employed well in advance tended to downgrade the seriousness of it in her mind, but the fact was, people were dying out there, and a lot more would die before the end of the day.

William and his army were long gone when that realization hit her in relation to herself. She might be perfectly safe being left behind with the ships, but Thorn had marched with the army down the road that connected Hastings with the town of Battle. He might not be able to die, but he could still get hurt, especially since he wouldn't actually be fighting to kill anyone, merely defending.

And she knew that William's scouts had reported in the middle of the night that Harold had arrived with his army, that the Normans had broken camp and were marching to meet the English, and the battle would begin this morning by nine o'clock.

That was no more than an hour away. And it didn't take more than moments for the thought of Thorn being hurt and her not being there to help him to drive her crazy. She had to get to the battlefield. She knew the layout of it, and that the English would be contained on the ridge where they took their stand, that every Norman assault would be against that containment, so the battle wouldn't be spread out where it might reach her if she sneaked in on the sidelines. And she could at least keep an eye on Thorn then.

Making the decision to go was so much easier than accomplishing it, because she happened to get stuck with Guy of Anjou, who had been charged with guarding her. He liked it no better than she, but he was staying close to keep her in sight. He took his duty very seriously since he'd nearly lost her the last time.

She had little doubt that he'd prefer to be in the thick of the battle, guarding Thorn's back, as was a squire's duty. But he wasn't a squire yet, so here he was with her instead. And she couldn't see any way to take off without him this time – which meant convincing him to come with her.

It was incredible how stubborn that lad could be, and how condescending. He laughed, of course, when she broached the subject with him. And he stood fast in his refusal to budge from that ship for a good hour, even when she had him convinced that through a dream, it had been revealed to her that it was a certainty the battle would be met today. Medieval folk were too superstitious not to credit things like dreams and omens.

It was an appeal to his own importance that finally enabled her to get through to him, when she said, 'If England is conquered, other Normans will come to settle here. And they will all be eager to hear about the glorious battle that won them this prize. It's going to be one of the most famous battles in history, Guy. Wouldn't you prefer to be able to say you were there and speak of it with authority? Or will you have to admit that all you know of it, you gleaned from others' accounts?'

He didn't *immediately* change his tune at that

339

point, but she'd hooked him through his vanity, so it wasn't long after that that he grudgingly agreed to fetch his horse – about the only one that had been left behind – and take her a ways down the road, not too near the battle, he'd stressed, but merely close enough for them to be of assistance when it was over.

'*Oh, sure*,' she felt like saying, but refrained from doing so. But she knew damn well he wouldn't be able to resist taking a peek at that battle if they got close enough to hear it. And she was right. He did it by playing dumb, pretending he didn't hear any of the various sounds of combat until they were nearly right up on the Normans' flanks.

Only then did he say in exaggerated surprise, 'Verily, we have come too close.'

Yet he didn't turn his horse about. He sat there and waited for her to convince him that they'd be safe where they were. Trouble was, where they were, she couldn't see much of anything with all those tall Norman backs in front of her, even if the fighting was taking place up the gradual slope of the ridge where Harold had taken his stand. But to the west was another hill, probably the one where William had first sighted the English.

So she told him, 'Nay, this is much too close. I think yonder would be much safer, don't you?' She pointed to the hill. 'And we might even have an unobstructed view of the battle from there.'

He needed no further encouragement to swing their horse in that direction. And soon they were both dismounted and somewhat concealed by the underbrush, with a clear view of the ridge. Harold's standards could be seen near the lone apple tree at the topmost point of the ridge where he'd planted himself, both the dragon of Wessex that he fought under, and his own personal banner of a Fighting Man.

It was a tightly contained mass of men, just as the accounts had claimed, a very strong defensive position that could have won Harold the war if his men hadn't broken rank to chase the retreating Normans when they lost hope. She didn't know what point the battle had reached – and then she did.

Disheartened, Guy said, 'We are retreating.'

Indeed the Normans were, but she knew that to be the beginning of their triumph. 'Yes, they've heard that William has been killed, they've tried to break through the English shields all morning with no success, but look there,' she told Guy, excited. 'That's Bishop Odo swinging his mace, exhorting the men to take heart, assuring them that William is hale and hearty.'

'But the English are now attacking!' he exclaimed as the English started rushing down the slope after the Normans.

She grinned. 'Don't worry, Guy, that is their

greatest mistake. Watch and you will see William's knights turn to make mincemeat of them.'

He looked at her aghast when that was precisely what began to happen. Roseleen didn't notice. She was too busy now trying to locate Thorn, and finally found him at the base of the ridge near William, neither actively fighting yet.

She sighed in relief, and then realized belatedly that of course he'd stay near William, and thus out of the attacks of the mounted knights. It was why he was there, to find out why William didn't give the order for the arrows to be fired into the air later.

They had a long wait yet, so she remarked offhandedly, 'That retreat was genuine, but there will be other feigned ones that will yield the same results.'

'How do you know?'

'Ah, I told you, I dreamed it,' she replied.

She couldn't tell whether the boy accepted that lame excuse, but she noticed that he was looking at her differently now, impressed that she knew so much about what was going on before them. 'Do we win?' he asked her hesitantly.

A good question that demanded a yes, she thought, unless the Normans failed to fire those arrows this time, and the answer would be no. So she said, 'My dream didn't get that far, though it certainly looked hopeful.'

He nodded, satisfied, and went back to watching the carnage. She averted her own eyes from that, and simply kept track of Thorn. So she was quite surprised when she later saw him talking to Sir Reinard, and not in an angry or threatening way. She even saw him throw back his head and laugh, which surprised her even more.

She was so bemused over that, that time passed without her noticing much of anything. Then suddenly it was late afternoon, and she saw the arrows flying through the air. She blinked, and her eyes flew up the hill. Sure enough, Harold Godwineson had been struck by one, just as the accounts claimed. She cringed and looked away in time to see the Norman cavalry charging up the hill.

The battle would be over soon. Harold would die by sunset at the very spot in which he had held firm since morning, the Normans would quit chasing any survivors from his army by nightfall, and an intimate of Harold's, Edith Swan-neck, would be brought in to verify which body was his. By William's order, he would then be buried on the shore that he had defended. Only much later would the new King of England permit Harold's body to be moved to consecrated ground at the church of Waltham.

History had finally gotten back to its correct course, ensuring that Roseleen's time in the future would once again be familiar to her. She didn't know what had changed to get William to give that order to his archers this time around, as he was supposed to, but why he had didn't matter all that much now, as long as the outcome was what they had sought.

She vowed that there would be no more time hopping for her after this. It was too nerve-wracking, and far too easy to change things without even realizing it. If she hadn't had the history books to tell her what to look for . . .

'Verily, did I suspect I would find you near.'

Roseleen and Guy both started and swung around to see Thorn towering over them, his expression not so much disapproving as exasperated.

Roseleen merely grinned, but Guy began to stammer his excuses, 'My lord, I – I can—'

'Be easy, Guy,' Thorn cut in. ' 'Tis easily guessed why you are here. I know how the lady doth browbeat and nag until she has her way.'

'Nag?' Roseleen snorted. 'I take exception—'

'So you may, but to little avail this time. How else are you here, when this is not where I left you?' She decided to play dumb on that one and clamped her mouth shut. 'As I thought,' Thorn added, then to Guy, 'They will be setting up camp soon and need assistance with the wounded. Go you and give what aid you can. I will attend to the lady.'

Guy got out of there fast, while the getting was good. Roseleen had to wonder if the scoldings would come now that she was alone with Thorn, but she didn't think so. He looked a bit weary – he'd been roused in the wee hours of the morning when William's scouts had made their report – and still exasperated, but he didn't look as if he would be lifting her up for some hard shakings.

In fact, all he said was, 'Are you ready to leave this time?'

Was she ever. She'd even brought her pillow-case of essentials along, just in case. But a kernel of curiosity got in the way first, and she asked, 'Did you happen to figure out what changed things here? Not that it's important anymore, but—'

' 'Twas your Sir Reinard who suggested the use of the archers in that particular way. Until I proved to him that he could not have you, he had been mooning over you, and cared not which way the battle went, he had been so lovesick. With his thoughts on the battle again, and the Normans nigh giving up, he made mention to William of that tactic with the archers that he had once seen previously employed.'

For some reason, her cheeks started to burn with heat. 'So it was my fault, indirectly – again.'

'Aye, yours indeed.'

'You don't have to rub it in. I didn't exactly encourage the man.'

'There is no need for you to encourage, Roseleen. You needs simply be present, for a man to fall in love with you.'

Her blush deepened. 'Well, you can't blame me for that.'

'Can I not? You would not have met Reinard de Morville had you not—'

'All right! That was a perfectly innocent . . . blunder . . . which just supports the conclusion I've reached. We have no business tampering with the past in *any* way. So I'm going to withdraw my permission for Blooddrinker's Curse to be used for jaunts into the past – after you get me home, of course.'

He sighed and took her hand, bringing it up to his lips before he said, 'Aye, I did anticipate you wouldst say just that. Odin did warn me I may not like what I find in the past.'

She made a rude sound of disagreement. 'You've enjoyed every minute—'

'Nay, I do not like seeing you fret and worry, Roseleen,' he told her sincerely. ' 'Tis not worth whatever battle I might find here.'

Words like that made her want to kiss him till he begged for mercy, but he didn't give her the opportunity to try. Even as her free hand reached for his neck, they entered that void that sent them through the realms of time.

39

'I like it not, being kept waiting, Blooddrinker.'

Roseleen heard the rasping voice behind her and swung around to try to locate it. They were back in her bedchamber in Cavenaugh Cottage, which meant no one else should have been there, at least not someone whose voice she didn't recognize.

But when she found the speaker, slouched back on her narrow desk chair across the room, her eyes flared wide, and she sucked in a breath so fast, she choked on it and started coughing. Unfortunately, that got her the palm of Thorn's hand slamming into her back, though he didn't even look her way to see whether he had knocked her off her feet or not. He hadn't, though it had been a close thing, which made her glare at him in return, but he didn't notice.

His blue eyes were riveted on the unwelcome visitor, and a slow grin slowly came to his lips.

'Ah, but you have naught better to do, do you?' Thorn said in response to the remark they'd heard, then as an afterthought added, 'Greetings, Wolfstan. You really must make a better effort to visit more often.'

A low growl came from the very obvious Viking. He was a ghost. Roseleen had a ghost in her bedchamber, not an assumed one this time, but a real one. And yet – he looked substantial enough, so substantial that the legs of the delicate chair he sat in bowed under his weight.

Long, stringy blond hair fell halfway down his chest. His eyes were so dark they defied color. And he was huge, easily as big as Thorn, with bulging muscles on the bare arms that presently crossed his chest. The sleeveless vest he wore was some kind of untanned black furry hide. The same matted fur edged his boots at his thick calves. And strips of it, with only a patch or two of fur left, crossgartered his leggings.

Behind him, lying across the top of her desk, was the largest, ugliest ax she'd ever seen. A battle-ax, designed for chopping off heads and limbs, and if used by a wielder of great strength, it could even cleave a man in two. Wolfstan the Mad looked as if he had a lot of strength.

Thorn remarked on the same thing, but with a good deal of scorn. 'I see you still have that weak weapon Gunnhilda bestowed on you when you lost your own. You should have killed her when she gave it to you.'

'Think you I did not try, the many times she called me to her to exhort me to kill you ere she died? That ax is as cursed as your sword, Blood-drinker. 'Twould fall from my hand each time I did raise it against the witch.'

'A shame.' Thorn sighed. 'I would at least one of us had stolen a few years from her wretched life. 'Twould have been some small recompense for what she did to us, to send her to her devil's realm early.'

Wolfstan nodded in agreement, only to demand, 'Then why did *you* never try? You, at least, were not under her command, as was I.'

Thorn snorted at that. 'Think you I did not search for her to do that very thing? I had great hope that the curse bestowed on me would end with her death, yet was she more powerful than that. And she hid from me well ere I departed that realm for Valhalla.'

The name of that Viking heaven was obviously a sore subject between them, because its mention drew another growl from Wolfstan and brought him to his feet, the poor chair creaking with his movement. And he really was as big as Thorn, maybe even slightly bigger.

His reaching for the battle-ax on the desk was a fair indication that he was a little more than annoyed. Thorn's suddenly shoving Roseleen behind him made it a sure enough guarantee. And with Thorn's sword still in hand from their journey there, it was only seconds before the two men were joined in battle.

Roseleen stared at them aghast. They were actually battling, trying to kill each other, right there in her bedchamber. And then the blood drained from her as that word *kill* set off alarms throughout her whole system. This was the one being who could actually kill Thorn, not just hurt him, but really kill him. And that's exactly what Wolfstan the Mad was trying to do with every swing of that mighty battle-ax he wielded.

'Stop it!' she cried 'Stop it this instant!'

Neither of them paid her the slightest attention. She might as well have not been there. But she was, and she was utterly terrified.

Thorn had no shield to use in fending off the swings coming at him. He had to use his sword to deflect those quelling blows, if he couldn't get out of the way in time. And God forbid he should slip or fumble. Wolfstan likewise had no shield, but he was on the attack, had been since their blades first drew sparks, and he was giving Thorn no time or opening to mount an offensive of his own.

Without thinking beyond getting this horrible fight over with, Roseleen worked her way around the combatants until she was behind Wolfstan. There she picked up her desk chair and swung it at his back with all her might, uncaring whether Thorn might object to her interference in such a way. But she was forgetting that Wolfstan was a ghost. Unlike Thorn, he really did lack substance, so that the chair actually passed right through him, nearly hitting Thorn in the process, and she ended up swinging around with it, losing her balance, and falling to the floor.

She sat there for a moment, wondering how he'd managed to put weight on that chair to bend its legs and make it creak, if he lacked any substance at all. Or was it selective? Did he have the power to change the consistency of his body himself? His ax certainly didn't lack substance. Again and again she heard it clash with Blood-drinker's Curse. But if there was nothing but space and image to him, how could Thorn manage to kill him? Wouldn't his sword pass right through him as well, causing no damage at all?

Roseleen had to suddenly scramble out of the way as they neared her. She wasn't quite quick enough to prevent Wolfstan's foot from passing through hers, leaving an icy chill in that part of her body. She shivered as she got to her feet. She *had* to stop this fight. But short of calling the village priest to ask him to get over here on the double, she couldn't think of—

'You always were a weakling, Wolf, even when you lived. Come now, can you give me no better sport this time? A wench could withstand those puny blows of yours.'

Roseleen glanced sharply in Thorn's direction to see him all but laughing. He was *enjoying* himself. She was frightened out of her wits, and he was having the time of his life.

She could have taken an ax to him herself at that realization. And yet, she should have known he'd consider this battle fun-and-games time. Hadn't he mentioned just recently that he wished Wolfstan would find him more often?

'You are an overweening braggart, Thorn. If your family had not the power of Irsa giving you added strength, I would have had your head chopped off long ere the witch got around to cursing you.'

Mudslinging now? Roseleen wondered as she picked up the desk chair, sat down in it, and listened to them throw insults back and forth for the next twenty minutes, some of which had her ears turning pink. Her arms were crossed, one of her toes was tapping impatiently – she was actually getting mad. They were like a couple of kids playing cowboys and Indians, cops and robbers – in their case, the cursed one and the ghost. It was obvious that they had known each other prior to Gunnhilda's interference in their lives. She could imagine they had behaved much like this back then.

When they returned to some serious hacking and slashing, she merely sighed, no longer afraid that Thorn was going to get hurt. Obviously, he was the better-skilled fighter and he'd merely been toying with his longtime enemy to prolong the enjoyment they were both having. But when Thorn finally spared her a glance and noticed how obviously annoyed she was, he made quick work of ending it.

The next swing of Wolfstan's ax was deflected as before, but this time Thorn's wrist twisted and brought his blade quickly back for a slash that should have opened the ghost from one side of his belly to the other. Instead, it passed right through him, just as the chair had, with no blood to show for it.

But instead of Wolfstan's paying no attention to it as he had when she'd hit him with the chair, he behaved as if he'd received a mortal blow. His ax slid from his hand, he clutched his middle, and then he was gone, having vanished within a blink, and in the next second, his battle-ax was gone with him.

'Until next time, Wolf,' Thorn said quietly as he sheathed Blooddrinker's Curse.

Vaguely, as if from an echoing distance, Roseleen heard the sound of laughter. She gritted her teeth and just managed to refrain from rolling her eyes.

'Is this a weekly occurrence?' she asked him in one of her driest tones. 'Monthly? How long will it take him to find his way back to you?'

'He comes only once during each new summoning,' Thorn replied, choosing to ignore her sarcasm. 'Actually, he will not come again, as there will be no new summoning.'

He said that with a degree of sadness, having only just realized it. Roseleen heard only that there would be no new summoning, which meant he was going to stick around permanently, as he'd said.

Now would be the time to disabuse him of that notion, to send him away, to get her life back to normal – if that would ever be possible. But looking at him standing there, triumphant from battle, so handsome he took her breath away, she couldn't do it, not yet. It was too quick, too sudden.

Tomorrow. Yes, tomorrow she'd do it. Till then . . .

40

Roseleen dragged her feet for an entire week, coming up with one excuse after another to keep Thorn with her – just a little longer. She knew it was doing neither one of them any good to put it off, that she was merely being selfish in wanting to keep him near a bit more. All it was doing was allowing her to become even closer to him, which was making it that much harder to think of sending him away.

So for several days, she didn't think about it. For several days, she just savored his presence, and stored up memories that would have to last her a lifetime.

She gave John and Elizabeth Humes a vacation, suggesting they visit Elizabeth's mother in Brighton for a week or so. And she put David off on coming to see her when he returned to England. She didn't want anyone to disturb her last days with Thorn.

But the time finally came when she knew she couldn't procrastinate any longer. Knowing that she'd never see him again after she sent him away was making her so sick at heart that she just couldn't bear it any longer.

And yet, she still put it off by first asking silly questions that she didn't expect any positive answers to. They were in her bedchamber, not to make love, though that was where they'd spent most of the last week, but just lying on the bed holding each other. She got such pleasure out of just holding him, absorbing his heat, feeling his gentle caresses that weren't meant to stimulate, merely to communicate how much he liked touching her.

Roseleen's fingers were strolling slowly through the hair on his chest when she asked him, 'Is Blooddrinker's Curse breakable?'

'Nay, 'twas a finely wrought sword to begin with, but the curse has made it indestructible.'

'What about the curse?' She grinned up at him. 'Is that breakable?'

He became very still of a sudden. 'Why do you ask that now, Roseleen?'

She shrugged. 'I don't know, I'm just curious. I suppose I should have asked sooner. The laws of fairness usually allow one little out to correct really blatant injustice, and I was wondering if you had one.'

'Aye, the curse may be easily broken.'

'Easily?' She sat up in surprise, never dreaming

she'd get an answer like that. 'Then why haven't you broken it before now?'

'Because I have not the power to break it,' he replied, his tone somewhat chagrined. 'The curse wouldst not even allow me to make mention of it, unless I was first asked, as you have just done.'

'Then where does the easy part come in? If you can't break it, who can?'

'Whoever is in possession of my sword has that ability,' he explained, 'since the only way the curse can be ended is by returning the sword to me without reservation, granting me full ownership of it again.'

'Are you serious? That's all it would take to break a thousand-year-old curse?'

His nod was endearingly curt. 'Then wouldst I be in control of my own destiny again, and my sword would be but a sword, all power gone from it.'

'That would certainly guarantee that there would be no more time hopping, should you ever be tempted again,' she said thoughtfully.

But she already knew she would make that sacrifice too, that she would give him back his sword and his own destiny, whatever that meant. And she really couldn't put it off any longer.

The sword was in its protective case, back under the bed where she had previously kept it. She got up to pull out the case now and opened it, took the sword in her hands one last time. She imagined she could feel the power surging in it, in protest of what she was about to do – end its long reign of absolute, unnatural power.

She couldn't tell Thorn the truth, that her sending him away was best for him. That could produce arguments from him that she couldn't validate, since they'd deal with the future. So she'd decided it would be best to lie to him, to give him the old it's-been-fun-but-now-it's-over routine. She was certain that a man from any century would tend to accept that fairly well, or pretend to for the sake of his pride.

Considering the subject just under discussion, Thorn sat up and looked at her suspiciously. 'What do you with that, Roseleen?'

The smile she gave him was tepid at best as she sat on the edge of the bed, the sword grasped carefully in both her hands. She stared at it a moment, almost hating it now, wishing she'd never even heard of it. Who would have ever thought that something this old and deadly could bring her the love of her life? And who would have thought the fates could be so cruel in not letting her have the man that she loved permanently?

'Roseleen?'

She glanced at him, and a lump rose in her throat. She couldn't get the words past it, not while she was looking at him directly, so she dropped her gaze again and prayed she'd have the strength to stick to what she was doing for his sake if not for hers.

Her voice still sounded unsteady when she got out, 'It – it's time for you to go, Thorn.'

'Go where?'

'Back to your Valhalla.'

'Nay!'

'Yes,' she cut in, and said the rest in a rush while she still could. 'I'll be returning to America soon, getting back to the old grindstone – that means back to work,' she added, before he could ask.

His hand came to her cheek ever so gently. 'We were fated to be, Roseleen. It has taken me a thousand years to find you, and now I have, I will not leave you.'

She closed her eyes, fighting desperately to keep the tears back. It was the last touch she would have from him, the last . . . Oh, God, why was he arguing with her? Why didn't he just accept her decision and let it go at that?

'You don't understand,' she said on a rising note. 'I want you to go. It's been nice having you around for a while – you're a really great lover. But I have to get on with my life now, and you can't be a part of it.'

'You love me, Roseleen, just as I—'

'No, I don't. *Now* do you understand? And – and I don't even want a reminder of you around, which is why I'm going to give you your sword back.'

'Roseleen, nay!'

But she had already leaned forward to place the sword across his lap, and his shout startled her into dropping it on him. In the next second, both Thorn and the ancient weapon were gone.

She stared at the spot where he had been, which was so completely empty now, the mattress not even dented or slowly returning to shape to prove he'd been there but seconds ago. She touched the empty spot with her hand and burst into tears.

41

Roseleen had cried herself to sleep after sending Thorn away. When she awoke, she couldn't say if it was the same day or the next, but that deep ache was still there – and so was her brother, David.

She had to rub her eyes to make sure she wasn't seeing things, but he was definitely there, sitting in a chair pulled up beside her bed. And he was smiling at her, really beaming, as if he had some special news to impart that he couldn't contain any longer.

'Hello there, beautiful,' he said cheerfully and reached over to grab her hand for a gentle squeeze. 'Welcome back to the living.'

'Excuse me?' she said, blinking at him. 'Did I die or something?'

He chuckled. 'No, but it was damn close.'

At that point, she figured he was pulling her leg for some reason she couldn't begin to guess at, and so she feigned a yawn, leaned back against her pillows, and said in a bored tone, 'Okay, I give. Tired I might be, but half-dead with exhaustion?

No, I don't think so.' But then she remembered all the crying she'd done and added, 'On second thought, maybe I'll allow that I look worse than I feel.'

'I hope you're feeling better, because you're looking great – all things considered.'

'All things considered? Come on, David, explain yourself. I've never been very good at figuring out puzzles upon first waking.'

'Hmm,' he said thoughtfully. 'The doc said you might not remember.'

Her eyes narrowed on him at that cryptic remark. 'Remember what? And *what* doctor?'

'Now don't get upset—'

'David!'

'You really don't remember, do you?'

She sighed. 'Okay, what is it I'm not remembering that you think I should?'

'Rosie, you've been sick, so sick that Mrs Humes not only called a doctor, she was so worried that she also felt it was necessary to call me.'

She frowned. 'Don't be ridiculous. Elizabeth and John aren't even here, they're on vacation in Brighton,' she started, only to amend, 'Did they return?'

'I don't know about any vacation they've had recently, but they're both definitely here, and a damn good thing. You could have died if you'd been alone here.'

She crossed her arms over her chest, almost glaring at him. 'Okay, this is a joke, right? I can't wait to hear the punch line, so why don't you get right to it?'

He shook his head at her. 'No joke. And I don't mind telling you, I've been worried sick.'

'But *why?*'

'Rosie, you had a really bad case of pneumonia. You've been out of it for five days straight, not to mention delirious and even hallucinating at times. Your temperature reached 105 degrees at one point, scaring the hell out of us. I wouldn't let the doctor budge from your side.'

She stared at him blankly for all of five seconds before she blurted out, 'But I don't remember being sick!'

'You really don't?'

'No, not a bit.'

'I'd count that as a blessing.' He grinned at her. 'Some of those hallucinations you were having sounded pretty nightmarish.'

'But I feel perfectly fine,' she assured him. 'Just a little tired.'

And that was because all that crying she'd done had worn her out. Or was it? When had that been, exactly? If she'd been out of it for five days, how many days before that had she sent Thorn away?

And then she stiffened as another thought occurred to her. Maybe she and Thorn hadn't really made it back to the right time after all. Maybe some small little thing still needed to be corrected in the past, something so minor that it hadn't radically changed the present, just merely made things somewhat different – enough so she wouldn't remember being sick, because it was the other Roseleen living in this time who'd nearly died of pneumonia, not her. Just as it had been another Roseleen who'd married Barry, and another Roseleen who had had a prude for a brother that she couldn't tolerate . . .

Suspiciously, she said, 'Answer a dumb question for me. I'm not married to Barry Horton, am I?'

'Don't be absurd. You wouldn't give that bastard the time of day, and if you did, I'd kick his ass before he could set his watch.'

At that she had to grin. 'Okay, I believe you. I was just checking, as long as we're on the subject of things I can't remember.'

He chuckled. 'You must be feeling better. You're already back to teasing.'

David had insisted she rest for the remainder of the day, and wouldn't hear any arguments to the contrary. And when the doctor stopped by later to check on her, he added a couple more days to that. Though she'd apparently spent five days in bed already, according to everyone who'd kept a vigil over her, they hadn't exactly been restful days.

Roseleen still found it hard to believe that she could have been that sick and yet have no memory of it, not even of the onset of the pneumonia. She'd thought she'd remember some sniffles or coughing, a headache maybe, or the start of her fever. But there was nothing that she could recall in the way of illness. Her last memory was of sending Thorn away, and she was never going to forget that.

Of course, it was possible that she'd been so depressed and heartsick over that, she hadn't noticed something as minor as sniffles. And according to the calendar, she did have a few more days missing from the time she'd sent Thorn away than just those five spent with her bout of pneumonia, which she couldn't remember.

It *was* possible that she'd sunk so low into misery after Thorn had vanished that time and the mundane things in life had passed without her noticing it. And whenever she thought of Thorn now, she felt that depression coming on again, so she tried not to think about him – too much.

David helped in that respect. He spent most of each day with her, telling her jokes, telling her about his recent trip to France, playing simple card and board games with her to keep her from climbing the walls.

But the day finally came when she got back to her normal routine, and David returned to his town house in London. Besides filling her notebook with all the things she had seen in the past while they were still fresh in her memory, she had a few things yet that she wanted to research before she returned to the States. And one of the things on her agenda was to make the drive to Hastings.

She left early one morning to do that. She had seen the area in the past, but she'd never been there before in the present. It was mainly her curiosity that prompted the trip, to see how different the area was now from how it had been in William's day. And she found it greatly changed.

The swampy meadow was gone, replaced by fishponds. What had been open country before was now full of trees. And Battle Abbey had been built on the exact site where Harold Godwineson had fallen.

Roseleen walked the area, envisioning the battle as she'd witnessed it. Many things might have affected that battle before it occurred, yet it still could have gone either way. William the Conqueror had been a brilliant man, a seasoned professional fighter, and a great tactician, but he'd gained the throne of England through luck and circumstance.

Had anything happened differently, as she'd found out firsthand, William wouldn't have won against the English, because they had simply outnumbered his forces. And their defensive position would have remained unbreachable if they hadn't foolishly broken ranks.

She was glad he'd gained his crown. She was glad she'd been able to witness his triumph. Of course, for her to have her own time back, it couldn't have gone any other way.

42

David was taking Roseleen to the airport for her flight home. He picked her up a day early, because her plane was scheduled to depart so early in the morning, they'd figured it would be more convenient if she spent the last night at his town house right in London.

Lydia had flown in from France just to say goodbye to her. That last night, the three of them walked to a small pub around the block where the fish and chips came hot and delicious, and ice for drinks was given only upon request.

Roseleen had never understood the Englishman's propensity for warm drinks, and had never bothered to ask. Fancifully, she liked to think it might go back to the days of guzzling warm mead out of a barrel. The thought at least made her smile – a rarity these days.

She had debated long and hard whether to tell David about Thorn. It wasn't something that he had to know about, since Thorn was gone now, never to be seen again. It was more that she *needed* to talk about him, to share her memories of him with someone. And aside from Gail, David was the closest person in her life.

The only reason she was leery of telling him the whole story or even part of it was that he would very likely think she had gone off the deep end, and who could blame him? It was, after all, an unbelievable experience she'd had. She'd be the first to agree with that.

Time traveling, witches with supernatural power, curses, a thousand-year-old Viking who resided in what the world considered a mythical place where time practically stood still. Very, very unbelievable. And yet, it had all happened, and she really did need to talk about it.

David and she were on the way to the airport early the next morning before Roseleen finally got up the nerve to broach the subject of Thorn with him. And she began in a roundabout way, hoping to keep her brother's shock to a bare minimum – at least to start.

So she said in an offhand manner, 'David, I gave Blooddrinker's Curse back to its owner.'

He glanced over at her, his tone merely curious as he asked, 'What are you talking about? You weren't able to buy that sword, remember?'

Roseleen hadn't expected to be the one surprised here, or confused. Maybe he had misunderstood her.

'What are *you* talking about?' she asked him. 'You bought it for me.'

He shook his head before he assured her, 'No, I didn't. I suggested it, but you were so pissed off at Sir Isaac Dearborn because he wouldn't deal directly with you that you told me to forget it. Dearborn still has the sword as far as I know, and he'll be lucky if he ever finds a buyer for it, it's in such bad condition.'

'It was in excellent condition!'

At that point, he turned to give her a really perplexed frown. 'Rosie, what the devil's gotten into you? You never even got a chance to see the sword.'

She sighed, deciding he'd either forgotten and needed his memory jogged a bit, or they were talking about two different swords. 'David, you bought me the sword. You sent it to me in the States, and I brought it here. And those dreams I told you about? About meeting the sword's original owner? Well, they weren't dreams after all, they were quite real. The sword turned out to be cursed. It came part and parcel with the original owner, Thorn Blooddrinker, whom I was able to summon just by touching the sword. And I got to know him so well that I – I fell in love with him.'

After a few moments of staring at her as if she had grown a second head, he said, 'That's quite a dream you had there, Rosie.'

'But that's what I'm trying to tell you, David. It wasn't a dream, it was all real.'

'Okay, to repeat a phrase that you threw at me not too long ago – I can't wait to hear the punch line, so why don't you get right to it?'

'I wouldn't joke about something like this, David. Didn't you hear me? I said I fell in love with the man. And it's hurting like crazy that I sent him away for good by giving him back his sword. But he would have been miserable if I had allowed him to stay here. His thinking was antiquated, his profession was antiquated. He was happiest when he was swinging a sword at someone.'

'Rosie, stop and think for a minute, will you? If you never owned the sword to begin with, and I promise you that you didn't – I wouldn't lie to you about that – then none of what you've just told me really could have taken place, could it?'

'But—'

'Just think for a minute, and you'll see I'm right. It was just a dream you had while you were so sick, the high fever you were running at the time probably making the dream much more vivid than your usual dreams, which would account for your thinking it was real. But it couldn't be real, because you never got your hands on that sword in the first place, so you couldn't have used it to summon anyone, or given it to anyone to send him away.'

A dream? How could her heart ache over a dream? How could she remember nothing of a serious illness, but everything about a dream? And yet, if she never had possession of the sword to begin with . . .

Then she had never really met and known Thorn Blooddrinker, let alone loved him. He wasn't real, any more than her dream was.

43

Roseleen fretted about it during the entire flight home. She had agreed with David and assured him that she'd adjust her thinking and try to put the whole thing behind her. But it wasn't going to be that easy, not when a dream seemed more real than what was apparently real. And telling herself to forget about it was fine, except her emotions weren't paying attention.

When she arrived back in the States, she decided to rent a car and drive to see Gail first, before she went home. She could tell Gail anything, and she did, recounting the whole experience, every single incident, from Thorn's first appearance in her classroom to her dropping the sword across his lap. And as she talked to her friend, she knew she wasn't recalling a dream, she was confiding her memories, and they were crystal-clear, every one of them. But Gail, just like David, swore she'd never owned the sword to begin with, that Roseleen hadn't shown it to her that last time she'd visited.

Afterward, exhausted, but feeling somewhat better for getting it all out, she said, 'I know it has to be a dream, Gail, but how is it possible to remember such details? Like the day Thorn discovered television, during that last week I spent with him. I never laughed as hard as I did at his reactions when I showed him what a remote control could do. Imagine *commercials* being fascinating.'

'Oh, stop it.' Gail giggled. 'What do I have to do, get pneumonia to have dreams like that? Why don't you just be glad you had the experience, dream or otherwise, and let it go at that?'

Feel glad that she'd had the experience? Roseleen mused. She would if she could just stop hurting and missing Thorn so much. As dreams went, this one had been a royal pain in the neck as far as her emotions were concerned.

And before she left, Gail had remarked about the whole tale, 'Sounds like a book I read recently. Maybe you read it too, and that illness you had made you think you lived it instead. Damn, what a neat concept. I've got a bookshelf full of books I'd love to live through. I think I'll go stick my head in the freezer for a while. How long do you think it takes to catch pneumonia?'

Trust Gail to make her laugh. Roseleen was glad she had decided to go see her friend before returning home. She was at least encouraged to think she would get over her dream man eventually. But it really would have helped if that expensive glass display case she'd had made for Blooddrinker's Curse weren't still hanging in the center of her weapons collection.

When she discovered it later on the afternoon that she arrived home, her confusion returned in spades. Was she supposed to have ordered that merely on speculation, because she *hoped* to own the sword? It wasn't in her nature to be that frivolous. Yet there was the case – empty. Of course, that would explain why she was so angry at Dearborn, since she'd already wasted money on a weapon he refused to sell her. But why couldn't she remember it that way, instead of only the way it had been in her dream?

She was in the middle of sorting out this new confusion when the doorbell rang and a measuring cup was practically shoved in her face when she opened the front door.

'Borrow a cup of sugar, ma'am?'

'Excuse me?'

'Roseleen White, isn't it?' the man holding the cup asked. 'I'm Thornton Bluebaker. Our neighbor on the other side of you, Carol What's-her-name, told me all about you.'

She took her eyes off his cup then so she could focus on him, and nearly went into shock. As it was, all she could do was stare. His light brown hair was short, falling only just below his ears, and in a style that was currently fashionable. His clothes were completely modern, tight black jeans with a tank top and a short suede bomber jacket full of American flag patches. But his face was Thorn's. His body was Thorn's. His lovely blue eyes were Thorn's. Even his name sounded too similar – Thorn Blooddrinker and Thornton Bluebaker.

Her mind was scrambling for an explanation before she broke down and cried. She wanted to throw her arms around him, shower him with kisses – but he was a stranger. A *stranger with her Thorn's face*. Apparently he was the new neighbor she had been worried about.

'I met you before I went to Europe, didn't I?' she asked him hopefully. 'I just can't recall exactly when or how . . .'

'No, I would have remembered meeting you, believe me,' he said with a look that set off heat waves in her belly. 'But it's possible you saw me. I was here a couple times while the movers were getting my things settled in. I think that was before your trip.'

She nodded. That had to be it. She'd seen him, his image had stuck in her mind without her realizing it, and since she found him handsome, very, very handsome, his was the image she'd put into her dreams. Maybe she wasn't losing her mind after all.

'I heard you're a college professor. That was the career I nearly chose myself, until someone steered me into writing instead.'

'What do you write?'

'Fantasy fiction. My last book came out a couple of months ago. Maybe you saw it in the airports during your recent traveling?'

The only memory she had of her trip to Europe was of being so rushed because she'd gone back home for Blooddrinker's Curse, that she'd snatched up a book in the airport newsstand without really glancing at it. But of course, that had been part of her dream. Her real flight to England must have been so mundane, she didn't recall it at all. So it was possible she'd seen his book. She just had no memory of it.

'What was it about?' she asked, merely to be polite.

'A fantasy about the Viking god Thor's unknown brother Thorn. Fascinating concept, dealing with a cursed sword and time traveling – what's wrong?'

Her knees had buckled. Her vision blurred for a moment. She came about as close to fainting as she ever had, and he'd reached to grab her when she'd started to sink to the floor. His touch, his closeness, only made it worse. Her system was going haywire, thinking he was Thorn, making her want . . . Oh, God, was she dreaming again?

377

'It's okay,' she got out, but it wasn't. Now she was certain that she was losing her mind. 'I just felt a little dizzy. . . . And I – I think I have read your book. I must have picked it up in the airport.'

'Really?' He beamed. 'How'd you like it?'

'It was – very unusual. There was a love story in it too, wasn't there?'

'Yes. I don't usually do love stories – just not my thing. But it seemed appropriate for this book.'

'I don't recall finishing it. How did it end?'

'Odin told my hero that his lady lied. She did love him. She loved him enough to send him away, because she thought she knew what was best for him. She thought he couldn't be happy in her time.'

She knew that she was imagining that his expression was now somewhat reproachful, as if he were actually blaming her . . .

'I hear the phone ringing,' she lied. 'Why don't you ask Carol for that sugar.'

She closed the door on him before he could make a reply and leaned back against it, closing her eyes as she groaned. Her heart was pounding erratically. And then she felt utterly foolish.

Of course he hadn't been looking at her reproachfully. She'd only imagined it because she deserved it. And she really must have read his book on the way to England. Gail had even suggested something like that. And nothing else made sense. Somehow, when she'd been sick, she'd lived the book in her delirious dreams, put herself in the heroine's shoes, and because she was so sick, her mind had somehow obliterated some of her real life in order to substitute those dreams, making her think *they* were real, rather than what really was real.

The doorbell rang again, drawing a startled gasp from her. It was him again. She knew it. She counted on it. Thorn would never have given up that easily . . . Oh, God, what was she thinking? She had to stop that. He wasn't Thorn, he was a complete stranger.

But as soon as she opened the door again, that complete stranger pulled her into his arms and kissed her. And it was no how-do-you-do-ma'am type of kiss, if there was such a thing, but a deep, welcome-home-I-missed-you-like-crazy type of kiss that she found very, very familiar.

When he let go of her, setting her back on her feet – she hadn't realized they'd left the floor – all she wanted to do was leap back into his arms. There was no thought of slapping him for his audacity when that kiss had been so damn familiar to her.

'I'm not going to say I'm sorry for that,' he told her, his expression now looking seriously posses-sive. 'I hope you don't think this is a come-on, but for some reason I can't begin to explain, I felt I had the right to kiss you.'

She knew why *she* felt she had that right, but him? Better not to even discuss that kiss, so she merely nodded and changed the subject. 'I forgot to ask how the love story part of your book ended.'

He grinned. 'My hero couldn't stay in Valhalla, of course. He'd only been a guest there, thanks to his brother's intercession, but that was a place for the dead, and he was still very much alive. So Odin took pity on him – he really had a bad case of the broken heart – and granted him his choice of times to live out his life. You can guess what time he picked.'

She managed a grin herself. 'Oh, I don't know. Considering how much he loved fighting and war—'

'He loved her more, Roseleen,' he said, and he was suddenly looking at her so seriously, so intently, her heart skipped a beat. 'He would have done anything to get back to her, even if he had to live his life over again in her time, and wait until he reached the age at which she knew him, before he could finally find her and make her his again.'

'Is – is that what he did?'

'Oh, yes, and he considered it well worth the wait. Don't you agree?'

Her smile came slowly, but soon it was blinding. She wasn't going to question how it happened. Either she had really lived those dreams and her own life had been somewhat altered, so that at least she could retain her memories of him after she'd sent him away, which Odin could have easily seen to, she supposed. Or a glimpse of him and a fantasy story had so impressed her, that she'd actually fallen in love in a dream, because her illness had made that dream seem so real.

Did she agree? 'Actually, I think she should spend the rest of her life making it up to him, for being so foolish as to think she knew what was best for him.'

His curt nod was achingly familiar. 'A woman's opinion. Not bad. I'll have to consult you about the ending of my next book.' And then he was smiling at her with promise in his eyes. 'I kind of like the idea about her making things up to him, though.'

She lifted a brow. 'That's not the way you ended it?'

'No, my ending was rather abrupt. They find each other again and she invites him to dinner.'

Roseleen took the hint and laughed. 'Speaking of which, how would you like to come to dinner tonight – to further discuss your book?'

'Careful, Roseleen,' he warned, managing to sound both teasing and serious. 'Once you invite me in, it's hard to get rid of me.'

As if she'd want to get rid of him. She wasn't about to make that mistake twice, and the smile she gave him assured him of that. She had her Viking back. And she wasn't going to let him go again.

THE END

YOU BELONG TO ME
by Johanna Lindsey

No man existed who could tame Alexandra Rubliov. Fiery, wilful and beautiful, Alex defied her father's wish for her to marry until, in desperation, he recalled a long-forgotten agreement between him and his oldest friend that Alex should marry his friend's only son, Count Vasili Petroff. Vasili, overbearing, arrogant and unbelievably handsome, was forced to take the unwilling Alex back to the kingdom of Cardinia – as his bride.

While the unwilling pair travelled through the snowy mountains back to Vasili's home they did their best to remain aloof from each other – but the passion which flared between them was too strong to be denied, and the fires of their love blazed fiercely for all to see.

0 552 14383 9

A SELECTED LIST OF FINE NOVELS
AVAILABLE FROM CORGI BOOKS

13992 0	**LIGHT ME THE MOON**	*Angela Arney*	£4.99
12850 3	**TOO MUCH TOO SOON**	*Jacqueline Briskin*	£5.99
13266 7	**A GLIMPSE OF STOCKING**	*Elizabeth Gage*	£5.99
14231 X	**ADDICTED**	*Jill Gascoine*	£4.99
13872 X	**LEGACY OF LOVE**	*Caroline Harvey*	£4.99
14220 4	**CAPEL BELLS**	*Joan Hessayon*	£4.99
14207 7	**DADDY'S GIRL**	*Janet Inglis*	£5.99
14262 X	**MARIANA**	*Susanna Kearsley*	£4.99
14045 7	**THE SUGAR PAVILION**	*Rosalind Laker*	£5.99
14025 2	**PRISONER OF MY DESIRE**	*Johanna Lindsey*	£4.99
14222 0	**THE MAGIC OF YOU**	*Johanna Lindsey*	£4.99
14292 1	**LOVE ONLY ONCE**	*Johanna Lindsey*	£4.99
13210 1	**HEARTS AFLAME**	*Johanna Lindsey*	£4.99
13075 3	**FIRES OF WINTER**	*Johanna Lindsey*	£4.99
14289 1	**SURRENDER MY LOVE**	*Johanna Lindsey*	£4.99
14383 9	**YOU BELONG TO ME**	*Johanna Lindsey*	£4.99
14002 3	**FOOL'S CURTAIN**	*Claire Lorrimer*	£4.99
13737 5	**EMERALD**	*Elisabeth Luard*	£5.99
13910 6	**BLUEBIRDS**	*Margaret Mayhew*	£5.99
13569 0	**A KINGDOM OF DREAMS**	*Judith McNaught*	£4.99
13252 7	**ONCE AND ALWAYS**	*Judith McNaught*	£4.99
13478 3	**SOMETHING WONDERFUL**	*Judith McNaught*	£4.99
12728 0	**WHITNEY, MY LOVE**	*Judith McNaught*	£4.99
13826 6	**ALMOST HEAVEN**	*Judith McNaught*	£4.99
14354 5	**UNTIL YOU**	*Judith McNaught*	£4.99
13972 6	**LARA'S CHILD**	*Alexander Mollin*	£5.99
10375 6	**CSARDAS**	*Diane Pearson*	£5.99
14123 2	**THE LONDONERS**	*Margaret Pemberton*	£4.99
14298 0	**THE LADY OF KYNACHAN**	*James Irvine Robertson*	£5.99
14296 4	**THE LAND OF NIGHTINGALES**	*Sally Stewart*	£4.99